"Kristoff has proposed."

Katie held the ticket up for her to see. Hannah rushed over and grabbed it into her still-gloved hands. She squealed with delight, holding it under the candle to read the words inked in black across the page.

"Oh, Katie, I'm so pleased. You will tell him about the baby now, won't you?"

"Oh yes, of course," said Katie, feeling a flush of warmth travel across her features. "Do you really think I should marry him?" she asked, her voice betraying her anxiety.

Hannah knelt beside Katie and took her hands in her own, the wetness of the melted snow on the gloves coating Katie's hands. "I really think you should. I promise you that I believe you will be a good match—the best match. The two of you are suited to each other in so many ways. He is handsome, kind, hard-working, and good. You are pretty, sweet, compassionate, and good. And together, you'll be perfect. I wouldn't say it if I didn't truly believe it."

Katie looked deep into Hannah's earnest brown eyes, and knew what her decision would be.

Vivi Holt lives in beautiful Brisbane, Australia, with her husband, three children and their three guinea pigs. After a career as a knowledge manager, she is now living her dream of writing full-time. When she's not writing, she loves to hike, read, sing and travel. As a former student of history, Vivi especially enjoys creating unique and thrilling tales inspired by true historical events.

His Surprise
MAIL-ORDER
FAMILY

VIVI HOLT

Previously published as *Katie* and *Holly*

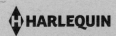

Recycling programs
for this product may
not exist in your area.

ISBN-13: 978-1-335-62999-9

His Surprise Mail-Order Family

Copyright © 2020 by Harlequin Books S.A.

Katie
First published in 2016 by Vivi Holt. This edition published in 2020.
Copyright © 2016 by Vivi Holt

Holly
First published in 2017 by Vivi Holt. This edition published in 2020.
Copyright © 2017 by Vivi Holt

This edition published by arrangement with Harlequin Books S.A.

For questions and comments about the quality of this book,
please contact us at CustomerService@Harlequin.com.

Harlequin Enterprises ULC
22 Adelaide St. West, 40th Floor
Toronto, Ontario M5H 4E3, Canada
www.Harlequin.com

Printed in U.S.A.

CONTENTS

KATIE

Chapter One

November 1870
Boston

Quincy Market stretched out long and wide, the vendor stalls blanketing the interior of the building like colorful pieces in a patchwork quilt. Its red brick walls reached skyward, meeting the domed archway of the ceiling where a series of rectangular signs hung, advertising the most prominent occupants of the space: Bolton and Hicks, Lanksey's, Hollands, Chapman and Co.'s. The gold lettering reached toward the cream expanse of the dome where decorative crown molding met inlaid floral designs in various colors. The building was impressive, and the sounds of conversation and vendors hawking their wares, along with the smell of cotton candy, fresh-baked croissants and seasonal fruits emanated throughout the cavernous space. The markets sucked shoppers into a cacophony that excited the senses and loosened the purse strings.

Katie Pearson clutched the basket that hung from

her arm and strode through the crowd with determination. She'd promised her husband Nicholas she would find an inexpensive steak for dinner that evening, and since they were rarely able to afford such a luxury, she was resolute in her mission to find one. Frowning, she stood on tip-toe to scan the marketplace.

"Maybe Lanskey's Butchery will have what you're looking for," offered Hannah Petersen, who hurried to keep up with Katie. Hannah was resolved not to run in the crowd, since that would be unladylike. She was older than Katie, and took her position of greater maturity in their friendship seriously. So, she scurried as quickly as she could while glancing about the crowded hall.

"Maybe. Let's go and see," said Katie, making her way toward the large Lanskey's pavilion. "Oh." Katie stopped still. Katie's features were pale, and her eyes widened in trepidation. She lifted a hand to her mouth, her face blanching.

"Katie, what is it?" asked Hannah, reaching for Katie's arm to steady her.

"I don't feel very well."

Katie lowered her head, pulled back the cover on her empty shopping basket and threw up in it.

"Oh dear," Hannah screwed up her nose, and patted Katie gently on the back. "Are you all right?"

"I'm not sure. I feel a touch dizzy. I'm also ravenously hungry and sick to my stomach, all at the same time. I feel very strange."

"Really?" Hannah looked at her with interest.

"Yes. Ugh."

"What about your bosoms, are they tender?"

"What?" asked Katie. She turned to face Hannah, her cheeks flushing with warmth. She tugged on her coat, pulling it more tightly around her.

"Well, are they?"

Katie wrapped her arms about herself surreptitiously, then squeezed gingerly as though she were hugging herself.

"Why yes, they are."

"Sounds like you're pregnant, my dear," exclaimed Hannah, a broad grin cutting across her rosy face.

"Do you think so? I guess that makes sense. You might be right." Katie beamed with delight. "Yes, I do believe you're right. I must be pregnant."

Her face paled, and she threw up quickly into the basket again, covering it back with the cheesecloth she had draped across the top to keep any produce they bought protected from the wind and insects.

"I think we'd better get you something to eat." Hannah grabbed Katie by the elbow and pushed her toward a nearby confectioner's stand. Fishing about in her purse, Hannah extracted two coins and handed them to the vendor who in return gave her two delicious looking bon bons.

"Mmmm, perfect," murmured Katie, slipping the chocolate between her lips and chewing happily on it. Her dainty face regained some color, and she pushed a flyaway lock of blonde hair behind one ear as she ate. "Nick is going to be so happy," she smiled at Hannah, "he's been wanting a son so badly he says he could almost taste it."

"Well, son or daughter, he'll be as pleased as punch. And you'll have everything you've always wanted since your parents died—a family of your own and a home to share together. I'm so happy for you Katie."

"Thank you, Hannah. What do you say we skip the shopping trip and head back home? I can't exactly fill this basket with groceries now, since I'll have to clean it out. Also, I really want to see Nick and tell him the good news."

Hannah laughed, nodding her head in agreement. The two women linked arms and hurried from the market and into the street beyond. The roads were slick with the ice of an early winter freeze. Katie wrapped the scarf hanging loosely about her neck more tightly, and buttoned her coat with a shiver. She couldn't wait to see Nick and tell him about the baby. They'd only been married a few months, but they'd been sweethearts for almost as long as she could remember. She'd never been courted by anyone else. They'd grown up on the same street, attended the same school and played together with the other children on their block. He was everything to her, and now she could give him the one thing he'd always wanted—a child.

They ducked around a horse cart, its red and yellow wagon trundling steadily down the street full of passengers and pulled by a set of black and bay horses, tossing their heads gaily and lifting their legs in unison. Katie and Hannah bustled onto the sidewalk, avoiding an icy puddle, and headed for their nearby apartment building. Hannah had once been Katie's teacher at the small school on the corner of their block and had been there to comfort her when both her parents died in a carriage accident in downtown Boston. Then, when Katie moved into her building with her new husband,

Nick, a few years later, the two of them had become fast friends, sharing everything together.

"You'll have to get some maternity clothing before too long," said Hannah, her voice catching with emotion.

"Yes, of course. I'm sure one of the ladies from church will have some to spare."

"No doubt."

They arrived at the squat building where they lived. Several sturdy oak trees filled the small garden in front of the building, their long branches reaching across the busy street, shadowing the passing wagons, buggies and pedestrians. Winter was almost upon them, and leaves fell about them as they hurried up the steps. The ground was covered in a blanket of the pointed oak leaves in various shades of orange, red and yellow, and the stoop hadn't escaped the deluge either. Their landlord was busily sweeping the troublemakers from the top step, his brow furrowed in frustration.

"Good evening Mr. Hungerford," chimed both women simultaneously as they hurried past him. He harrumphed at them grumpily, and continued working.

Inside the building, Katie stopped to unravel the long, red scarf from around her neck. She was beginning to feel overly warm and queasy again. It was then that she saw the two men at the bottom of the staircase speaking quietly together and looking her way. One of the men wore a bowler hat. It sat jauntily on top of his head. His faded suit jacket was missing a button. The other man held his hat in his hands and his small eyes squinted at her through a pair of spectacles that had slipped down his long nose.

"Mrs. Pearson?" asked the taller one, removing his hat and holding it at his side as he walked toward her. The other man followed, a few strands of greying hair combed over the top of his bald head.

"Yes?"

"I'm Detective McNamara, and this is Detective Constantine. We're with the Boston Police Department, Ma'am."

"Oh. Are you looking for me?" asked Katie, her voice quavering.

"Yes, I'm afraid so, Ma'am. There's been an accident. I'm sorry to say that your husband has been killed."

Katie stared at them, her eyes wide. "No!" she whispered. Then she fell to the floor in a heap, unconscious. Hannah screamed and ran to her side. She took Katie's head off the hard, tiled floor and placed it in her lap. She stroked the pale cheeks gently even as Katie's eyes flickered open.

"Nick," she said, tears squeezing from her eyes.

"I'm so sorry, my dear," whispered Hannah, her own cheeks wet with tears.

Hannah leaned her head over to hover above Katie's curled figure, and the two women sobbed as the Boston sky fell dark about them, and an early snow drifted silently to the ground outside to cover the thick spread of leaves that lay there. The sounds from the street grew silent as neighbors hurried home for dinner. People returning home to their own apartments moved about them, shaking their heads and tut tutting, wondering what the two young ladies were about, laying on the floor of the foyer like that. As they rested there, the cold of the floor seeped up through Katie's coat and into her body, chilling her to the bone. She wondered how she would be able to go on without Nick. He had been her comfort, her friend, her lover, and now he was gone. What would she do?

Chapter Two

Sacramento

Kristoff Petersen strode down the main street of Sacramento, California, squinting into the morning sun rising over the distant Sierra Nevada mountain range. The sky was lightening to a subtle grey with blue tones near the horizon, and the dark shadows of the storefronts jutted sharply across the dusty street in front of him.

"Howdy, Kristoff. Woohee!" called a feminine voice from above.

Kristoff looked up, shielding his eyes with one hand. He saw Belle Waters leaning out of the top floor of the saloon, her bust spilling out of a bright red corset, her auburn curls loosely trailing across her bare shoulders.

"Hello, Belle, how are you today?"

"I'd be better if you were up here with me. When are you going to make an honest woman out of me?" She winked at him suggestively, and leaned further over the windowsill.

"You know you'd tire of me before sundown, Belle." Kristoff chuckled good-naturedly and waved goodbye to her as he continued walking.

"I'd like to give it a try," she called after him, her laughter echoing down the street as she slipped back through the window and closed it shut behind her.

Kristoff ran his fingers through his short, blonde curls and nodded to a busty woman sweeping the sidewalk in front of the Wesson Bakery. She wore a white bonnet on her head, and her floral print dress was buttoned high beneath her chin.

"Mornin' Mrs. Wesson," he called.

"Mr. Petersen, how are you on this fine morning?" She paused her sweeping for a moment to smile at him.

"I'm doin' well, Ma'am and you?"

"Just fine, just fine. I saw Mayor Jones has started pasting flyers about town already, you gonna run against him this time? You'll get my vote."

"Why thank you, Mrs. Wesson. I appreciate it. I'll let you know, I haven't quite decided yet—not sure if politics is for me."

"That's why you gotta run. You're just the kind of people we need in office."

"I'll keep that in mind. You have a good day now." He tipped his hat, and spun on his heel to continue down the street. Kristoff stopped beneath a hanging sign that read, Petersen Mercantile and Grocery. He studied it for a moment, his hands on his hips, then walked into the store.

"Good morning, sir," called a middle-aged woman who was standing on a step stool dusting a high shelf containing bolts of variously colored and patterned textiles.

"Good morning to you, Mrs. Hutchins," said Kristoff, slipping off his coat and folding it carefully over his arm.

"It's a beautiful day, that's for sure. I hope you didn't stay too late last night taking inventory."

"No, I was out of here by seven o'clock. Did the sugar order come in this morning?" Kristoff strode toward the back of the store. Mrs. Hutchins called after him, "it arrived promptly at six. It's out back where Steve left it."

"Thank you."

Kristoff stepped into his office, and closed the door behind him, looking for a moment through the glass pane at the top of the door to the shop floor beyond. The store was filled with barrels of goods—flour, sugar, apples, oranges, nuts and grains. The outside of the room was lined with shelving holding reams of linens, pre-made clothing, boots, tools, candy and other miscellaneous items. Kristoff scanned the goods with pride. He sold almost everything a person could need within the four walls of his mercantile. And he was known throughout the region as a man of integrity who stocked quality goods at a reasonable price.

He smiled at the clean and ordered efficiency of the layout in front of him. Then he turned on his heel and walked to the desk to sit down. His mind kept wandering back to the same line of thinking that had been occupying his thoughts for months now. On the surface he seemed to have everything a man could desire in life. He was successful, the owner of a reputable business in downtown Sacramento. He was well respected throughout the community, even being considered for the upcoming mayoral election. A deacon at the local Baptist church, he never missed the weekly Bible study.

Yet there was one thing absent in his life. He had no one to share it with. His entire extended family still lived either in Norway or Boston. His parents had emigrated from Norway to Boston when he was four years old. They'd both since died and he'd travelled out to California alone, to try his hand at the pioneering life. Focused on building his career, he hadn't found a lady who'd captured his heart. And now, many years later, he knew that all the success in the world couldn't change the way that he felt deep down inside. Alone.

Chapter Three

Katie lay silently in bed, looking up at the sloping ceiling above her head. Her eyes traced the line of a crack as it snaked through the paint, across the crown molding and down one corner of the wall. Tears trickled over her cheeks, and her hands lay limply on her forehead as she sobbed. Darkness still blanketed the cold room, but dawn was approaching and fingertips of sunlight snuck beneath the curtains.

Today was the day she would say farewell to her husband—Nicholas's funeral was to be held in the small chapel where they'd attended church every Sunday. Katie didn't know how she was going to get through the day. How could she be expected to stand by and watch them bury her husband? It wasn't right. He was too young. They had so much more life to live together. They'd had plans, and dreams. And there was a baby on the way. A baby that Nick had longed for, and now would never know. She buried her face into the downy pillow, and let out a long, low wail. The muffled sound filled the silence of the chilly apartment, and Katie heard her mother-in-law stirring in the living room where she was sleeping on a spare feather bed Katie had borrowed from Hannah, who lived alone down the hall.

"Are you all right?" Elsie whispered from her bed.

"Fine, thank you."

"Shall I make some coffee?"

"Yes, please."

Elsie Pearson, Katie's mother-in-law, was a seamstress. She lived across town on her own in a small boarding room in a working class area of Boston. She had insisted on staying with Katie for the funeral, and Katie was glad of the company. The two women had talked and cried together the previous evening before bed. Katie's eyes felt sore and puffy—she wiped them dry with a handkerchief she'd hidden beneath her pillow. She didn't want Elsie to see her crying. Elsie had enough grief of her own to cope with, she didn't need to shoulder the burden of Katie's grief as well. Katie took a deep breath and rolled out of bed. It was time to face the day.

"We are gathered here to celebrate the life, and to mourn the loss, of one Nicholas Pearson. A beloved son, devoted husband and faithful Christian, he was taken from us all too soon." The minister wore a black suit. His hair was parted in the middle and slicked down against the sides of head. His face was somber as he spoke.

Nicholas's funeral was a small affair. Nick's mother was the only family he had. Some of their friends had taken the day off work to attend the service. A few

men from the construction company were there, along
with several members of their church. Katie scanned
the sanctuary, attempting to take in the rows of faces
since she would be expected to thank them later.

The church building was narrow, with a pointed bell
tower above the chapel and a rectangular hall standing
beside it. Katie sat in the front pew beside a sobbing
Elsie, and stared at the floor as the minister delivered
a blessing over Nick's red cedar casket.

"Yea though I walk through the valley of the shadow
of death, I will fear no evil…"

As his voiced droned on through the ceremony, his
long face regarding the congregation with sympathy,
Katie couldn't shake the feeling that Nick was seated
beside her. They always sat together here, every Sunday morning. Not in this same pew, but in one further
back. They shared a Bible, and stood side-by-side to
sing their favorite hymns in loud voices. They listened
to the sermon with interest, remembering the best parts
to discuss with each other after lunch. And when Nick's
hand grazed hers, she would be transported back to
their evenings, alone, in their apartment, where they
could express their love for each other without holding back.

A tear skidded unimpeded down Katie's cheek, and
she dabbed at her eyes with a blue tartan handkerchief.
Nick's favorite handkerchief. She stashed it back in the
inside pocket of her coat, next to her heart, and patted
it gently before returning her hands to her lap, where
she held them demurely.

The church was decorated only with a few simple
flowers taken from the gardens of those in attendance,

along with long piece of black chiffon draped around the bottom edges of the casket. Katie couldn't afford much for the funeral, but thankfully Nick's mother was helping to cover the costs.

When it was finally over, Katie drew in a deep breath. She had to brace herself for what was coming. She made her way to the front door of the church and stood resolute and strong, as each person paid her their respects. It was a well-intentioned tradition, but she felt as though a thousand knives were digging at her heart. Their sorrow-filled features, their polite remarks, their pity, and their intrusion into her personal grief—it was all too much. She didn't want to share this moment with anyone. It was hers, and she held it close to her chest, burrowing herself deep down into the darkness of it, while smiling dimly at each mourner as they shook her hand and shared with her their words of encouragement.

The burial service afterwards at the graveside was brief, and Katie linked her arm through Elsie's as they walked back to the apartment, their grief echoed in the black of their thick dresses and the lace veils covering their faces. Elsie cried loudly, her arm shaking in Katie's. Katie patted her hand, and thought about the future.

What would she do when the baby came? How would she support this new life? She couldn't keep working with a baby to care for, could she? Would the Sommers family allow her to bring the baby to work with her? Katie worked as a maid for the Sommerses, and they'd always treated her fairly. Maybe they would allow it, and Katie could work and care for the young one. She had to believe that there was a way for her to survive this.

"It's going to be all right," said Elsie, sobbing loudly as she turned her forlorn face toward Katie. She wiped her tears, and clasped Katie's hand in her own.

"Is it?" asked Katie.

"It doesn't seem that way now, but the pain will fade. Not for me—a mother should never have to bury her child. But a wife can move on. I know, I did it. I've lost two husbands in my life, and the pain feels as though it will kill you—but it doesn't. You will endure, my darling, and one day you'll remarry."

"No, don't say that Elsie."

"It's all right, Katie dear. I don't mind. I know that you'll never be able to replace my Nicholas, but he loved you and would want you to be happy. I do so hope you will be again, one day."

Katie considered Elsie's words. In her anguish she had forgotten that Elsie had lost two husbands. She had persisted and had made her own way in the world as a seamstress. It was a hard life, but she had managed to live these past years on her own. Katie couldn't even imagine getting remarried someday. It seemed like a betrayal to Nick for her even to consider the thought. But even as she pushed it out of her mind, another disturbing thought sprang into its place.

The baby.

If she didn't remarry, how would she support and raise her baby? She would speak to her employers tomorrow. If they would let her bring the baby to work with her, perhaps she would be able to manage it all somehow. She patted Elsie's hand again. She had to be strong now, for the baby's sake. She couldn't fall apart, that wouldn't help anyone. She had to focus on finding a way to ensure that she could provide a good life for her baby. That's all that mattered now. That's what Nicholas would want. It's what he would have done.

When they walked into the apartment, Katie noticed Nick's boots sitting against the wall. They still had mud on the toes from when he'd tramped through the park after the last heavy rainfall. Above the boots, his hat sat on the top of the coat rack, and his Sunday coat hung beneath it. The room was cold and empty. Never again would Katie walk through that door to the sound of Nick humming as he polished his shoes. Never again would she be surprised by Nick giving her a hug from behind and a kiss on the cheek as she stirred their supper on the stove top.

Oh God, please let everything be all right. I don't know what to do. I don't know how to fix this. Please help me.

Chapter Four

It had been four weeks since the funeral, and Katie's morning sickness had only gotten worse. Only it wasn't just in the mornings, it was all day long. The smell of food, the sight of it, the feel of it on her tongue—everything sent her running to find a container into which she could throw up. And yet she remained voraciously hungry all of the time. The only thing that made her feel any better was to eat, and so the cycle continued. Her face had become pale and gaunt, and her skin was sallow. She stumbled through each day, wishing she could rest, or at least get a break from the constant nausea.

Elsie had returned home the day after the funeral, waiting while Katie dressed for work. They walked to the coach station together, and it was there that they parted ways. Katie hadn't told Elsie about her pregnancy. She had meant to, but there never seemed to be the right moment for it. She didn't know how to bring joy into the ever-present grief which consumed them both. The only person who knew about the baby was

Hannah, and only then because she had found out before the accident. Katie had told no one since, not even the Sommerses. She had finally worked up the courage to tell them today, and was on her way to work now, her stride steady with resolve.

"I thought pregnant women were supposed to glow," she hissed at Hannah as she passed her in the hall.

"But you are glowing, my dear," replied Hannah, one eyebrow cocked in amusement.

Katie pulled a face at her and opened the foyer doors to step outside into the biting wind. Winter had fallen upon Boston with force now, and a thin layer of frozen snow coated everything about her. The street was white, the bowing branches of black-limbed trees held a deposit of the icy whiteness from the trunk to the tip of each reaching branch. Carriages that had not yet moved in the morning light were blanketed with it, and Katie's feet trudged through it, leaving a trail of dainty dark footprints in her wake.

She shivered and pulled her woolen shawl closer about her thin body. She'd never liked Boston winters. The cold was so biting she could get no comfort. It permeated to her very bones, leaving her in a constant state of unease. The pot-bellied stove in their apartment warmed the small rooms well each evening, but by morning it was frigid again, and Katie couldn't afford to light the fire before work. So, breakfast was a cold piece of bread with a glass of freezing water, and she dressed quickly while her body shivered in the intense cold, her breath leaving small puffs of steam hanging in the air before her.

The Sommers family owned a large house in an

upmarket part of town. It was a long walk for Katie, but she didn't mind. It gave her time to think and the exercise warmed her. She carried an extra piece of bread in her pocket to munch on as she walked, which kept the nausea at bay. She climbed the stairs at the back of the house to the service entrance, and rapped quietly on the door. It was opened shortly by a portly, older woman, Mrs. Pierce. As the housekeeper, Mrs. Pierce lived with the family and managed the household staff. She was a brusque but kindly woman. She walked with a slight limp after a childhood accident left one leg shorter than the other.

"Good morning, Mrs. Pierce," said Katie, reaching for a peg by the door where her apron was hung.

"Good morning to you, Katie dear. And how are you today? It's a cold one, isn't it?"

"Yes, Ma'am. I'm well thank you."

"You best get started with the breakfast tray. Mrs. Sommers is expecting hers early today, since she has the meeting of the Booster Club over at the church this morning."

"Yes, Mrs. Pierce." Katie hurried to the kitchen counter where a tray filled with coffee, milk, croissants, jam and a thick slice of yellow butter stood waiting. She picked it up, and pushed her way backwards through the swinging doors and out into the main house. Walking smartly to the stairs, she paused at the bottom, fighting back a wave of sickness. The scent of the croissants wafted around her, and her stomach growled in complaint. She breathed slowly, then climbed the stairs, her black heels clacking on the marble.

Even though Katie had worked for the Sommerses for three years, she never tired of marveling at the beauty of their home. Above the marble staircase hung a set of three matching canvases. Each one was painted in dark colors, with a likeness of the three most recent generations of Sommers men. Every corner of each room in the house was decorated with a vase, a table or a statue of some kind. Luxurious rugs, imported from exotic places like Turkey and Italy, graced the floors, and fresh hothouse flowers filled the house with an enticing fragrance. Katie smiled as she summited the staircase, and turned down the hall toward Mrs. Sommers' room. She rapped gently on the door.

"Enter," came a high voice from within.

"Good morning, Mrs. Sommers," said Katie, walking into the bedroom, and placing the tray down on a sumptuous cedar dresser.

Mrs. Sommers was standing in front of a full-length mirror, holding an emerald dress in front of her silk nightgown.

"Katie dear, what do you think of this gown?" she asked, spinning right and left as she studied herself.

"It's beautiful," said Katie, pouring coffee into a china cup that squatted upon a matching saucer on the breakfast tray.

"Do you think it would suit New York society though? Oh, of course you wouldn't know, would you? You've never been there?"

"No, Ma'am. I never have, but I'm sure it would do well there just the same."

Katie sliced open a croissant and buttered it thickly,

then dabbed the fruity jam across the butter. "Are you going to New York, Ma'am?" she asked.

"Yes, we're moving there next week. Didn't Mrs. Pierce tell you yet? Oh dear, I thought she would have mentioned it by now. The whole family is moving. We're selling this house, you see. Mr. Sommers has been transferred to the New York office, and we've taken a house just outside the city. I declare, I have so much work to do I don't know where to start. Men don't think about these things, you see. They say, 'I'll take this job, and I'll take that house', never stopping for a moment to consider how much work it will cause their poor wives."

Katie stood still, her mouth open, and she gasped. "Do you mean—will you be selling this house? Will you still be needing me?"

"I'm afraid we have to sell. I'm sure you'll find something else to suit you in no time though. I wouldn't fret. A pretty young girl like you…you'll be snatched up as quick as a wink."

"Oh," was all Katie could think to say. Her face felt flushed, and nausea swept over her again. She rushed from the room and down to the kitchen, before throwing up in a clean bowl sitting on the bench awaiting the ingredients for the day's baking.

"What's wrong with you?" asked Mrs. Pierce suspiciously.

Katie wiped her mouth with the back of her hand, tears pricking her blue eyes.

"Mrs. Sommers says they're moving to New York."

Mrs. Pierce walked to her, and lay one hand on

Katie's arm. "I'm sorry Katie. I was going to tell you this morning."

"I need this job, Mrs. Pierce."

"You'll find another, my dear."

"I hope so."

"I'm sure you will. I wish I could have given you more notice, but the whole thing has been rather last minute. I'm the only member of staff to keep their job since I'll be moving with the family. Other than me, they're hiring an entirely new staff when we get to New York. I'm sorry. I will give you a reference, my dear."

Mrs. Pierce left the room, and Katie stood in the quiet, her thoughts jumbling together as panic gripped her. What would she do now? She had been counting on this job to support her and the baby. Now, in a moment, that hope was gone. If she didn't find another job before her pregnancy started to show, she'd never find one. Even if she did find one, they'd be unlikely to keep her on after the baby came. Katie lay one hand protectively across her stomach. It wouldn't be long before she would be unable to hide the swell of her growing abdomen. She considered the young life budding inside her. What kind of life would this baby have? What would it be like? How could she give this child everything she wanted to? She was an unemployed widow. All her life she'd seen women begging on street corners, their children starving, unwashed and even abandoned, and she'd wondered what had happened in their lives to bring such destitution. Now she knew. Katie gripped the edge of the counter, and leaned on it, loud, heaving sobs wracked her thin body and as she let them out they echoed in the empty kitchen.

Chapter Five

Trudging up the front steps to the stoop of the apartment building, Katie paused to knock the snow from her shoes. The landlord was there, sweeping out the foyer again. He tipped back his bowler hat, and stared at her through beady, dark eyes.

"Evening, Mrs. Pearson," he said.

"Good evening, Mr. Hungerford."

"Everything all right?" he asked, no doubt sensing her fear and frustration.

"Yes, everything's fine, thank you. I might be a bit late with rent next month, though."

"You know, I've got a job for you, if you need it." He watched her closely, leaning on the end of the broom.

"A job? What kind of job?"

"All ya have to do is keep some nice gentlemen company—that pretty face of yours, it'll be a piece of cake."

"Keep gentlemen company?" Katie's eyes clouded over, and she sighed before heading for the staircase to her apartment. "No, thank you, Mr. Hungerford. I'm not interested in a job of that kind."

"Well, never mind. I'm sure you'll come around sometime. You just let me know when you're ready to take that step. There'll be no extensions on the rent 'round here Missy. And there ain't many jobs about these parts for a young girl on her own neither. You'll get hungry one day, you just remember me when you do."

Katie shot a look of disgust over her shoulder, and continued toward her apartment.

"Don't forget rent is due Monday, not a day later," he called up to her, before returning to his sweeping, his loud chortle echoing about the cold foyer.

When Katie reached her front door, she found Hannah bent down on one knee, sliding something beneath the frame. Hannah's soft brown locks were caught up in a ponytail and curled into thick ringlets. She wore a short brown cloak around her shoulders over a fashionable green velveteen dress. Katie's heart warmed to see her there.

"Hannah," cried Katie, her face breaking into the first smile of the day.

Hannah stood to her feet and the two women embraced.

"I was just leaving you a note asking you to come for dinner this evening, but since you're here I can ask you in person."

"I'd love to," said Katie, relaxing her shoulders and reaching for one of Hannah's hands to squeeze it. "I've had a horrible day, and dinner with you is just what I need to make it better."

"Well then, get washed up and come right over. I've made a fresh jug of iced tea, and I even bought a lemon to squeeze into it, so you're in for a treat."

"I'm looking forward to it." Katie took her apartment key out of her purse and opened the door as Hannah disappeared down the hall. She pushed the door open, and walked inside. She dropped her purse on the foyer table, and the sound of it echoed hollowly about the room. The cold emptiness of the apartment hit her like a slap across the face, and she slumped into a wicker rocking chair. Smoothing fly-away strands of hair back into the bun that was curled tightly at the nape of her neck, she sat still for a few moments and sighed into the stillness. Then, she reached for the nearby washstand. The washbasin contained cold water from that morning, and she used it to wipe down her face and wash her hands and arms. Patting herself dry with a towel that hung from a thin wire on the washstand, she stood to her feet and took a deep breath.

The silence of the apartment sent a shiver through her body. She'd have to get used to coming home to a quiet, dark room. She didn't know how she could ever become accustomed to being completely alone in the world. For the first time in a long time, the pain of missing her parents had come back to roost in her chest. It perched heavily alongside her grief over Nicholas. The pain of it seemed to squeeze the breath from her lungs. Katie shook her head. She didn't want to burden Hannah with her grief. She pushed a smile onto her face and walked into the hallway, then pulled the door closed and locked it behind her.

Hannah's apartment was just like Katie's. She was always in awe that Hannah lived so happily on her own. She'd always been too afraid to live by herself, not that she could have afforded to on a maid's wage. But now she was alone as well, and having Hannah just down the hall was a big comfort to her.

The living room was small but cozy, and Hannah had knitted and crocheted colorful cushion covers, throws and rugs to decorate the space, making it feel warm and homey. Her furniture had been purchased second-hand, but it was sturdy and functional and Katie felt a sense of peace settle over her for the first time since Nicholas' accident, even if for just a moment.

They sat down to a meal of chicken and dumplings, along with a tall glass each of iced tea with a luxurious slice of lemon. Katie smiled at Hannah, her stomach rumbled and lurched as she breathed in the tasty aroma.

"This looks delicious, Hannah. Thank you for inviting me, I feel much better already."

They said grace together, linking hands across the small round table, and then each of them dipped their spoons into the steaming soup, sipping gently so as not to scorch their tongues.

"Now tell me, my dear, why was your day so horrible?" asked Hannah.

Katie chewed slowly, savoring the flavor of chicken, and the richness of the dumpling in her mouth. She swallowed and the ill feeling passed, for the moment.

"I lost my job," she whispered, staring down into her bowl.

"Oh no! What happened?" asked Hannah, dropping her spoon into her bowl with a sudden splash.

"Oh dear, the soup has splattered all over your lovely dress," said Katie, handing her napkin to Hannah who wiped herself dry. "Well, the Sommerses are moving to New York. There was nothing I could do about it, they're moving and don't need me anymore. And of course, they know nothing about the baby so they assume I'll be fine. They assured me I'd find another job in no time at all, which of course I know is almost an impossibility—especially finding something before I start to show. And anyway, even if I do, as soon as they see my growing belly I'm sure they'll fire me. No one wants to see a pregnant maid plodding about their house and kneeling to scrub the floorboards." Katie gave a hollow laugh, and ladled another spoonful of soup into her mouth.

"What are you going to do?" asked Hannah, sipping her tea.

"I don't know. The only family I have is Nick's mother, and she's barely making ends meet as it is. I don't want to burden her with having to look after me and a newborn as well. I really don't know what to do. I'm completely overwhelmed; it's an impossible situation."

At that, Katie burst into sudden tears, and Hannah sat across from her, her eyes full of pity. She stood to her feet and carried her chair around to sit beside Katie. Taking her friend's hand in one of her own, she patted her gently on the back.

"Why don't you stay here, then?"

Katie looked up at Hannah, her big, blue eyes full of tears, her face red and covered with blotches. "With you? Really?"

"Yes, really. It's just a quick move down the hall… simple. You can live here as long as you need to. Maybe you'll find a job, but even if you don't you can stay here. I have a steady job at the school, and my wage covers the rent here as well as enough food for both of us. We'll have to share a bed for now so it'll be a squeeze, but we can do it. Please, won't you consider it?"

"I don't want to bother you. You have your own life, and I'm just about to bring a small, screaming baby into the world. I'm afraid you'd not get much sleep, and you need your rest so that you can teach your students. I know first-hand how challenging those students can be, since I was one of them not so very long ago."

"I don't mind. Really—what choice do you have? Where else can you go? And I'd love to have you here. It would be such fun."

"If you'll have me, I'd really like that," said Katie, embracing her friend and sobbing into her shoulder.

"That's settled then. You can tell Silas Hungerford that you're giving up your apartment before the rent is due on Monday. We'll gather your things and move them in here. It will be perfect."

"All right. I'll do it. Thank you, Hannah, you're a true friend."

Hannah returned to her seat, and Katie dug into her meal with gusto. Somehow it seemed to taste richer, fuller, and more appetizing than it had a moment ago. She drew in a deep breath and smiled. Things were looking brighter already. She didn't have a way to support herself and the baby when it finally came, but at least now they'd have a roof over their heads. She knew that she wouldn't be able to take advantage of Hannah's hospitality forever, but Hannah's offer had lifted a heavy weight from her tired shoulders, and she'd figure the rest of it out later. She sent up a silent prayer of thanksgiving as she scraped her bowl clean and coyly asked Hannah for more.

Chapter Six

Kristoff pushed a pile of letters to one side of his desk. Reaching for the top drawer he pulled out a ledger, and set it on the desk in front of him. Selecting a quill, he twirled it between his fingers for a moment, lost in thought. One of the letters caught his attention. He picked it up and flipped it over. It was from his cousin, Hannah Petersen, in Boston. He poked about in the drawer again and pulled out a letter opener, slipped it into the opening at the top of the envelope, and deftly sliced the paper open. A piece of stationery decorated around the edges with a lush green vine sprouting pink flowers fell out onto the desk. He picked it up and began to read.

Dearest Kristoff,
I was so glad to receive your letter yesterday. I couldn't wait to respond, but had to visit Aunt Agatha after church, and spent the afternoon reading to her from Milton's Comus. She sends you her regards, and asks me to inform you that

her lungs are not what they used to be and she is unlikely to be able to visit over the summer as she had promised you.

I was sorry to hear of your loneliness. We wish you could return to Boston to be with the rest of the family. But since that seems unlikely, given your great successes in Sacramento, I recommend you find a wife. You mentioned that there is a lack of suitable prospects in your current circle of acquaintances. I have a potential mate I would urge you to consider.

A former student of mine, a Mrs. Katie Pearson, has been recently widowed when her husband was killed in a construction site accident. She has no family of her own, and I'm sure would consider an engagement to an upstanding gentleman like yourself. I have not approached her about this matter, but first wanted to hear what you thought of the idea.

I know that it is somewhat unusual to consider an engagement to someone you have never yet laid eyes upon, but in this case I believe it would be a good match. Katie is sweet, intelligent and thoughtful. She is as pretty as a peach on a summer's day, and I consider her my closest friend. I would indeed miss her if she were to leave, but her happiness and yours mean so much to me that I would be willing to bear it.

Please write in reply to let me know if I should ask her about it.

Your cousin,

Hannah

Kristoff folded the letter and returned it to the envelope, his face thoughtful. He selected a clean sheet of paper from the second drawer, and lifted the quill to dip into the ink pot at the top of the desk. His chest hammered loudly, as he considered his cousin's proposition. The longer he contemplated it, the more it made sense. For generations people had been selecting spouses for family members. It was a sensible way to ensure that a potential match met all the requirements of temperament, birth and values that were so important in a marriage. He trusted Hannah's judgement implicitly. Perhaps this young widow might be the answer to his prayers. He lowered his head to write a response, the pen moving quickly across the cream-colored page leaving a trail of sloping black letters in its wake.

Chapter Seven

Hannah Petersen hoisted the bag of groceries over her shoulder, and braced herself against the frigid wind that howled about her. She wrapped her scarf around her head and over her hair, then shoved her hands back into a warm fur muffler that hung from her matching fur-lined brown cloak. The trees banking the street were bare. Their dark branches looked dead against the grey sky, but she knew that in a few months' time green shoots would work their way out and a new season of life would begin.

As she approached the apartment building, she pushed her way through the front door. The wind whistled loudly as it skidded through the small opening, and a flurry of leaves blew in at her feet. She pushed the door closed behind her, locking out the noise and cold.

Square mail boxes lined one wall in the foyer, and she lay the groceries on a table beside them. She opened her box and pulled out a thin stack of letters, flicking quickly through them and scanning the return address on each. There was a letter from her aunt in

Philadelphia, a bill from the gas company, and a letter from her cousin, Kristoff Petersen, in Sacramento,
California. She flung the strap of her grocery bag over
one shoulder and tramped up the stairs as quickly as
she could. She couldn't wait to open the letter from
her cousin.

They'd always been close as children. She remembered fondly a tree house he'd built in the back yard
with his father, and he'd let her climb up there with
him to play. He was always so kind to her, pretending
to sip tea from floral china cups whenever she wanted.
In return, she joined in his hunting expeditions around
the base of the large oak tree that housed his cubby,
always making sure to miss her target since even in
her imagination she couldn't bear to kill one of God's
creatures. Kristoff was so kind and patient with his
older cousin. She could still picture his cute little face
peering over the top rung of the ladder as he climbed
into the tree house carrying his stick rifle in one hand,
his blue eyes wide as he described his latest adventure
to her in detail.

Hannah unloaded the groceries down on the counter
top, then hurried to her rocking chair. She slid the mail
onto the coffee table and sat down with the letter from
Kristoff in her hands. She tore it open, and pulled out
the thin sheets of paper that were covered with Kristoff's familiar scrawl. Just as she finished reading the
final line of the letter, she heard raised voices in the
hallway. She crept to the door and inched it open, focusing one eye through the gap between the door and
the doorframe. She could see Katie standing in the hall-

way, her back to Hannah. The landlord, Silas Hungerford, stood on the opposite side facing her.

"I told you that rent was due Monday, and I still haven't seen it. I've got a feeling you haven't got it for me, ain't that right honey?" He grinned lasciviously at Katie.

Hannah's stomach lurched. She'd never seen this side of her landlord before, and it sparked her anger.

"I told you last Saturday that I was moving in with Hannah Petersen. I won't be keeping my apartment. You can let it to someone else. Thank you, Mr. Hungerford." Katie turned to leave, but he frowned angrily at her and grabbed for her arm, tugging hard on it.

"Hold on there, Missy. What if I can't find someone to let it on such short notice? You'll still owe me rent, since you didn't give me time to look for a new tenant."

"My lease expired a year ago, Mr. Hungerford," sighed Katie, pushing his fingers from her forearm. "I don't owe you anything."

"You'll come work for me one day, honey. I can see it in your future," he called after her retreating back.

Hannah hurried to sit in her rocking chair as Katie walked through the door and into the apartment, her face flushed red. Hannah's heart was pounding in her chest. How dare he speak to Katie that way? She wondered if he'd done it before. Katie kept so many things to herself, and rarely confided in anyone. Hannah had been surprised that she even let her know that she lost her job, since Hannah usually had to pry to get even the slightest detail through Katie's closed lips.

"How was your day?" asked Hannah, slipping the

letter from Kristoff back into the envelope and placing it on the coffee table with the other mail.

"OK." Katie smiled wanly at her, and set about making coffee in the small kitchen. She opened up the stove and stoked the fire within. Adding another piece of wood, she stoked it again and then lay the poker back in its stand beside the stove. She filled the kettle with water, then sat it on top of the stove to boil. Standing on tip-toe, she reached high and opened a small cabinet above her head to retrieve the coffee, sugar and condensed milk.

"Coffee?" she asked Hannah.

"Yes, please." Hannah cleared her throat. "What did Mr. Hungerford want?"

"Oh, he was only telling me I owed him rent on the other apartment. It's nothing. He can't make me pay. I didn't have a lease with him. He's just trying to pressure me into taking a job with him is all."

"A job. Well that's great. Isn't it?"

Katie's face colored as she lifted the singing kettle from the stove top with a rag to keep her hand from burning.

"No, he wants me to—entertain gentlemen."

"Entertain gentlemen? Oh dear," said Hannah, realization causing anger to boil inside her again. "The hide of that man. As though you are the sort of woman…"

"Well, in a way, I suppose I am," whispered Katie, as she spooned coffee into their cups.

"What on earth do you mean?" sputtered Hannah.

"I mean, those ladies no doubt started out with good intentions. Then circumstances beyond their control pushed them to the point of desperation. They must have had no other choice. Don't you think? At least, that's the way I see it. If it weren't for you, I could be one of those ladies. I would like to think that I wouldn't do it, but really—what would someone do if they were homeless, starving and pregnant and didn't have a friend like you to turn to?"

Katie looked at Hannah with wide eyes, her face full of gratitude toward Hannah. Until that moment, Hannah hadn't realized the weighty burden that Katie must have been shouldering all this time. She'd never really thought through what would have happened to Katie if she hadn't stepped in to help her. But of course, now that Katie pointed it out, Hannah knew she was right, and she was glad that she'd been able to help keep Katie away from the grasp of men like Silas Hungerford.

"Well, you're not going to be in that situation as long as I have breath in my body, my dear. You'll stay with me for as long as you need to."

Spotting the letter from Kristoff out of the corner of her eye, Hannah smoothed her hair and strolled to the other side of the room and back again. Katie was sweetening the coffee with sugar and stirred a spoonful of condensed milk into each one. She handed Hannah a cup, and the two women stood together silently for a moment, savoring the warmth of the strong drink.

"Speaking of the future, have you ever considered that you might re-marry one day?" asked Hannah.

Katie's face blanched, and she choked on a mouthful of coffee.

Gathering herself, she responded, "I've thought about it, but it's really a bit soon for me to consider seriously. I know it would probably be what's best for the baby, to have a father to provide for us. And if I can't find a job, it may be that I'll have to think more about it. But it's just so hard for me to comprehend the idea, with Nick buried so recently. I still feel so wretched, really, and the idea of loving another man— well, I just can't imagine I'll be able to do that for a long time, if ever again."

Hannah hid her disappointment and forged ahead.

"I understand dear. But can I broach the subject for just a moment longer? Would you mind very much?"

Katie nodded reluctantly, so Hannah continued.

"I don't know if you remember me speaking of my cousin, Kristoff Petersen, in Sacramento—do you?"

"Yes, I remember you talking about him very fondly. He was your childhood playmate, wasn't he?"

"That's right—that was Kristoff. Well, he's living out in California. He has his own mercantile store there. It's very successful from what I understand, and he's even considering running for mayor. The towns-folk there hold him in very high regard."

"Oh, that sounds exciting," said Katie, sipping her coffee slowly.

"The only problem is, there are very few eligible young ladies out there in California. It's pioneer country, you know, so most of the women are married. They've travelled out there with husbands to start a new life. Very few single women travel out there alone, and those who do aren't usually suitable for someone like Kristoff. He's lonely. He wants to get married, but he can't find anyone he feels would make a good wife and mother to his children."

Katie watched Hannah's face, sudden understanding dawning.

"I told him about you," said Hannah.

"What do you mean? What did you tell him?" asked Katie.

"That you were newly widowed, and living with me. That you're clever, funny and beautiful, and that I thought the two of you would make an excellent match."

"Is that all you said?"

"I didn't tell him you're pregnant, if that's what you mean."

Katie blushed. "And what did he say?"

"I received this letter from him today. He'd like for you to write to him. He says he trusts my judgment, and that you might just be the answer to his prayers."

"He said that?"

"He did. What do you think?"

"I don't know. It's so soon."

"It is very quick. I know that. But I also know that you'll be showing soon, and your options will change very quickly after that. I want the best for you, Katie, you know that, dear. And I think that Kristoff would be the very best for you. He's the kindest, gentlest, most handsome man I've ever known. If he wasn't my cousin and childhood friend, I'd have married him years ago. I don't want you to leave. You're a dear friend. But I honestly do believe that he'd make you happy. I know you may not be able to love him right away, because your heart still aches for Nicholas, but I also believe with everything that's in me—that you will grow to love him, given time."

Katie listened quietly to Hannah's words. She turned the coffee cup around in her hands and watched the fire in the stove cracking through the open door. Walking to the stove, she closed the cast iron door quickly, and then turned to face Hannah.

"You're right. I don't have many options. It may be that I will have to re-marry, but I can't think about it yet. I'm going to do my best to find some work. Maybe I can do this on my own. Or, maybe I'm being naïve to think that I can do it. But either way, I can't imagine loving again. Not yet."

Hannah nodded silently. "I thought you might feel that way. Will you consider writing to him anyway? I know he will enjoy having someone to share letters with, at the very least."

"I would be happy to," said Katie, taking Hannah's hand in hers. "You're so kind to me, Hannah Petersen." She smiled. "And who knows, maybe one day I'll be ready to love again."

"If not, at least we have each other," grinned Hannah.

Chapter Eight

The weeks passed by slowly, and Katie spent every waking moment walking the streets of Boston looking for work. She called at every house that she knew employed a staff; she applied at restaurants, and she even asked at a garment factory. But everywhere she went, she received the same response: they didn't have any current openings and would keep her in mind if something came up. It didn't help that she looked thin and pale, and often had to run from the interview to throw up. Within not much more than a few weeks, she would no longer be able to hide her swelling abdomen under full skirts, and then job hunting would become impossible.

After a full day of job searching, Katie was on her way home when she spotted Hannah standing with Fred Tundrell in the park. The light about them was growing dim as the sun set behind the Boston skyline. Street lamps from the surrounding park cast a dim glow over the green grasses, dormant flower beds and steel benches. The remnants of a thin snow lay about them on the ground. Dressed in her long, brown coat with the fur-trimmed collar, Hannah was standing with her back to Fred. Her mahogany hair was caught up in the front with pins, and then flowed down her back in the modern style. She was laughing at something he'd said and throwing pieces of bread to a few squirrels that darted about her feet, their tails twitching back and forth as they begged for food. Then, Katie saw him grab her by the arm, spin her about and kiss her full on the mouth.

Katie gasped in surprise. She knew that Fred had been courting Hannah recently, but the kiss between then took her breath away. She turned her back on them, her face flushing with warmth. Hurrying home, she couldn't get that kiss out of her mind. The impulsiveness, the tenderness, the urgency—and most of all, the love behind that kiss reminded her so much of Nick that her stomach twisted into knots. She was certain of one thing, that kiss signaled the end of her stay with Hannah. There was only one place where a kiss like that led, and it was directly to the altar. She ran toward the apartment, choking back tears. Tears of grief, jealousy, joy and fear over the unknown future that lay stretched out before her.

Hannah had offered to let her stay even after the baby was born, but that wouldn't be practical if Hannah was to be married. A newlywed couple wouldn't want a widow and her newborn living with them. Suddenly everything in Katie's world was shrouded in uncertainty again. Where would she go now? She had to take matters into her own hands. She had to do what was best for the baby, no matter how badly it made her feel. She didn't have the luxury of doing what she wanted to do anymore. The unborn child within her deserved more than that, and she would do whatever it took to ensure that the baby was born into a safe, secure and loving world.

Katie sat at the table, a blank sheet of paper in front of her. Then, holding the pen steady in her hand, she dabbed the nib into an ink pot, and blotted it on a scrap of envelope near her elbow. What should she write to a man she'd never met? Where could she even begin? She'd been trying so hard to find work, but nothing had panned out yet. She knew that given time she'd be able to find some kind of employment, but time was something she didn't have much of. It was possible she could court a gentleman in Boston, but that too would take time. She'd never be able to hide her pregnancy throughout a courtship, and who would want a pregnant fiancée? Since the Civil War ended, there was a short-age of men in the east anyway. Those who had sur-vived the war and returned to Boston could take their pick of eligible wives—they weren't likely to choose a pregnant widow.

Every corner she turned in Boston, something re-minded her of Nick and their life together. Every way she spun it, the idea of marrying a handsome and kind gentleman from California made rational sense. It scared her half to death, but it appealed to her de-sire for security at the same time. She needed a change of scenery, and the excitement of an adventure in the west sent a throb of adrenalin pumping through her veins. A marriage of convenience could be undertaken quickly without raising suspicions, and she'd have plenty of time after the wedding to share her condition with Kristoff. No doubt he'd be displeased with her secrecy, but he couldn't turn her away once she was his wife, could he?

Katie hated to be dishonest with anyone, and the idea of hurting Kristoff, even though she'd never met him, sent a pang of anxiety through her chest and into her stomach.

What really matters is the child growing inside of me. I'll do anything to keep it safe and secure. If wounding someone or being untruthful protects my child, I'll do it. I'll even marry a stranger if it means that I won't have to give up my baby to be raised by strangers, and I'll be able to provide a roof over my child's head and food in its stomach. I will do what I have to in order to look after my child, and Kristoff may just be the answer to all my problems.

Katie lowered her pen to the paper, and began to write.

Dear Mr. Petersen,

I'm delighted to be able to write to you. Hannah has told me so much about you. She sings your praises all day long. I must admit that I'm intrigued to find out more about California and your life there. Tell me, do you attend a church?

Hannah and I attend the local Baptist church. It's a small gathering, but we enjoy it and also attend Bible Study on Wednesday evenings at the pastor's house.

I have lived in Boston my whole life, and I love

it here. Losing my husband recently, though, has given me reason to desire a change.

I was working for a family nearby until a few weeks ago, but they have since moved to New York, so I am currently searching for a new position.

I hope that we can correspond and be friends. Hannah has convinced me that you are one of the very best of men.
Yours sincerely,
Katie Pearson.

Katie closed the envelope then dripped hot wax from her candle onto the back of it. She reached for her seal, and pressed it into the wax. After sealing the envelope she held it to her chest, her eyes closed. She felt so unsure about this courtship, but at the same time she couldn't see any other way forward. Hannah was such a trusted friend and Katie was certain that she wouldn't lead her astray. As confusion overwhelmed her, she clung to that fact. She stood and grabbed her shawl, wrapped it around her shoulders and carried the letter to the Post Office. She'd just have to trust God with her situation. There was nothing more she could do.

Kristoff stared at the letter in his hands. The writing on the front of the envelope was neat and simple, the lettering clean and perfectly formed. It was the writing of a woman, and his heart raced as he read the return address. Katie Pearson. He knew so little about her, yet every little piece of information his cousin revealed about her made him want to know more. She sounded kind, funny, compassionate and tender. Everything he wanted in a wife. And according to Hannah, she was quite beautiful as well. He found it hard to believe that a woman could be all of those things at once, and yet he found himself excited at the prospect of reading her letter.

He opened it quickly and pulled out the single sheet of paper. He drew in a deep breath, taking in its scent. It smelled of rose water and something else, perhaps lavender. He read the letter and then dropped it onto his desk. The note was sweet but not particularly revealing. He felt as though he knew little more about the author of the letter than he did before reading it. Yet still, there was something about Katie Pearson that niggled at him. He wanted to meet her, he wanted to know more about her, but how could he? They lived on opposite sides of the country.

The only way to meet her was to send for her, since he couldn't leave the shop for the time it would take him to get to Boston and back. And, if he sent for her—a single woman, travelling alone to meet him— he'd have to make a commitment. Was he ready for that? Could he trust his cousin's word enough to take on a wife? What if they didn't get along? What if she was completely unappealing in every way? Surely Hannah wouldn't recommend someone like that—she knew him so well. No, he trusted her judgment. He knew that she wouldn't have given such a glowing appraisal of anyone unworthy of it. Katie Pearson must be everything Hannah said she was, and if that were so, then he just had to meet her. He'd send a train ticket with the next letter, and a proposal along with it.

Kristoff shivered at the prospect. He was a man of common sense. He always carefully considered every decision he ever made. He dwelt upon life-changing decisions for the length of time that befit the situation. How could he marry someone he'd never met on the recommendation of a cousin he hadn't seen in years? He shook his head and rested his arms on the desk, his heart pounding. What was he about to do?

Whatever the outcome, one thing was certain—his life would never be the same. But whether or not that would be a good thing remained to be seen. He lifted his hand from the desk, and pulled a clean sheet of paper from the stack in the drawer. It was time to write a proposal, and then what happened next would be in God's hands.

Chapter Nine

Katie's hands shook as she held the letter from Kristoff. A train ticket had fallen to the table beneath the letter when she pulled it from the envelope, and she knew what it meant the moment the gold lettering caught her eye.

Boston to Sacramento—One Way.

The ticket was clear. Kristoff wanted her to come to California, with no prospect of returning. That meant one thing—marriage.

She opened the letter and read its contents. It was a gentle, loving and romantic proposal, and her heart thumped in her chest as she read the words.

I would be honored if you would come to California and be my wife.

Be his wife. Be someone's wife other than Nicholas's. Katie shivered, and dropped the letter to the table where it covered the ticket. What would her answer be? She'd been working toward this outcome with their correspondence, yet now that it had arrived she wasn't sure what she should do—what she wanted to do. It had happened faster than she'd expected it to, she'd only written to him once. But considering her expanding waistline, faster was better than slower. And really, did she have any other choice? There was really no other option that made sense. Not if she wanted to keep her baby and raise it herself. And in her mind, that wasn't a question. She'd sooner die than let her child be raised by anyone else. She picked up the ticket and held it close to read it over again.

Boston to Sacramento. No return date.

Just then, Hannah pushed open the apartment door and tramped in from the cold, stamping her feet as she wiped them enthusiastically on the door mat.

"Hi, Katie," she said, brushing snowflakes from her coat onto the floor about her. "Brrr, it's frosty out there. It's started snowing again, and I do believe it will be a white Christmas. I love it when the ground is covered in a carpet of white for the Christmas holiday, don't you? Although, I do have to say that when it begins to melt and the entire ground beneath starts to show through and becomes muddy, I always wish it hadn't snowed after all."

She stopped when she saw Katie's pale face. "What is it?"

"Kristoff has proposed." Katie held the ticket up for her to see. Hannah rushed over and grabbed it into her still-gloved hands. She squealed with delight, holding it under the candle to read the words inked in black across the page.

"Oh Katie, I'm so pleased. You will tell him about the baby now, won't you?"

"Oh yes, of course," said Katie, feeling a flush of

warmth travel across her features. "Do you really think I should marry him?" she asked, her voice betraying her anxiety.

Hannah knelt beside Katie and took her hands in her own, the wetness of the melted snow on the gloves coating Katie's hands. "I really think you should. I promise you that I believe you will be a good match—the best match. The two of you are suited to each other in so many ways. He is handsome, kind, hard-working and good. You are pretty, sweet, compassionate and good. And together, you'll be perfect. I wouldn't say it if I didn't truly believe it."

Katie looked deep into Hannah's earnest brown eyes, and knew what her decision would be. "OK, I'll do it. I guess this means I'm moving to Sacramento. Although I'll miss you, my dear Hannah."

The two women jumped to their feet and embraced. Both crying tears of joy, and also tears of grief over parting. Katie wondered what it would be like to leave behind everything and everyone she knew and loved in the world, and move to the other side of the country—to the frontier of civilization. Even though it made her heart quicken at the prospect, it didn't sadden her the way she'd expected it to. Perhaps she was more ready for this change than she had realized. Either way, she was certain it was going to be an adventure she'd never forget.

Chapter Ten

Katie stood in front of the stove, her apron snug about her waist, and stirred a bubbling pot of pea and ham soup. Her eyes were dreamy, and as she secured a loose strand of hair into a hair pin, she soaked in memories of Nicholas. The day they met on the school playground, when he ran past her trundling a hoop with a short stick. The hoop had knocked against her foot, and landed on the ground before her. Nicholas bent down to retrieve it, and glanced up at her with a smile before going on his way. His green eyes flashed with mischief, and she was smitten.

If only they'd been able to grow old together, like they planned. It didn't seem fair to have him taken from her when they were still so young, and with a baby on the way. A baby he didn't even get a chance to find out about, let alone know. Katie felt the warmth of a tear trickling down her cheek, and used her apron to wipe it away. The sound of a key in the lock startled her, and she pinched her cheeks with her fingers to draw some color into them, pasting a smile on her face.

Hannah rushed into the room, her hair in disarray, her eyes shining with joy.

"Well, look at you," said Katie, taking the soup from the stove and placing it on the countertop. "You look like you've got something exciting to share."

"You'll never guess what's happened."

"No, I won't, so go ahead and tell me."

"Fred proposed! We're getting married in the Spring!"

Katie stood still for a single moment and grief flitted across her face. She banished it with a grin and walked to Hannah with wide open arms. As she threw her arms around Hannah's tall frame, she whispered in her ear, "That is such great news, my dear. I'm so happy for you."

Hannah bounded away, spinning about the room.

"I'm so excited, I just can't contain myself. I mean, I'm getting on in years you know, I'll be eight and twenty this year. And for some reason, I thought that perhaps it was never going to happen for me. That maybe I'd never find that special person. But Fred is— well, he's so very special and so wonderful. I can't quite believe I'm going to be his wife. He chose me!"

"Well, I can." Katie returned to the soup, ladling it into two enamel bowls. "You are warm, and beautiful, and generous—what man wouldn't love to call you his wife. Fred is a lucky fellow."

Katie carried the bowls of soup to the table, and returned to the kitchen to fetch spoons.

"I'm sure the two of you will be ridiculously happy together, and I can't wait to hear all about the wedding."

Hannah's face dropped. "You won't be coming?"

Katie sighed. "I just don't know. Will Kristoff want me to return to Boston so soon after we're married?"

"I don't think he'd mind. Although, I know it is a long journey for you to take twice in such a short space of time, especially in your condition. I will understand if you can't make it—although I hadn't really considered that when we agreed to a Spring wedding. Perhaps we should get married before you leave, or we could do it after the baby comes."

Katie took Hannah's hands in her own and stared into her large, brown eyes. "No, dear Hannah. You should get married in Spring. Before I leave is too soon, and after the baby comes is too long for you lovebirds to wait. I will promise to do my best to be here. And if I'm not, then you'll know my thoughts and prayers are with you."

Hannah slumped into her seat at the table, and lay her chin in her hands. She looked deflated.

"Please don't let it upset you. This is a big day—you should be ecstatic."

"I am ecstatic, honestly I am. It's just that I'm finally realizing this is how it's going to be from now on. We're going to be living separate lives—we'll hardly ever see each other again."

Hannah's mouth turned downward, and tears filled her eyes.

Katie's eyes glistened too, and she felt a thick lump forming in her throat. She pushed it down and said, "That is true. But we'll write, all the time. So it will seem as though we're never apart."

"Yes, all the time—do you promise?"

"I promise."

***

It was Christmas Day, yet Katie didn't feel particularly festive. The day had arrived, cold and dark, and Katie had welcomed it with tears and a nose that was red from blowing into Nicholas's old, blue handkerchief. Hannah was determined to make the day as enjoyable as they could, given that Nicholas wasn't there to enjoy it with them. She welcomed Katie into the warm kitchen, and served her a bowl of spiced oatmeal, steaming hot, and covered with dried raisins and brown sugar. Setting a cup of scalding hot tea in front of her bowl, Hannah sat opposite Katie and watched her eat, smiling with encouragement and telling her entertaining anecdotes from the final days of school before the holiday break. Stories that usually made Katie smile, but not today.

After breakfast, they rested in rocking chairs before the fire that Hannah had built in the stove, to exchange gifts. Katie sat and stared at the small, square package in her hands.

"Go on, open it," said Hannah, prodding her with an elbow.

"OK, all right," Katie smiled at her, then pulled the yellow ribbon from the gift. She tugged gently to release the wrapping paper, and unfolded it slowly to reveal a small box. The box had a lid, and Katie lifted it to peer inside. Her eyes widened, and she pulled a silver chain from the box, with a small silver locket attached.

"Oh Hannah, it's beautiful."

"I'm so glad you like it. I wanted you to have something to remember me by. I've hidden a lock of my hair inside. I know that's probably silly, but I couldn't think what else to do." Hannah's cheeks blushed pink, and she furrowed her brow as she watched Katie slipping the chain around her own neck.

"Here, let me help you, dear."

Hannah jumped to her feet and hurried around to help fasten the clasp of the necklace. She patted it happily. "Show me!"

Katie spun to face her, and they both laughed with delight. Hannah pleased to see Katie smile for the first time that day.

"It looks lovely on you. Perfect."

"I love it. And having a piece of you with me will give me the strength I need to face whatever is to come in California."

"Everything will be fine, you just wait and see. Kristoff will make sure of it. And I'll write to you straight away. You'll get my letter almost the moment you arrive. That reminds me—you never mentioned what Kristoff said about the baby when you told him in that last telegram. Is he excited?"

"Oh yes, of course. He sent right back that he was a little shocked, but that it will all be fine." Katie's lie made her quiver inside. She'd never lied to Hannah before—she was used to keeping the truth from people, but had always tried not to lie outright. It felt so wrong to lie to her friend, but she convinced herself once again that it was for the right reasons.

"Oh good. I knew it would all work out. Now hurry and get ready, or we'll be late for Christmas dinner at Fred's parents' house."

Katie rushed to the looking glass hanging over the dressing table in Hannah's bedroom and stared at her own reflection. The silver locket dangled gracefully across her pale neck. She'd never owned a piece of jewelry like it before in her life, and she ran her hand across it again just to make sure it was real. It opened when she pressed on it with the tips of her fingers. She regarded the brown lock of hair inside, then pushed it shut again. She didn't know what California would be like, but at least having the locket around her neck would remind her of Hannah, and their lives together in Boston.

Her stomach churned with excitement and trepidation as she considered the week to come. What would the future hold for her and her unborn child? She combed her hair back into a ponytail, then twisted it into a tight bun. She pried open a handful of hairpins between her teeth and secured her hair with them before saying a silent prayer asking God to help her through the journey that lay ahead.

After ten days of travelling on the steam train, Katie's face was more pale and angular than ever. Once Christmas was over, she'd left Hannah standing on the platform at the station in Boston, waving at the retreating train, the steam from its smoke-stack obscuring her face even as it pulled away. Katie sat comfortably in the first class cabin, watching the scenery flash by with the occasional stop at various towns along the way. Instead of running to the wash room every time a wave of nausea hit her, she'd taken to using brown paper bags provided by a kind conductor.

She stared out the window at the landscape beyond. The view had changed dramatically throughout the journey from the east coast to the west. From thick woods with green fir trees, to open plains and rolling prairies, and finally the dry wilderness of California.

Just then the conductor walked through the swaying berth, smiling at the passengers. He wore a navy jacket, trimmed with gold brocade, and a small navy cap. A silver whistle poked out of a tidy pocket on his jacket, and two golden lines ran down the sides of his navy pants. He stopped beside Katie and shouted loudly to the group, "Sacramento!" before continuing on his way to the next cabin.

Katie's hands flew to grasp her locket in glee, and she grinned as she stared out the window at clumps of fir, cedar and oak trees, smatterings of hemlock, and other shrubbery, and in between pockets of various hardy flowers that caught the eye with a dash of color here and there. She had made it to Sacramento, finally, after such a long journey. It felt to Katie as though she had lived on this train for half her life, and the clattering of the tracks beneath it echoed constantly in her head, even while she slept.

Soon, she could see a group of buildings huddled together in the dry and dusty landscape ahead of the locomotive. They pulled closer, and the brakes engaged, slowing the train with a squeal and a sigh as it approached the station. As they lurched back and forth with the rhythm of the wheels, Katie heard the shriek of the whistle—the driver announcing their approach to the station ahead. Then, the brakes held tight, pulling the train to a stop and a burst of steam hissed from the engine, blanketing the platform in a smoky veil.

"End of the line. End of the line. Everyone out, it's

the end of the line," shouted the conductor, stepping quickly through the cabin.

Katie stood unsteadily to her feet. She gathered her things, then made her way to the exit. She climbed down the stairs, and with a hop she was on the platform. She swayed, slowly gaining her balance on the still ground beneath her feet. It was mid-morning, and the sun was high in the sky. The chill winter weather had not followed them from the east, and she felt the warmth pricking at her skin under the thick, woolen clothing. She unwound the scarf from her neck, and began undoing the large buttons on her coat before slipping it off and laying it over one arm.

The brakeman deposited her luggage by her feet with a nod, and she thanked him before looking anxiously up and down the length of the station. Kristoff was supposed to be meeting her here, but she couldn't see anyone who matched his description. Within a few minutes, all of the passengers who'd alighted from the train had left the station, and Katie was alone with an elderly woman who was studying her from the other end of the platform. She started toward Katie, her eyebrows furrowed in concentration.

"Katie Pearson?" she asked.

"Yes, that's me," said Katie, shifting her coat to her left arm and sticking out her right to shake the woman's outstretched hand.

"I'm Imelda Hutchins. Kristoff sent me to get you. He's sorry he couldn't come himself, he had to deal with a little issue down at the store, but he wants me to take you straight to him."

"Oh, thank you."

The woman was all matronly bustle. She beckoned to a porter, who hurried over to them with a dip of his hat.

"Yes, Ma'am?"

"Please ensure this luggage is delivered to Petersen's Mercantile over on Elm Street."

"Will do, Ma'am." He nodded, and began gathering Katie's luggage and loading it onto a layered trolley.

Mrs. Hutchins smiled at Katie with a twinkle in her blue eyes. Her gown was practical, yet well made. It was a pale yellow calico covered in sprigs of red cherries with green leafy twigs. Her hair was pulled neatly into a bun at the back of her head, and her cheeks were rosy and round.

"Follow me, dear," she said. She turned and walked back down the length of the platform. Katie picked up her hat and satchel, and followed. As they walked, she scanned the township in front of her, taking in her surroundings with wonder. It was so very different to what she was used to. Boston was an established city, but Sacramento was little more than a pioneering town. Wooden facades loomed high above shop fronts, whose small structures sat hidden behind them, and covered boardwalks made a pathway for pedestrians between the buildings. Katie could see people scurrying hither and thither down the wide streets, the dust of passing wagons obscuring their path.

"The store is this way. It's not far, so we'll walk. I didn't want to bother with getting the horses out for such a short trip. It's nice to stretch one's legs after a train ride, don't you think?" Mrs. Hutchins chattered amiably as they walked.

Katie nodded her head, and stared about her with wide-eyed wonder at the foreign-looking surroundings. They turned at a busy intersection across from the train station and down a dusty thoroughfare. In the distance, a bell clanged, its sound muffled by the distance.

"What was that?" asked Katie, standing on tip-toe to peer in the direction from which the sound had come.

"The bell? Oh that'd be the old barge leaving the banks of the river and heading downstream. We're not far from the river here. See these boardwalks, how high they are? They had to raise them due to the terrible flooding some years back. It happens every now and then, but at least now most of the town is high enough not to be drowned by it. Watch your step."

Katie almost stumbled over a cowboy lying drunk at her feet. His body stretched across the entire sidewalk and his bone colored Stetson covered his face, stifling a loud snore. Mrs. Hutchins barely broke her stride as she hopped over him. Katie followed suit and stepped gingerly over his legs, her eyes wide.

Next they passed a hardware store, then a baker's where the smell of fresh baked goods wafted out to greet them. Katie's stomach grumbled ominously, and a wave of nausea rolled through her body. What she wouldn't do for a sweet bread roll. She licked her lips and looked back at the bakery wistfully as they moved on at a brisk pace. Before long she found herself standing under a swinging overhead sign that announced "Petersen's Mercantile and Grocery". She stood under the sign for a moment, watching Mrs. Hutchins retreat into the store through a narrow door that was held open by a small bucket filled with pebbles.

As Katie walked into the store her heightened sense of smell was bombarded by scents of fruits, vegetables, flour, sugar, candy, fresh herbs and more. The entire floor of the large store was covered with barrels of various sizes containing foodstuffs. Along each wall were rows of shelving and on the shelves sat shining pots and pans, brightly colored linens and fabrics, ribbons, shoes and candy. Tools filled one corner of the room, along with a small selection of chairs and stools, and yet another section was covered with dolls and toys.

Katie scanned the room slowly, her eyes finally resting on a man standing behind the counter. He was serving a customer, and he smiled warmly at her as he finished wrapping the woman's fabric selection in brown paper. Handing it over to the lady, who was wearing a green dress decorated with flowers and a straw hat, he wished her good day and turned to face Mrs. Hutchins.

"Mrs. Hutchins, you're back already. That was fast. Is this Mrs. Pearson?"

Katie felt his gaze land on her. She returned his stare, and the blue depths of his eyes took her breath away. His left cheek housed a mischievous dimple, and his blonde hair swept back in waves away from his tanned face. Dressed in a simple suit, with a white apron tied neatly around his waist, he walked toward her with a grin, reaching out his hand to grasp hers. Just as he took her hand in his, nausea overwhelmed Katie, and she rushed to the nearest barrel, throwing up the contents of her last meal with several violent heaves. Mrs. Hutchins and Kristoff watched her in surprise and dismay.

"Oh dear me!" exclaimed Mrs. Hutchins, rushing to her side. "Well I never. Are you all right, my dear? Whatever could the matter be? Oh the flour. Mr. Petersen, the flour!"

Katie wiped her mouth with the back of her hand, and felt her face flush as the realization of what she'd just done dawned on her with stark clarity.

"I'm so very sorry, Mr. Petersen. I've ruined your lovely flour."

"Never mind. I just hope you aren't too unwell. I think maybe you should go into the back and lie down for a while. Perhaps the trip was too much for you."

"Thank you. I would like to lie down if I could."

"Mrs. Hutchins, would you please take Mrs. Pearson into my office? She can lie on the settee."

"Of course, come with me, dear. My, my, what a way to introduce yourself child," she chortled under her breath as she led Katie to the back of the shop and into a small but comfortable room. The office held a large desk, a chair, a settee and a cabinet that no doubt contained papers and files. Katie dropped down onto the settee and laid back with her head resting against a soft, plump cushion. She sighed loudly, and closed her eyes.

"Can I get you anything, my dear?" asked Mrs. Hutchins, hovering over her.

"I'd love something to eat. I'm absolutely famished."

Mrs. Hutchins looked startled, "Are you sure, my dear? You might want to give your stomach a moment to recover."

"Oh yes, I'm sure. I think some food would do the trick, actually."

"Well, if you think so. I'll see what I can rustle up for you."

"Thank you kindly, Mrs. Hutchins."

Mrs. Hutchins hurried from the room, and Katie could hear her boots clacking across the store and out to the street beyond. She remained still for a moment, one hand on her forehead. What would Kristoff think of her? She'd only been here for a few minutes, and already she'd ruined a perfectly good barrel of flour in his store. She remembered the look on his face, and shook her head with a groan.

She had hoped to make a good first impression, but the journey had been draining. She was exhausted, and that made her feel even more ill than usual. When she thought about it, if you added the fact that she hadn't eaten anything since her breakfast on the train hours earlier, she was only surprised that she hadn't thrown up sooner. If she was to keep her pregnancy a secret from Kristoff until after the wedding, she'd have to be more careful to eat regularly and get plenty of sleep, otherwise someone would figure it out sooner or later. If he found out she was pregnant with another man's child, there was no way he'd still want to marry her and then what would she do? She would be stranded in California on her own with no one to help her.

At least in Boston she'd had Hannah to turn to. Why, oh why, did she come to Sacramento? If Kristoff turned her away, she had no one else to help her. Panic pricked at Katie's stomach and she felt the nausea returning. Just then, Mrs. Hutchins bustled in with a bowl of steaming hot soup and a plate covered in small, sweet bread rolls. Katie's mouth watered and her stomach growled at the sight.

"Chicken soup, with fresh rolls coming up," chirped Mrs. Hutchins, pulling a small side table over to the settee and placing the meal on top of it.

"Oh, that looks marvelous," exclaimed Katie. "Thank you so very much."

"You're most welcome, my dear. Eat up now, you need your strength after a journey like that. It's no wonder you're unwell, all those hours on board a train filled with strangers. Rocking back and forth, stopping and lurching and heaving. You poor thing. Eat up now, and I'll be back to check on you shortly."

Mrs. Hutchins poured a glass of water from a pitcher that was sitting on the desk, and handed it to Katie. Then she swept from the room and back into the store.

Katie dug her spoon into the soup, and shoveled it into her mouth, burning her tongue in the process.

"Ouch!"

She chugged a quick mouthful of water to soothe the burn, then bit into one of the soft bread rolls. It was delicious. Before long, her hunger had been satiated, and Katie stretched out on the settee again, closing her eyes. The sounds of the street carried through the store and into the office. Hooves beating rhythmically on the road. Animated conversations echoed through the walls, along with laughter and the occasional shout. Finally, the whistle of the dusty train, as it pulled away from the nearby station reminded Katie that she was here to stay with no prospect of going home anytime soon. Dreaming of home, she drifted off into a deep slumber.

Chapter Eleven

Kristoff finished counting out the day's take into the sturdy, metal cash box and closed the latch. Locking it carefully with a small key, he pushed it beneath the counter ready to take to the bank. He returned the key to a pocket in his waistcoat, and leaning back in his chair, he laced his strong hands behind his head and sighed. It had been a busy day in the store. Mondays were always his busiest day, and today had been no exception. He closed his eyes and ran through the day's business in his head.

Mr. Smythe had ridden in from the renowned Statesboro Ranch, a day's ride from town, to buy his usual three months' worth of supplies for a full staff of cowboys, maids, cooks, nannies, tutors and their families. Diane Clempton had ordered everything the Rainier Hotel would need for the week to feed their many guests. And other out-of-towners from smaller ranches along with the regular townsfolk had buzzed in and out of the store all day long. The lesser orders placed by ranchers, settlers and cowboys were often made in exchange for pelts, skins, bear grease for styling hair, reams of leather, barrels of honey or other such goods, which Kristoff could resell in the store.

After today's sales, Kristoff's supplies were running low, especially on things like sugar, oats and of course flour, since Katie Pearson had thrown up in a full barrel. He'd have to call on his suppliers tomorrow to restock all of the necessities.

He shook his head and chuckled. What a way to start their lives together. She certainly had caught his attention—in more ways than one. He recalled how he had finished serving Mrs. Clempton and had looked up to see Mrs. Hutchins returning from the train station. He knew who Katie was immediately—the beautiful, petite, blonde woman. Her large blue eyes were staring up at him as though he might bite her if she came too close. Her hands twisted together in front of a cornflower blue dress that made her eyes seem impossibly blue. She had to be Katie Pearson, since his cousin's description matched her perfectly. His heart had thumped loudly in his chest as he greeted her. When he stepped forward to take her hand in his, he watched in dismay as she slipped past him and threw up in the flour barrel.

It was most disturbing to have to discard such a large amount of flour—Kristoff hated to waste anything, especially food. But it couldn't be helped. He hoped she wasn't seriously ill. No doubt just a stomach bug she'd caught on the train. Perhaps he should take her to see Doctor Arden tomorrow. He could ask her about it the next time they spoke.

Kristoff hadn't seen Katie since Mrs. Hutchins had

bundled her into the office earlier that day. He wasn't sure what he should do—why didn't she come out of there? Would it invade her privacy if he were to open the door and walk in? I mean, it was his office, after all. He cracked open the office door and peeked in. Katie was curled up on the settee fast asleep. She looked like an angel with her hair spread around her shoulders, but he knew he shouldn't linger even though he would have liked to. He crept over to the desk to retrieve his accounting ledger, quill and ink pot. He had to do his accounts in the store front, since Katie was sleeping in his office.

Before long he'd finished working on the accounts, swept the entire store from front to back, tidied up a stack of cans that had been knocked askew by some enthusiastic children, and wiped smudge marks from the front windows. He had nothing left to do. He wondered when she might stir. The rest of the staff had gone home, and now that he'd finished up, he had to decide whether to leave her where she was until she woke by herself, or go in there now and wake her up. He walked to the front of the store, and flicked the "Open" sign around so that it read "Closed" to anyone who might walk by outside.

Kristoff admired the modernity of the town that had grown up around him over the past few years. He loved Sacramento—it was fresh and vibrant. It felt to him as though it had unlimited potential for anyone with a bit of nous, and the people who came here were generally adventurous and fun-loving by nature. The town had thrived under the influx of miners and fortune hunters after the Gold Rush near Coloma, only thirty-six miles southwest of town.

Now that the rush was over, many of the surrounding hamlets had dried up and faded away, but not Sacramento. It was thriving. Buildings and businesses had popped up in a haphazard fashion. Carts and wagons hurried down its busy streets, throwing up clouds of dust in their wake. New money had come to town, and the townsfolk celebrated its arrival in garish style. Saloons thrived, and the best saloon girls quickly became the toast of the town, soliciting a kind of celebrity that only those in the west could truly appreciate. And Kristoff had benefited from the town's growth as well, moving from fisherman, to store clerk, to store owner in less than four years. He smiled, considering the journey he'd taken to get to where he now stood.

Ambling back through the store with his hands in his pockets, Kristoff decided to see if Katie was awake yet. He shrugged out of his apron, and hung it on the wall behind the counter, then strode to the office and slowly pushed the door open. He spied her on the settee, still fast asleep. He stepped carefully over to her, and squatted down beside her, watching the steady rise and fall of her chest. A few stray strands of hair had fallen across her face, and he resisted the urge to push them behind her dainty ear. Her face was almost doll-like in its beauty, and for the first time in his life he found himself feeling protective of a woman he barely knew. He realized in that moment he wanted to get to know her. He wanted to know everything about her.

"Mrs. Pearson," he whispered.

Her blue eyes opened with a few slow blinks, and

focused on his face. She flushed red, and hurriedly rose from the settee.

"Steady, no need to rush." He smiled at her.

"Oh dear, how long have I been sleeping?"

"A few hours."

"A few hours? I'm sorry, I didn't mean to fall asleep. I hope I haven't inconvenienced you at all."

"No, you haven't. Really, it's no problem. I hated to wake you. You were sleeping so peacefully. You must be tired after your journey. It's devilishly hard to sleep on those locomotives, all the clacking and the swaying. I hope you're feeling better now. Do you think you should see the doctor tomorrow?"

"The doctor?"

"You were sick earlier."

"Oh yes, of course. No, I don't think I need to see the doctor. I feel fine now. I think I just needed something to eat and a rest."

"Well, if you're ready to go, I'll take you to Mrs. Hutchins' house. She has kindly offered to let you stay there until the wedding on Friday."

"Thank you that would be fine."

Kristoff gathered up Katie's belongings and followed her out of the store. A buggy was waiting out front, and a bay gelding relaxed in the traces. A young boy stood feeding him handfuls of hay and scratching under his forelock as the animal munched happily.

"Good evening Mr. Petersen," said the boy, dropping the hay to the ground and rushing about to open the door of the buggy for them.

"Good evening, Ralph," said Kristoff, helping Katie inside and climbing in behind her.

Ralph closed the buggy door. Katie turned her head to see her luggage already stashed behind the chassis of the buggy. Ralph checked the tailboard to ensure it was secure, and climbed up to the driver's seat. With a click of his tongue, he set them moving at a brisk pace as the bay trotted down the long street.

Kristoff fidgeted with a loose thread on his pants leg as they sat in the buggy, jostling against each other with the movement of the vehicle. Katie appeared to be fixated on the scenery passing by on her side, and she sat silently with her head turned away from him. Their hands brushed against each other for a moment, and it felt to Kristoff as though a bolt of electricity had run through her and into him. He trembled as Katie quickly moved her hands into her lap, folding them together neatly. He couldn't deny the chemistry between them. He wondered if she felt it too, or if it was all on his side.

"Hannah mentioned that your family are also originally from Norway, is that correct?"

Katie glanced his way, then back out the window. "Yes."

"What a small world." He chuckled, then frowned when he got no response.

"Where in Norway?"

"Oslo."

"Really, that's where my family are from also. I was born there, but we moved to Boston when I was a teenager. So, I've lived in this country for some time, although, according to folks around here, my accent is still so strong I may as well have just arrived."

Still nothing but a quick nod. Kristoff scowled in frustration. How could they get married if they couldn't even hold a conversation? He'd initially been hesitant about the idea of marrying someone he'd never met, but had decided to trust his cousin's judgement. Kristoff believed she knew him well enough to select someone who would suit him. Someone he could love. And when Katie had arrived at the store, looking beautiful and vulnerable, he'd thought for a moment that his cousin had made an even better match than he could have imagined. But now, this taciturn woman seated beside him was making him re-consider the whole idea. He believed the most important thing in a marriage was the ability to get along, and to be open and honest with each other. That's how his parents had lived, and that's what he wanted in a marriage for himself.

He decided to try again. "Can you tell me anything about your family?"

"My parents died when I was young. I have no other family."

Katie's answer was clipped and brief. Peering around to catch a glimpse of her face Kristoff saw her purse her lips tightly as though she was unhappy having to answer so many questions. He rubbed one hand across his forehead and through his hair, sending it spiking in several different directions at once.

"And are you feeling well now? Do you know what might have caused your illness?"

"I am well. Thank you."

Kristoff gave up trying to draw her out, and settled back into his seat in defeat. Katie sat silent and tense beside him. Her eyes were fixed on the horizon ahead, and her back was turned to him, straight and taut. Her thin waist barely bending with the pitch of the buggy, she looked as though she were ready to jump from the vehicle and run for her life.

He sighed, and lay his head against the seat cushion behind him. It would certainly be difficult to send her back after bringing her here from Boston. He had everything set up and ready to go for the wedding on Friday. But, if they couldn't even hold a simple conversation, how could they get married as planned? He couldn't imagine committing himself to a silent marriage. It was almost as if she couldn't stand to be in his presence. Well, if that was the way she felt, perhaps she'd be relieved when he told her he didn't think they should go through with it.

On the other hand, Hannah did lead him to believe Katie's situation was fairly dire in Boston. He was sure it couldn't possibly be as bad as Hannah had insinuated. He twisted his head to look at her, taking in the long waves of blonde hair neatly pinned away from her face, the trim figure, the subtle tan of her glowing skin. He was sure she'd be able to find a decent job working in a nice home with very little effort. And if it truly was marriage she wanted, no doubt she'd find someone in Boston to marry in no time. He couldn't believe her situation was as bad as Hannah thought it to be. Perhaps Hannah was simply being melodramatic, or maybe she just wanted to help Kristoff find a wife.

He sat in silence, letting the movements of the buggy rock him back and forth as they trundled down a narrow, country road toward Mrs. Hutchins' yellow farmhouse. Her husband, David Hutchins, stood at a simple slatted gate leading into the property and waved to them as the buggy passed by. Kristoff leaned out the window and gazed at the house as they approached. With two full stories, the square house had been built from store-bought siding. Its tin roof glistened silver in the shimmering reds and oranges of the setting sun. A spiral of smoke wafted from a thin chimney, and a large porch wrapped around the lower level, with a short staircase leading up to a robust front door.

"Evenin', Kristoff," said David Hutchins, tramping over to them and extending his hand toward Kristoff.

"Good evening to you, sir."

Kristoff climbed from the buggy and shook hands with David.

"Your house is as warm and welcoming as always. Thank you for your hospitality. I'm sure Katie will enjoy staying here."

Katie climbed out behind Kristoff, who held up his arm to steady her.

"This is Katie Pearson. Katie, this is Mr. David Hutchins."

David took Katie's hand in his, and shook it gently. He smiled shyly, and Katie beamed at him.

"So pleased to meet you, Mr. Hutchins. What a lovely farm you have."

"Why thank you."

"I'm so grateful to you for letting me stay here. Is Mrs. Hutchins about?"

"Mellie's inside fixing supper. Why don't you go on in while I see to your bags?" said Mr. Hutchins.

Katie turned to Kristoff, and grasped his hands in hers.

"Thank you, Kristoff. You've been so thoughtful and kind. I do hope to see you soon."

Her eyes were so full of sincere gratitude as she squeezed his hands gently between hers that Kristoff felt quite confused.

"You're welcome, Mrs. Pearson. I know you'll enjoy your stay here. I will call on you tomorrow if that suits?"

"Yes, please do. I look forward to it." She smiled warmly at him, and her eyelashes fluttered dreamily against her cheeks as she dropped her eyes demurely to the ground, still holding his hands in hers.

Kristoff was astonished. She had gone from cold and unresponsive in the buggy, to effusive and affectionate only moments later. What would cause her to act in such a way? He was certain he had no idea, and had never met anyone like her before in his life. He nodded his head at her before she spun about to walk into the house in search of Mrs. Hutchins. He stood staring after her, his lips parted as though he were about to say something. David chuckled softly, reaching for Katie's luggage.

"Well, I'd say she has your attention, Kristoff." He shook his greying head, and his eyes twinkled merrily.

Kristoff grunted and frowned. "I don't know about that. She's the most confounded woman I've ever met, and I've only known her a few hours."

"That sounds about right." David grinned.

"I don't know what she's thinking. She's cold one minute and warm the next. I don't have any idea what to make of it."

"Well, I'm sure you'll figure it out in thirty years or so."

"I can't marry someone who's up and down like a yo-yo," protested Kristoff.

"No doubt she has her reasons. Why don't you ask her about it?"

"How in tarnation would I do that?"

"Just ask, 'is something botherin' you?' Then you listen to what she says. It's pretty simple. Took me a few decades to learn, but I've found it works wonders with Mellie."

Kristoff scratched his head and stepped back into the buggy. It couldn't possibly be as easy as that, he was sure of it. "Well, have a good evening. Give my regards to Mrs. Hutchins."

"Will do, Kristoff. We'll be seein' you."

Kristoff could hear him snickering all the way up the stairs as he carried Katie's luggage into the house. He slumped down in his seat overcome by dismay at the whole situation as the buggy darted down the long driveway and back toward town. His own property was closer to Sacramento, but not far from the Hutchinses' farm. Night was falling fast and he looked forward to getting home and relaxing for a few minutes before supper. He'd almost decided to call off the wedding, but maybe he was being too hasty. Perhaps if he gave it a few more days he'd be able to make up his mind.

He knew he couldn't postpone things forever, but what was the use of rushing it? They could put the wedding off if he needed more time to think it through. There was no harm in that, was there? What would he say to Katie though? How would he break it to her without it sounding like he was backing out of mar-

rying her? Surely that would hurt her feelings, and he
certainly didn't want to do that.

He stuck his head out the window and took in the
distant lights of the dusty town. The hoot of an owl
swooping overhead could be heard faintly above the
noise of the wheels on the road, and a blanket of brilliant stars emerged one by one in the sky above its
outstretched wings. Turning around to look behind, he
saw the dark outline of the Sierra Nevada. The brood-
ing peaks were barely visible now that the sun had set,
but Kristoff knew their shape by heart. He felt a warm
peace slipping over him and he sighed with satisfaction.

Kristoff loved California. The massive dark sky full
of twinkling lights, the wide openness of the valleys,
the dramatic ravines, the warm breezes that swept in
from the desert leaving everything dry and full of grit
in their wake. The hint of adventure in the air as though
anything were possible. He never wanted to leave this
place, there was something so alive about it all. He
pulled his head back inside the buggy, and furrowed
his brow. Whatever was he going to do about Katie
Pearson? He was lonely, and had been for a long time.
The idea of spending his life with someone was so appealing, and yet what if marrying was a mistake? What
if they weren't suited to one another? They might well
spend a lifetime regretting their decision.

He couldn't figure it all out now; he'd have to give
it some time. If only she had been open with him, he
might have a better idea of what to do. They could postpone the ceremony. It wouldn't be too hard to do. And
surely she would see the wisdom in the idea. There was
one thing he was certain of, as they swung into his long

driveway and headed past the sumptuous stables, unless something happened to change his mind, he wasn't going to marry Katie Pearson on Friday.

Chapter Twelve

Katie woke to the sound of a woodpecker hammering at the trunk of a nearby tree. The air was full of the call of birds, the low of grazing cattle and even the buzzing of bees. Compared to the cacophony of city noises that Katie was used to, and the clackety-clacking of the train over the past ten days, the gentle sounds of country life were a welcome change. The shrill call of curlews had interrupted her sleep throughout the night, startling her into partial wakefulness each time. Yet she felt as though she'd slept for days when her eyes opened and her mouth gaped in a wide yawn.

The sun was high in the sky, and the aroma of freshly baked bread wafted up the staircase to greet her. Katie lay on her back, relishing a rare lazy moment. For the first time since Nicholas's death, the anxiety that had brought a constant tingling sensation to her chest was gone, and she smiled at the ceiling before throwing back the covers and standing to her feet.

Traipsing to the window in her nightgown and cap, Katie leaned on the ledge and peered out at the farm below. In the distance she could see David leading a brown cow with a white head into a large, red barn. A fluffy dog bounded around his legs, chuffing and yapping in delight. Further down the field, a small herd of cattle with the same brown and white markings were grazing on the green grass. Other than the single field of grass, the rest of the property on every side was covered in swaying fields of golden wheat. The half-grown crop reached skyward, tall and straight, ready for the thick heads that would sprout and grow heavy when the weather turned warm.

Katie dressed quickly, and washed up in a wash-basin that Mrs. Hutchins had kindly filled with clean, fresh water and left by her bedroom door. She looked around for a mirror and found one inside the wardrobe, where she was able to smooth her hair back into a chignon, check it for stray wisps and pinch her pale cheeks before she hurried downstairs. She was starving, and if she didn't eat soon she'd be sick all over again.

Mrs. Hutchins might not be suspicious after she threw up once at the store, but she was bound to catch on quickly to Katie's condition if she continued to be sick. Either that, or she and Kristoff would insist that Katie visit a doctor and she couldn't do that without them discovering she was pregnant. She just had to make it to Friday without anyone guessing what was going on. After that, she'd be married and would tell Kristoff the truth.

It had been difficult to keep her condition a secret the previous evening in the buggy. All the way to the Hutchinses' farm, she'd been so ill. The boy driving the vehicle had pushed the horse into a canter almost as soon as they set off. They weaved, swayed, lurched and careened around corners at top speed. It was all Katie could do not to throw up directly into Kristoff's lap. She sat as still as she could, staring out the window and breathing slowly and deeply, but he kept peppering her with questions about her family. She gritted her teeth, and answered him as best she could, while striving desperately to hold the nausea at bay.

Katie hoped that she'd hidden her discomfort, but she wasn't sure he was convinced by her performance. She got the impression he could tell she was hiding something. She hoped he hadn't figured out just what her secret was. If he had, she could forget about him wanting to marry her. Even though her heart was still hurting from losing Nick, there was something about Kristoff that intrigued her.

She felt drawn to him, with his handsome face, the deep dimple in his cheek and his waves of golden hair. But it wasn't just his looks that attracted her. He was confident, and had an aura of authority about him. At the same time he seemed so kind and gentle. It was an intoxicating combination, and Katie found herself hoping he'd come by the farm to see her soon. Perhaps he'd visit before work. If he didn't, she supposed she could ride to the store with Mrs. Hutchins and would see him there.

"Good morning, Mrs. Hutchins," called Katie, skipping into the generous kitchen. Fresh herbs hung drying on a rack in a corner of the room. Bright curtains in white with green leaves adorned the windows. Cedar benches lined two walls, and were covered with bowls, bunches of vegetables, candles and various kitchen implements. A brick oven occupied one wall of the kitchen, and a large, black stove stood in the center of the kitchen with a tall chimney, giving the room a warm, cozy feel. On the stovetop sat a fresh-baked loaf of bread, the scent of it filling the entire house. Katie's stomach growled threateningly, and she swallowed a wave of nausea.

"Good morning, Katie dear. Please, call me Mellie." Mrs. Hutchins smiled kindly at her.

"All right, Mellie. This bread smells divine."

"I'm so glad, would you like a slice?"

"Yes please. I'm famished!"

"Coming right up. Butter and strawberry jam? I made both myself, and I do believe they're quite delicious, although I may be biased." She laughed merrily as she cut the loaf cleanly with a long, sharp knife.

"That sounds perfect. Thank you."

"How did you sleep?"

"Like I hadn't a problem in the world."

"Good to hear."

"Mellie, do you think Kristoff will stop by before work this morning? I only ask because I like to plan out my day in the morning, and if I should expect him, I'd like to prepare." Katie felt a flush of warmth rising to her cheeks, and she ducked her head as she sat at a long table made from thick, cedar planks that matched the benches. A green and white checked tablecloth covered the table, and two tall candlesticks stood in the center beside a vase containing a small bunch of lavender.

"Oh no, dear. He won't be coming by this morning. He'd already be at the store meeting the suppliers. He has to meet the deliveries in the morning. Someone has to be there to check and sign for them. Maybe he'll come by after the store closes this evening."

"Oh." Katie tried to hide her disappointment. She was surprised by her own reaction of dismay to Mrs. Hutchins remarks. Had she really been counting on seeing him so soon?

"Never mind, my dear. He won't have forgotten about you, I can assure you of that. You'll see him soon enough, and after Friday you'll be husband and wife so you'll get to spend every morning and evening together."

"Yes, of course. Although, perhaps I could come to town with you. Are you going to the store today? I could ride with you, and maybe I could take a walk about the town, just to look around. I don't want to bother Kristoff, but I would like to get a feel for the place."

"I'll be heading into town in the wagon after breakfast. You're welcome to come with me if you like. Although I'm not sure Kristoff would want you traipsing about town on your own, seeing as how you've only just arrived and don't know your way around."

Mrs. Hutchins looked at Katie with concern, pausing with a butter knife poised above a thick slice of warm bread. Red, berry-filled jam dripped from the knife onto the buttered bread, and Katie felt her stomach spasm at the sight of it.

"Oh, I'll be fine. Boston's a much bigger place than Sacramento. Don't worry about me, I'll have no trouble finding my way back from wherever I roam to."

"Well, all right then. Let's eat and we'll get going."

* * *

The toll of a bell broke through the noise of the docks. The barge was coming to shore, and wanted a clear path through the crowd of vessels. Determined to see more of the town, Katie had walked down to the Sacramento River to stroll along its banks and watch the buzz of activity on the water and the shoreline. The town itself was flat and low set. The wide river formed its western border, and fingers of river water drifted into a swampy lake to form yet another border.

The buildings across the street from the river were built up high, and elevated boardwalks joined the storefronts across town. A faded timber sign showed the flood levels from 1862, only eight years earlier. Katie stood beside the sign, peering up at the mark—the water would have been well above her head. She shivered at the thought of all that brown, muddy water inundating the town, floating along streets and creeping into buildings.

The banks of the river were riddled with docks where boats were currently berthed, or were pushed away from the shore by dock workers, drifting off to begin a new journey. A fishing skiff sang through the water close by, the weathered looking fisherman driving it along heartily with a set of chipped oars. Katie watched it all with a smile on her face. It was good to get outdoors and breathe some fresh air after all her time indoors lately. The air was chill, but not as cold as Boston had been, and the sunshine warmed her face as she lifted it skyward.

After circling the block once, Katie had seen enough of Sacramento for one morning. She couldn't believe how quickly she tired now that she was pregnant. All she wanted to do was lay down and take a nap, right after she ate something of course. A savory treat would really hit the spot. Perhaps another piece of warm bread, or a baked potato still in its jacket, or maybe she'd be able to find some cheese to slice over crackers. She licked her lips at the thought of it, and scurried toward Petersen's Mercantile.

Katie walked through the front door, waving to Mrs. Hutchins. She couldn't help feeling at home in the welcoming atmosphere of Kristoff's store. Mrs. Hutchins smiled at her and pointed her toward the back. That must be where Kristoff was working. Katie strode through the store, noticing how well the products were organized and displayed on the sturdy shelves, how neat and tidy the floor was, and how friendly the staff were who served customers at the long counter that ran along the entire length of one wall.

Kristoff ran an impressive business, and Katie was filled with sudden pride for her husband-to-be. The feeling was followed quickly by a pang of guilt over her secret. If she told him now about the pregnancy, maybe he'd still marry her. He seemed like a man who would keep his word. No, she couldn't risk it. If this didn't work out, she'd be back in Boston within the week, with no prospects.

Hannah was engaged to be married, and Katie had nowhere to live, no job to return to and no way to support herself or her baby. The best possible scenario involved her giving up her child for adoption, and she couldn't even think about that without a shudder of grief ripping through her body. She'd just have to keep her pregnancy from Kristoff for a few more days, and pray he'd be understanding when the truth came out.

The sound of Kristoff's deep voice echoed from the back of the store, and Katie made her way toward it with a grin. Just then, she heard a woman's voice answer him. The voice was silky and sultry, and whatever she said made Kristoff laugh. Katie stopped and listened intently. She scurried closer and peered around a stack of ladders leaning against the back wall. She spotted Kristoff talking to a beautiful woman in the storage room behind the shop front.

The woman was dressed in a queer outfit. Her gown was made of garishly colored silky fabrics, and her hat had several long feathers protruding from its peak. Her lips were colored red, and her cheeks looked flushed. She had one gloved hand resting on Kristoff's arm, and as she spoke to him she leaned forward as though she were telling him the most delightful secret. Katie's hand flew to her mouth, and she watched them in alarm. Kristoff appeared to be enjoying the woman's company a little too much, and Katie felt a twinge of jealousy rising in the pit of her stomach.

"So, what do you say, Kristoff? Are you going to run away with me, or what?"

"Come on now Belle Waters, you know I'm engaged. I just told you not five minutes ago." Kristoff chuckled with apparent delight, and patted Belle's hand where it sat on his arm.

"You don't want to marry that prudish, cold fish from Boston. She's probably going to make you do it through a sheet, I know the type well."

Katie glowered at the woman's remarks, her cheeks

blushing at the woman's crudeness. Cold and prudish indeed. Is that what Kristoff was telling people about her? Or was this horrible woman drawing her own conclusions?

"Belle!"

"Oh don't act shocked, Kristoff. You know you love it when I speak to you like that."

"I most certainly do not," Kristoff said, but Katie could see his grin widening.

"Well, anyway, what you need is someone with passion and experience. I'd give it all up you know, everything for you, if you just gave me the word. I only have eyes for you." Belle's face had changed expression, from jesting to serious as she spoke. She leaned forward and, for just a moment, she seemed to be pleading with him.

Kristoff eyed her with suspicion, he looked unsure of how to take her confession. "Belle, I…"

"Forget it champ, I can see you'd never have me. I'm damaged goods. Don't worry, I won't hold it against you. You're one of the few good men in this whole godforsaken town. I never see you at the saloon, and you're not even a married man yet. I get it. I just wish— well perhaps in another life, things might have been different."

Just then, Mrs. Hutchins tugged on Katie's arm, startling her.

"Oh, Mellie, you frightened me."

"What are you doing?" she whispered, raising her eyebrows as though the two of them were involved in some kind of secret conspiracy.

"Nothing. I'm not doing anything. I was just admiring these ladders. They're so solid, and such a unique design. I…"

"Really, the ladders? Hmmm. Well, if you decide to buy one, please come and see me, I'm sure I can get you a discount," Mrs. Hutchins kidded, chortling. "You wouldn't be eavesdropping now, would you?"

"Of course not, Mellie." Katie pretended to be indignant, drawing her eyebrows together in consternation.

Mrs. Hutchins nodded knowingly. "Nothing good can come of it, you mark my words. Best to just come out with your questions for Kristoff, if you have any. Honesty—that's the only way, my dear."

She ambled off with a snort. Katie watched her leave impatiently, then returned to her post, her ears pricked toward Kristoff and Belle. She could no longer see them, they must have moved behind the stacks of hay and boxes layered across the back of the storage area.

"I can't follow through with it. I know we had an agreement, but it's just not how I expected it to be. I'm afraid I can't do what I promised."

Kristoff's voice was fading. There was a low murmur in response, but Katie couldn't make out what else was being said as the speakers moved further away. Katie's heart sank. She buried her face in her palms, and felt the tears come. Wet and warm, they filled the crevices between her fingers. Kristoff wasn't going to marry her. He'd just told Belle as much. Hope crept from her chest, leaving a hollow emptiness in its place.

Katie stifled a sob, and pushed away her grief. She lowered her hands and used her sleeve to dry her face and eyes. Katie grasped the silver locket hanging around her neck, rubbing it absent-mindedly, and she became lost in thought. He'd likely send her back to Boston on the next train, and she'd be all alone again. In that moment, she realized just how happy and secure she'd felt since she arrived in Sacramento—as though her future wasn't without hope. That happy façade was stripped away in a moment, and she saw herself lost, afraid, and without hope all over again.

What would she do now? She plodded to the office, and threw herself down on the settee. As her eyes drifted closed, she prayed for hope. She asked God to give her and the baby a future together, to provide her with a way forward. Then she floated into a deep sleep, her appetite forgotten.

Chapter Thirteen

Kristoff scratched his head and leaned casually against the office doorframe. Katie was sleeping on the office settee again and he had no idea how she'd gotten there or when she'd arrived. She hadn't even sought him out to say hello. He wondered what was going on in that pretty head of hers. And why was she so tired? She should have caught up on plenty of shut-eye last night out at the Hutchinses' farm, but maybe she hadn't slept well for some reason. He couldn't imagine why someone would need so much sleep. Unless she was seriously ill. She had thrown up the moment she arrived, after all. Perhaps she really was sick. He'd have to talk to her again about visiting the doctor.

Katie's eyes flicked open and lighted on Kristoff's smiling face. He felt a tremble course through his body, when for a moment it seemed her soul lay bare as she held his eyes with her gaze. Then she blinked and the moment passed. He straightened, and sauntered toward her, ruffling his hair with one hand and breathing deeply in an attempt to slow his heart rate and underplay the chemistry he felt between them.

"Sleeping again?" he asked.

"Mmmm. Sorry, I didn't mean to sleep for so long." Katie sat up and smoothed her skirts. Her hair was mussed in the back where she had lain on it, poking out in every direction. Kristoff hid a grin; he thought she looked adorable with her messy hair and sleepy eyes. Her compact but curvy figure was outlined by the line of her brown corduroy dress, and the blue ruffles around her arms and waist accentuated the hue of her eyes.

"You are welcome to sleep as much as you'd like. Although I am a little worried about you. Are you feeling all right?" Kristoff squatted down on one heel beside her, and regarded her with concern. He liked the feeling of being close to her. He wanted to take her hand, but she rose from the couch and moved quickly away from him, her hands closed across her abdomen.

"I'm fine, really I am. Don't worry about me."

"It's just that you seem to be awfully tired, and you were ill yesterday as well."

"Most likely it was the travel, I'll be well in no time. I rode into town this morning with Mrs. Hutchins and took a little walk around town. It's an interesting place. Very rustic. I even strolled along the riverbank, and watched the big steamers, and the small fishing skiffs coming and going. So much activity, people rushing here and there. Sacramento is becoming quite the metropolis."

Kristoff wondered if she meant to compliment or criticize his town. Compared to Boston he was sure that Sacramento seemed small and uncouth, but he'd hoped she would see the potential that he saw in the place. He couldn't tell. Thinking for the umpteenth time that she was a difficult woman to read.

"Oh. I'm glad you like it. I love it here. It has an air of potential—as though anything is possible. And it is, for someone with gumption and a bit of know-how. I arrived with barely a penny and nothing to recommend me, and only a few years later I'm operating a successful store. I might even be running for mayor in the next election. It's a wonderful place, truly it is."

Kristoff rose to his feet as he spoke, and walked toward Katie. Her back was to him, and she was studying a newspaper clipping from the Sacramento Times that hung on the wall of the office beside his desk. It was a framed story about the opening of his store from four years earlier. She lifted her hand to trace the outline of his face in the photograph. He looked younger, filled with hope and inspiration. Wearing a dark, ten gallon hat, he stared earnestly down the camera lens—all seriousness and ambition. Kristoff watched her with interest, wishing he could read her thoughts.

Katie turned to face him, and he heard her breath catch when she realized how close he was standing. Leaning forward to look at the clipping himself, he had her boxed against the wall, and Katie had nowhere to turn. She looked up at him again and he met her gaze, wondering at the fear he saw there.

"What is it?" he whispered, lifting his hand to brush his knuckles against her cheek. "What's wrong?"

"Nothing. I'm fine," she dropped her eyes, and he

could see the heave of her chest as she gulped deep breathes of air.

If only he could understand what it was that made her afraid, and why she was being so cagey with him. They were supposed to be getting married on Friday, as far as she knew. Why wouldn't she open up to him? There was something she was keeping from him, he could tell, and it was aggravating him no end that she refused to confess it. He was frustrated with her, but at the same time had an almost uncontrollable urge to kiss her. Placing his finger beneath her lowered chin, he lifted her face to his and looked deeply into her eyes.

"You can tell me what's bothering you. I wish you'd trust me."

In response, she closed her eyes. Her dark eyelashes made half circles on her pale cheeks. A single tear fell from beneath one of those half-moons, and drifted slowly down the side of her face. Kristoff was startled, unsure of how to respond. He had no experience comforting a crying woman, and such a sight usually sent him scampering in the other direction. But as the tear reached her chin, he lifted his finger to catch it.

Leaning down, he kissed her gently on her upturned mouth. Her full lips met his, responding softly at first, then she pushed into him with greater urgency, curling one hand around behind his neck and pulling him closer. Kristoff felt a pleasant warmth travel from his mouth and down through his body, as though a tide was sparking life within him. Her mouth was so small and soft. He drew her body to his, her supple curves melding into the line of his hard body.

In a moment, she pulled away from him, a barely

perceptible frown on her delicate face. Kristoff protested, and pulled her back toward him, but she lifted her hands against his chest to stop him.

"What's wrong, Katie dear?"

"I just don't think we should, that's all."

"Why not? We're to be married, what's the harm?" His heart was pounding loudly in his ears, and his body screamed out for more of her. He couldn't clear his head to think, all he knew was that he needed Katie, every part of her.

"We're not married yet, Kristoff," she said it snidely, and it stabbed him to the core. The way she said it, it sounded as though she had doubts about marrying him at all, and he wondered what he had done to cause a change of heart.

"Don't you want to marry me?" he asked, backing away from her, feeling a dull pain building in his chest. Katie didn't answer him, only ran from the room with a sob. Kristoff slumped down onto the settee, laying his head back on a soft throw pillow. He would be darned if he could understand that woman. She had kissed him back as though he was the one man in the world she wanted. Their kiss had been deep and passionate. It was a kiss unlike any other he'd ever had in his life.

There was a connection between them that couldn't be denied. They shared an intense attraction, there was no doubt about it. But when she pulled away from him, she'd looked at him with a mixture of despair and anger. He couldn't comprehend what he'd done to cause her to see him that way.

How could they build a solid relationship based only upon attraction? He had to know her, what made her who she was. And importantly, he wanted her to re-veal what it was she was hiding from him and why. He had to find a way to get her to talk to him, or there was no hope for them as a couple. Any marriage without openness or honesty would be doomed from the start, and Kristoff was determined not to foster that kind of relationship.

He wanted to build a loving family with someone, based on trust. If they couldn't do that, he'd rather remain single. He had a good life here, and he was content, if somewhat lonely. He could continue living that life if things didn't work out between them. He'd be disappointed, that was certain, but surely he would be able to get her out of his mind without too much difficulty. Just as the thought passed through his head, the realization dawned on him that it wouldn't be as easy as that. Katie Pearson had already worked her way into a place in his heart that would make her hard to forget.

"Women!" he huffed in frustration, pulling the pillow from behind his head and burying his face in it to muffle a yell in the downy stuffing.

Katie sat solemnly on a bench outside the front door of the store chewing nervously on a jagged nail. Kristoff had kissed her, a kiss that made her dizzy with desire, after telling Belle Waters he didn't want to marry Katie. Was he toying with her feelings? Surely he wouldn't do that, not given Hannah's description of his character and after having brought her all the way from Boston.

Katie's reverie was interrupted by Mrs. Hutchins,

who strode through the door her gaze sweeping the street and landing on Katie's hunched figure.

"There you are, my dear. Well, well, what are you doing out here?"

"Just getting some air, Mellie."

"I meant to mention it earlier, but it completely slipped my mind. Kristoff has invited us to his ranch for supper tonight. So, we'll head home now to get ready."

"I've got a bit of a headache, actually and…"

"Nonsense child, he's invited his friends over to give them a chance to meet you before the wedding. You're the guest of honor, you can't miss it."

Mrs. Hutchins looked horrified at the prospect of Katie missing out on what seemed to be a kind of engagement party. Funny that Kristoff hadn't mentioned anything about it to her, although she supposed she hadn't really given him much of a chance. It did seem strange to go ahead with a dinner party, introducing her around as his fiancée, if he didn't intend to marry her. But perhaps he didn't want to cancel the engagement celebration at the last minute, and still intended to back out of the wedding.

"Oh, I didn't realize that, Mellie. Of course we'll go then."

Katie stood to her feet reluctantly and followed Mrs. Hutchins' wide, swaying hips back into the store. Katie sighed. The last thing she wanted to do was to face a bunch of strangers and pretend to be happy about a wedding that was never going to happen. It didn't seem like she had much of a choice about the matter though, so she might as well try to enjoy herself. And it would be a treat to see Kristoff's house. She wondered what kind of place a man like Kristoff would have. Even if it was never to be hers, it would be interesting to see it, just the same.

Katie sat beside Mr. and Mrs. Hutchins on the wide plank seat atop their rocking wagon. She watched with growing excitement as they drew closer to Kristoff's property. Mrs. Hutchins kept up a rolling commentary about his ranch, his house, the horses, the neighbors and every piece of idle gossip she could think of as they trundled along.

Set in a lush hollow of the Sacramento Valley, his ranch was a small one that joined onto the edge of a much larger property owned by a well-known rancher, Mr. George Smythe. Apparently his house was a day's ride away, but the edge of his behemoth property touched on the border of Kristoff's and he'd sold the small patch of land to Kristoff two years earlier as a favor to the potential new mayor. Mrs. Hutchins said that Mr. Smythe was determined to see his friend and neighbor in the mayor's seat, and had pledged to back his election campaign.

As they approached the house down a short winding drive, Katie could see Kristoff had placed candles around the entrance of the house illuminating the gardens and entryway with a twinkle of lights. She spotted wagons, coaches and buggies of all shapes and sizes parked neatly in lines in front of what appeared to be a large stable. Stable hands busily rubbed and bedded down horses in the stable, and folk from town and the surrounding properties, stepped through the gardens and into the house, the buzz of their conversations and laughter carrying loudly on the night air.

Suddenly Katie felt nervous. Kristoff's house was grand, his stables impressive and the people attending the party were obviously the "Who's-Who" of Sacramento society. She had never rubbed shoulders with people like this before. In Boston, she had been first a well-educated but poor orphan, then a poor married woman, and finally a poor widow. The only people she'd known of this caliber were the ones she'd waited on at the Sommerses' house. Well, at least she knew how to behave, even if she was more comfortable serving them than socializing with them.

Mrs. Hutchins seemed to sense her discomfort.

"Don't worry, dear. Everyone is excited to meet you. We don't carry on with the airs and graces of the east coast out here. You'll fit in just fine."

Katie inclined her head gratefully and tried to smile. They pulled to a halt in front of the house, and a stable boy ran to meet them. He nodded his head, then reached for the horse's bridle.

"I'll take 'im from 'ere if ya like," he said.

"Thank you, Ralph, most kind of you," said Mr. Hutchins, stepping off the wagon and holding up his hand to help his wife down behind him.

Katie stood, and took Mr. Hutchins' hand to climb from the wagon seat, scanning the property with great interest. It was a lovely ranch, kept very tidy and in good repair. The gardens were dormant at this time of year, but hedges remained green and vibrant, and looked to be nicely established and trimmed. The driveway was smooth and well maintained. The house itself was a two-story farmhouse, similar to the Hutchinses' home, but larger. It was painted a light blue color, with white trim and a tin roof. A tall chimney divided the roof, and lazy smoke drifted into the darkness, a welcome sight on a cool night.

Just then, Kristoff's tall frame appeared in the doorway.

"You're here," he cried, stepping out to meet them. He took Katie's hand in his own and kissed it gently.

"I'm so glad you came. I wanted you to have a chance to see my home, and meet my friends, before the wedding."

Katie felt her face grow warm under his gaze, and she smiled.

"Thank you for being so considerate. Your home is quite lovely."

Kristoff led them up the front stairs and into the house. It was already full of partygoers. The din of their conversations reverberated loudly throughout the house, and Katie was sure she wouldn't be able to hear herself think let alone converse with anyone else.

"You know all of these people?" she shouted above the noise of the crowd.

He simply nodded and grinned. Then he went about the room, pulling her along by the hand behind him, and introduced her to each person, one-by-one. Katie did her duty, smiling, nodding and answering questions as politely as she could. Whenever a tray of food passed her by held by a smartly dressed waiter, she made sure to grab something from it to eat, since she was becoming more and more exhausted with each passing moment. By the end of the night, she had met and spoken with everyone there. She walked onto the verandah for some peace, trying to recall the names of the people she'd met, matching them with faces in her mind's eye.

Standing outside staring in at the party through the window, Katie nibbled on a sandwich she had grabbed from a tray on her way out. Inside, people were chattering and laughing together. Some people were gathered around an upright piano, and a woman was belting out some raucous tunes which a few of the others attempted to sing along to as well. The woman's red hair was piled high on her head, and ringlets cascaded down and across her peaches-and-cream shoulders. She finished the song, and turned her head to say something to Kristoff, who stood by her side watching her play with a drink in his hand.

It was Belle Waters.

Katie's stomach clenched into a tight knot, and she leaned forward against the window pane, almost pressing her nose against the glass in her haste. What was Belle doing here? From what Katie could tell, the party was made up mostly of politicians, business owners and church folk. How did Belle fit into that particular crowd?

Belle stood and lay her hand on Kristoff's arm, laughing heartily at something he said. Just then, she spied Katie watching her. Belle grinned scornfully at her, and turned her back to Katie as she linked her arm through Kristoff's. Both Kristoff and Belle were faced away from her now, so she couldn't see what they were saying or doing, but they stood that way for several minutes before Katie pushed herself away from the window and wandered down the stairs and into the yard.

What was the relationship between Kristoff and Belle? If indeed there was one. Was Belle simply hopeful, or did Kristoff reciprocate her feelings? No doubt Belle must be the reason that Kristoff had decided against marrying Katie. But how could a man of his stature consider marrying a woman like Belle? He certainly wouldn't be able to run for mayor with a saloon girl on his arm. Or would he? The way that Belle was dressed tonight, in an understated cream and gold gown, with minimal jewelry and no makeup, she looked every bit the mayor's wife. Perhaps a town like Sacramento was more forgiving and accepting of people who made a change to their lifestyle than those in Boston would have been. Maybe Kristoff did intend to marry Belle after all. And even if he didn't, and he married someone else, would his wife want to share him with Belle? Katie knew she certainly wouldn't. When she married, whomever she chose to marry, she wanted him to be all hers—body, mind and soul.

I have to put it out of my mind. There's nothing to be gained by worrying about something I have no control over. Kristoff will do what he wishes, and I will be fully occupied taking care of the baby.

Katie felt a spark of curiosity when she noticed the stables. She wondered what kind of horses Kristoff might have. She'd always loved horses, but had never owned one herself, and had rarely had the chance to ride one. She wandered across the lawn toward the stables, opened a thick, timber door, and stepped inside. The building was divided in two, with stalls along each side, and a walkway down the middle. Katie closed the door behind her, and ambled through the stable, stopping to speak to, and pet, each horse she found there. Obviously a much larger number of horses were stabled there this evening than normal. With several to each spacious stall, she wondered which of them could be Kristoff's.

"You like horses?" Kristoff's voice startled her from behind. She spun about to see him standing in the doorway, watching her with a smile.

"I love them. I've never owned one, but I've always admired them."

"My favorite rider is down the end on the right. His name is King. He's a beauty."

Kristoff walked past Katie to the stall he had indicated, and she followed close behind him. A tall, black horse stuck its nose over the stall door and nibbled at Kristoff's chest. Katie giggled.

"Maybe he's hungry."

"He's always hungry for treats, aren't you boy?" Kristoff rubbed his forehead vigorously, and smoothed his forelock. "I'll take you for a ride sometime. If you like?"

"I would love that. Although King looks a bit much for me to handle."

"Oh don't worry about that, I've got just the horse for you. Her name's Merry. She'll be perfect, she's right over here."

Kristoff crossed to the other side of the stable, opened the stall door and slipped through; he whistled softly. A small, white mare nickered to him and walked over for a scratch.

"See?" He grinned up at her.

Katie gasped, clapping her hands together with glee. "She is beautiful! Oh, I'd love to ride her. Merry, what a wonderful name for her."

Kristoff looked pleased. "She's yours, if you want her."

"Really?"

Katie's eyes filled with tears. Her very own horse. She couldn't quite believe it.

"Katie, dear. Are you in here?" Mrs. Hutchins' voice echoed through the stable.

"Yes, I'm in here."

Katie dashed the tears away with the back of her hand, and turned to face Mrs. Hutchins with a forced smile.

"We're ready to leave whenever you are. Oh, hello Kristoff, sorry to interrupt. Thank you so much for including us in your lovely celebration."

Kristoff slid from Merry's stall into the corridor and grinned at Mrs. Hutchins, closing the door behind him. "Don't mention it. Good evening, Mrs. Hutchins."

He nodded at Katie, who turned to leave. "Good evening, Katie. Thank you for your company this evening. I hope you've had a nice time."

"Goodbye, Kristoff. I have thoroughly enjoyed myself. But I have to say, I think my favorite part of the evening was getting to meet your gorgeous horses."

As she walked from the stable, she turned back for one last look at Kristoff standing beside Merry, her pretty head hanging over the door of the stall watching Katie's departure. The sight sent a shiver of emotion through Katie's tired body. If Kristoff had no intention of marrying her, why would he give her a mare? It seemed too cruel for a man as kind as he was to offer a gift he had no intention of giving. Katie couldn't help wondering again as she climbed into the wagon, what her future might hold. If only she could find some kind of certainty to cling to.

Chapter Fourteen

The next day dawned late, with grey skies keeping the countryside bathed in a pre-dawn light. Katie rose early anyway, unable to sleep any longer, and pulled a letter from beneath her pillow. It was from Hannah and had arrived with yesterday's mail. Katie had been so excited to see it sitting on the mantle downstairs when they returned home from the party. She had said her goodnights quickly and scurried upstairs to open and read it in private. It didn't tell her anything she didn't already know, since Hannah had no doubt posted it the same day, or soon after, Katie left Boston. But one paragraph in the scrawl of letters had stood out to her and sent a tremor of loneliness through her body.

> *Katie, my dear. Do let Kristoff in, won't you? I know you like to keep us all at arm's length, and I love you just the same. But he will want more than that. I hope you can find it within yourself to give it to him. He's a good man. You can trust him with your tender heart.*

How she missed her friend. Katie lay on the bed for a few minutes, re-reading the letter and considering her friend's wise words. She fingered the locket about her neck and wished she could follow Hannah's advice. She wanted to open up to Kristoff, but she knew it was impossible. If she opened up to him and became truly vulnerable, he'd see the lies she held tightly in her fists. She dressed quickly, and, wrapping a shawl about her shoulders, made her way downstairs in the silent house. She felt like taking a walk around the property, but it was drizzling outside. Katie found a white umbrella by the back door and headed outside. A misty rain fell about her, dampening the usual sounds of morning in the country, and giving her surroundings a clouded, wet look.

The curlews had remained hidden in their nests throughout the night, no doubt sheltering from the rain and cold, and the woodpecker had given up his work for today. The cattle were huddled beneath a large oak tree in the center of the field, and David had not yet ventured out of the house to tend to the morning's chores.

Katie wandered down a well-worn cattle track through the rain-dampened grasses, over a little rise and down a short hill. At the bottom of the hill, she discovered a clear creek. The gentle water bubbled over black rocks and around fallen logs. Squat fir trees hugged the banks of the creek, and she could see the beginnings of a beaver's dam on the opposite side. The water rushed around the small dam wall, and the soothing sound of its journey enveloped Katie.

The misting rain had ceased, and all about her the signs a new day were beginning to emerge. She sat down on the stump of a felled tree, and snapped the umbrella closed. With a loud sigh, she scanned the surrounding landscape. It was a soothing sight, and she soaked in it, reveling in the feeling of peace that crept up about her heart.

Her head was filled with troubling thoughts. Katie had felt the need to get away from the farmhouse for a few minutes to think. She had decisions to make—such as what she was going to do once she returned to Boston. If she returned to Boston. It was all very confusing. First, she'd heard Kristoff telling Belle that he wouldn't go through with the wedding. Then, he'd kissed her. A heart-wrenching, body tingling, life changing kiss, and Katie hadn't been able to think of much else since it had happened. She pulled away from him of course, because his kiss had awakened feelings in her that she thought had died with Nicholas. And knowing, as she did, that he didn't intend to marry her, she knew she had to stop him before it went any further.

She wanted desperately to keep kissing him, but she had to think about her future with a clear head, and being around Kristoff made that almost impossible. Not to mention the fact that he was pulling her body so close to his, he was bound to feel the swell of her stomach through her skirts. Then he had thrown her an engagement party, at which Belle fawned all over him. Finally, he had given Katie a pretty little horse as a gift. So many mixed messages. It was all very vexing.

Katie's mood was pensive. She fretted about what she was going to do, and how she and the baby would survive. She had been so happy when she arrived in California, only days ago. It had seemed as though everything was going to work out. Kristoff was handsome, successful, kind and considerate. He was everything she wanted in a man—if only her heart were ready for love. He'd make a wonderful husband and father, from what she could tell and if everything Hannah had said was true. But he'd decided—too rashly to her way of thinking—that she wasn't what he wanted in a wife. Maybe he would reconsider. Maybe she could get him to change his mind and marry her. After all, he had kissed her with a passion that couldn't be contrived. He must have some feelings for her.

Katie rose to her feet and stretched her arms above her head with a yawn. Pregnancy certainly had a way of exhausting her. She'd never wanted to sleep so much in her life before. Not to mention all of the niggling aches and pains she experienced all over her body on a daily basis. On her way back up the hill toward the house, Katie noticed a buggy standing idle in the driveway, a bay horse grazing freely nearby. It was Kristoff's buggy. What on earth was he doing here so early in the morning? Katie stood frozen in place. What should she do? She didn't want to see him. Not after that kiss, and the party last night. Not when she hadn't decided yet how she was going to win him back.

Seeing her disheveled and bleary-eyed so early in the morning certainly wouldn't help her cause in that regard. And she hadn't even had her breakfast yet. Katie pulled a crust of bread from the pocket of her dress, and shoved it hurriedly into her mouth. She had grabbed a slice on her way out of the kitchen, knowing that she would need to eat as soon as she rose. She tried not to go anywhere these days without a snack on hand. Still staring at the yellow farmhouse, she chewed quietly and considered her options. She could just walk back down to the creek and sit on the stump until he left. No one knew where she was, and he would soon leave. It would be so much easier than facing him. Katie turned, and scurried back down the hill.

"Katie, my dear, there you are. We were quite worried about you. It's cold and wet outside, you must be soaked through," Mrs. Hutchins admonished, fussing about her. Katie stomped through the kitchen door, and wiped her feet on the doormat.

"I'm fine, I had an umbrella with me."

"Kristoff stopped by on his way to the store. He was hoping to see you, and I thought you were still in bed. You can't imagine my surprise when I found your room empty. Mr. Hutchins searched high and low for you. We didn't know what to tell Kristoff."

"I'm so sorry, Mellie. I hope Kristoff wasn't too disappointed."

"He was very disappointed, although he didn't say so, of course. I could tell though."

She handed Katie a dry cloth, and Katie patted her face, hair and dress to remove any dampness. Then she stood in front of the open door of the stove, allowing the heat emanating from the fire to complete the job.

"Do you know what he wanted to see me for? Did he say?" asked Katie, attempting to sound nonchalant.

"He didn't say, exactly. But he did hint at the idea that you were withholding something from him. I believe he wants to make sure that you're all right.

You're not keeping anything from him, are you? You are well?"

Mrs. Hutchins eyed her with apprehension, as she filled the coffee pot with water and set it on the stovetop.

"Of course I'm not keeping anything from him. Everything is well. I am well. He's being overly cautious, that's all. I couldn't sleep, so rose early to take a walk. I'm sorry I missed him." Katie pulled an apron from a peg on the wall beside the back door, and fixed it firmly about her waist.

Mrs. Hutchins nodded with relief, and smiled tenderly at Katie.

"You know, Katie dear, Kristoff is a good man. I've known him for four years, and in all that time he's never had a serious courtship, or a casual affair. He is honest and reliable, not to mention tender-hearted. I hope you can see that. I'd hate for you to miss an opportunity for happiness because you didn't realize what you had, standing right in front of you. He wants to marry you, and if you're having second thoughts about that, perhaps you should talk to him about it."

"I'm not having second thoughts," said Katie. She grabbed a bowl of freshly gathered eggs, and greased a frying pan with pork lard, then placed the pan on top of the stove. She cracked the eggs into the pan, one by one. As she stirred them, she watched the clear liquid of the eggs mix with the thick, yellow centers and grow firm beneath her spoon.

"Well, that's good news. I'm glad to hear it. I think the two of you will be very happy together."

"You're sure Kristoff still wants to marry me?"

asked Katie, her wide eyes following Mrs. Hutchins as she bustled about the kitchen.

"Of course he does, why wouldn't he?"

"I don't know," mumbled Katie, scooping the scrambled eggs onto three plates.

Mrs. Hutchins stopped her work, and placed one hand on her hip. The other held the handle of a hot enamel coffee pot encased in a thick cloth.

"Katie, my dear, is there something you'd like to get off your chest?"

"No, Mellie, everything is just fine. Although, I think I'll stay home today and read by the fire. It's the perfect day to sit by the fire with a good book, don't you think?"

"Yes, that sounds lovely." Mrs. Hutchins returned to her flurry of activity, the concerned look returning to her round face.

Mr. Hutchins stomped through the kitchen door, wiping his thick rubber boots on the mat. His morning chores complete, his cheeks held a rosy glow.

"Good morning ladies," he said.

He tipped his hat from his head, and slid it onto a peg by the door. Then he walked to the washbasin to wash up for breakfast.

"Good morning, Mr. Hutchins," said Katie.

Mrs. Hutchins shot him a warm smile. "Breakfast is ready, my dear."

"Fantastic!" he grinned at them both. "There is fresh milk in the outdoors pantry if you need it."

"Lovely," said Katie. She was enjoying the creamy white milk that seemed to be in unlimited supply on the farm. Along with the cheeses, butter and cream that the Hutchinses liked to use liberally, dousing all of their meals with one if not all of them. Katie still wasn't used to eating and drinking such rich and, to her mind, luxurious foods. Ever since she'd arrived in Sacramento there'd been good food to eat, and plenty of it.

They sat together at the dining table and Mr. Hutchins prayed a quick blessing over the meal. As she lay a napkin across the lap of her gown, she noticed her corset was sticking out at a strange angle beneath the fabric. She pushed at it to smooth it down. It felt as though she could barely breathe, it was pulled so tight around her middle. Every day, she'd been loosening it, but it seemed today was the day she'd have to give it up altogether. She sighed as deeply as she could, given the restrictive clothing, and lifted a forkful of eggs to her mouth.

It was just as well she was staying home, since without a corset it would be obvious to any observant person that her girth was growing. If Kristoff saw her like that, he'd know for sure she was pregnant and would never consider marrying her. She had to keep him in the dark for as long as it took to get him to fall in love with her and change his mind about backing out of the wedding. Then, when they were married, she could finally tell him the truth.

Katie wanted so badly to share her situation with Kristoff. To be open with him, to let him into her world and into her life. She didn't want to hold him at arm's length. But she had no choice. This baby couldn't be kept secret for much longer, and if Kristoff turned her away she wouldn't be able to secure a job or find a new beau. She'd be alone and vulnerable, and so would her child. And Katie wasn't certain she'd able to keep the child. Unable to even consider bringing her baby into such a situation, she set her mind to the task at hand—getting Kristoff to fall in love with her, change his mind and marry her, on Friday, without him finding out her secret. Simple.

Chapter Fifteen

Kristoff strode to the stables. The weather-worn timber structure stood just behind the house, and it was his favorite part of the ten acre property. Moving through the stalls, he patted each horse he passed. Their soft noses nuzzled his hands, looking for food, and their quiet nickering beckoned him to come back after he had moved on. King stood tall in the last stall. His sleek black coat was covered with a warm blanket, and he moved restlessly about the confined space, trampling the dense covering of straw on the floor.

"Time for a run, hey big boy?" Kristoff opened the door of the stall, and reached for King's halter. The horse's face was strong, and his eyes drooped closed comfortably as he pushed his nose beneath Kristoff's hand for a scratch. A long stripe of white ran down the length of his head, between his large, dark eyes and over the end of his snout.

"It's been too long, hasn't it?"

Kristoff disappeared back into the main stable, returning shortly with a saddle, saddle rug and bridle.

He pulled the blanket from King's back, and folded it carefully over the stall door. Then, he threw the saddle rug up over the horse's withers and placed the saddle on top. Securing the saddle in place with the girth, he slipped a shiny bit into King's pink mouth and pushed the bridle over his twitching ears. King lifted his legs impatiently, stamping in place as Kristoff finished up. Leading the giant horse out of the stall, Kristoff stopped outside to stare up into the magnificent sky. The clouds had lifted, taking the rest of the rain with them, and the crisp air felt freshly washed, the scent of grasses and damp earth hanging pleasantly about him. The stars were even more vibrant than usual, and the howl of a coyote sent King trotting sideways, pulling against the reins.

"Steady there, boy," said Kristoff. He reached for King's face, and rubbed his nose gently. He slipped the reins over King's head and up onto his neck. Then, taking them in both hands, he pushed his foot into a stirrup, and leapt up on top of the horse, as he pranced about the yard.

"OK boy, let's go," Kristoff leaned down to whisper in the horse's back-turned ears.

King took off, out of the yard at a gallop. They careened down the driveway, and out onto the country road. There was something so appealing about country life that Kristoff had never wanted to give it up, even when his store became successful and Sacramento society beckoned. He owned several horses, two cows for milking, and a handful of chickens for eggs. He hoped that Katie would enjoy living there too. She seemed to be enjoying the Hutchinses' farm, and his house was very similar in many ways, although his wasn't a working farm. She also seemed to have taken a liking to his horses the other night at the engagement party. He wondered whether Katie preferred country or city living. It was definitely something they should discuss before Friday. Perhaps he'd ask her tonight.

Kristoff had been frustrated that morning when he dropped by the farmhouse to see Katie. After deciding that he needed to get to know her better, he rose from bed even earlier than usual to spend some time with her before he had to be at work. But she wasn't there, and Mrs. Hutchins didn't seem to know where she might be. It was downright aggravating. They had such limited time to get to know one another, and Kristoff felt as though he was being foiled at every turn.

The sound of King's hooves pounding against the hard road filled the night's silence, echoing through the valley and up the sides of a nearby canyon, which sent the noise right back to Kristoff. He was determined to get to know more about Katie tonight. He still had reservations about marrying her, but that kiss had muddled his head. Kristoff wanted her. It was that simple. He could try to talk his way around it, and complain night and day about her vexing ways, but it didn't change the singular fact—he wanted to marry Katie Pearson on Friday. So, he was going to have to get her to open up to him before then, somehow. If he could see her again, perhaps it would assuage his concerns about marrying her. He wanted to know her—everything about her, but he was a patient man, and was willing to give it some time. If she would just give a little, let him get to know a small part of her. Surely she would let him in.

Katie was startled by the sound of hooves hammering down the drive and into the yard. The noise stopped at the garden path, and she heard a loud banging on the front door.

"Who could that be?" Mr. Hutchins exclaimed from his armchair.

Katie sat with Mr. and Mrs. Hutchins in the living room before a roaring fire. Freshly cut logs cracked and spat in the hearth the warmth of the blaze kept the cool night air at bay. Mrs. Hutchins was knitting a green shawl, and Katie was crocheting a tiny woolen hat. The yellow wool thread wove in and out, over and under, and Katie's fingers trembled as she watched the teeny bonnet taking shape before her eyes. Mr. Hutchins was smoking his post-supper pipe, and reading the newspaper, since a farmer rarely got to read it in the morning when the cows needed milking. Grunting unhappily, he pushed himself to his feet.

"Who would call unannounced at this hour?"

He opened the door to find Kristoff standing there. His long coat trailed almost to his feet, and he wore a black Stetson perched high on his golden curls. He grinned, showing off his dimple and pulled the hat from his head.

"Good evening, David, how are you on this fair night?"

"Good evening, Kristoff. I do hope everything is all right?"

"Fine. Fine. Yes, everything is fine. I'm so sorry to

stop by without warning, but as you know I don't get a lot of free time these days."

"Of course, won't you come in?"

"Please, sit down," said Mrs. Hutchins, hurrying to clear a place on the sofa next to Katie. She moved Katie's bag of wool and crochet needles to the floor, and kicked them deftly under the seat.

"Thank you, I will."

Kristoff removed his coat, which was quickly taken by Mrs. Hutchins who hung it by the door along with his hat. Then he ambled to the sofa, and sat down.

"Katie." He nodded at her, with a half-smile.

"Kristoff, how nice to see you." Katie carefully readjusted her gown so that it puffed out over her abdomen sufficiently.

"And you, I hope you've had a nice day. I was sorry to miss you this morning." He peered at her inquisitively, and Katie felt her face flushing red beneath his gaze. It was as though he knew she'd avoided him intentionally.

"I heard you were looking for me. I'm so sorry I missed you—I took a walk."

"In the rain?"

"It wasn't raining much."

"Still."

"It was lovely. I can't get enough of the countryside around here. It's so very beautiful. So wild and full of life." Katie smiled at Mr. and Mrs. Hutchins as she spoke, trying to avoid making eye contact with Kristoff.

"I'm glad you think so," he said, "I hope you liked

my place just as well. The two properties are very similar."

"Oh, I did. Even though it was dark, I could tell it was a beautiful home and property." Katie glanced up at him, wondering why he would care what she thought of his home if he had decided against marrying her.

"Would you like to take a walk?" he asked suddenly, standing to his feet and holding out one hand toward Katie.

Katie took his hand, and stood as well, still holding the small, yellow bonnet. Her dress no longer fit as well as it once did, and had inched upwards causing it to gather and scrunch together above her waist. She tugged at it, trying in vain to pull it down to where it was intended to sit on her hips. She lay her work down on the sofa, and followed Kristoff from the room.

Mrs. Hutchins looked up from her knitting and beamed at the pair, as they walked hand-in-hand past her and out onto the front porch.

"Have a nice time," she said.

Katie's heart was racing and felt as though it might catapult itself into her throat at any moment. The touch of Kristoff's large, warm hand in hers sent shivers pulsating through her body. The confident way he led her from the house made her feel giddy. What was he doing? Where was he taking her? He started down the porch steps, then turned and pulled her into his chest, kissing her abruptly on the mouth. Caught off guard, Katie whimpered. His hands crept around behind her back, drawing her closer still, and she melted into his embrace. Katie's arms stole around his neck, and she stood on tip-toe to kiss him back. He groaned, then pulled away from her, his mouth in a lop-sided grin.

"So, you do like me," he said with a chuckle.

"Hmmm." Katie's eyes were still half-closed, and she was reveling in the feel of his arms around her body. His hands felt their way around from her back to the sides of her waist, and she remembered her growing bump. She pushed him backwards, and he stumbled down the stairs.

"Oh dear, I'm so sorry, Kristoff. Are you all right?" Katie hurried down the steps to him.

"What on earth?" he stuttered. "What's going on? Something is wrong—don't say it's not. We were kissing and you were enjoying it. Then all of a sudden your face turned ashen and you pushed me away. Something is bothering you, and I think it's high time you tell me the truth Katie." He regained his balance and stood looking at her with his hands on his hips.

"I just don't think we should. You know…kiss like that. Not until we're married." Katie crossed her arms over her middle, and her gaze fell to the ground.

"And that's all?"

"That's all."

She heard Kristoff sigh loudly. "I still feel as though you're not telling me something, but if you say that's all it is, then I'll believe you. If we're going to be married on Friday…"

Katie's eyes flew to his face, and she stepped toward him with hope, "You still want to marry me?"

Kristoff looked confused. He frowned, and reached for Katie's hands. Holding them in his own, he watched her face closely.

"Of course I do. Isn't that what we planned? Nothing's changed, has it?"

"Well, I wasn't sure."

"You mean, you aren't sure about me?"

"No, nothing like that. Nothing's changed for me, I just wasn't sure you still wanted to get married. I overheard you talking to that woman, Belle Waters, in your store."

"Oh, her. Belle's had an interest in me for years. It's nothing. It's not reciprocal, I assure you. There has never been anything between us, and there never will be."

Kristoff twisted his hands in hers so that their fingers were interlaced. Her breath caught. Perhaps she had misheard him. It seemed almost like a dream, or a nightmare, now that she was thinking of it. Had it really happened?

"I also heard you tell her you didn't intend to go through with it. That I wasn't what you had expected, and…"

"I didn't say that. Oh wait, I did say that."

Katie felt a weight crushing her chest. Was he trying to hurt her? Without warning, Kristoff laughed heartily. His face turned red, and he laughed until tears squeezed from his closed eyes and onto his cheeks. Katie watched him in utter confusion. He looked as though he might be going mad? She giggled a little along with him, since his laugh was so infectious she couldn't help herself. Perhaps they were both mad. Finally Kristoff stopped laughing, and looked at her with affection in his eyes.

"What is it?" she asked him.

"I did say that." He whispered it kindly. "Is that what you've been worrying about all this time? Well, you needn't have worried. I was talking to my miller. He brought in a barrel of flour to replace the one you—well, he brought it anyway—and it was full of weevils. I told him I wasn't going to pay him for it. That's what I was talking about. It wasn't about you and I wasn't speaking to Belle. She had already left when he arrived."

He smiled at her, reaching up to push a stray strand of hair from her face. Katie's mouth dropped open. Could it be true? He wasn't speaking of their wedding at all, but talking to his supplier about some bad flour. He wanted to marry her still. She didn't have to go back to Boston to face the world alone. She drew a deep breath into her lungs and closed her eyes, drinking in the moment. She should tell him about the baby. He was happy, they were alone; it was the perfect time. Maybe he wouldn't be upset. She couldn't keep it from him any longer, not the way he was looking at her. Not the way she was feeling when she looked at him.

"Kristoff, there's something…"

Just then, he leaned in to kiss her again, and the passion between them ignited a fire deep inside Katie that surprised her. She forgot the words she was going to say, so carefully planned in quiet moments, and became lost in this moment, her head spinning and her heart pounding. The softness of his lips, his firm arms wrapped tightly around her. Nothing else mattered.

Chapter Sixteen

It was the day before the wedding, and Kristoff had arrived at the Hutchinses' farm in a weathered looking open wagon just before noon. Dressed in brown pants and a blue, button-down shirt with a tan Stetson perched on top of his blonde curls, he grinned down at Katie before leaping to the ground. Katie's heart fluttered at the sight of him. After last night, she felt an intense and growing attraction to him. She was standing in the yard playing fetch with one of the Hutchinses' two black and white dogs, when he pulled in, and her heart raced when she realized who it was. She reached up to straighten her wind-blown hair, and ran her palms down her wrinkled and dusty skirts in an attempt to smooth them.

"I thought you might like to come and have a picnic with me. It's such a beautiful day, and it would be a good chance for us to get to know each other a little better. What do you say?"

"That sounds lovely," said Katie, thinking again how considerate Kristoff could be.

"Great! You don't have to bring a thing, I've already packed everything we need. Just bring your sun bonnet, and we'll go."

Katie hurried inside to grab her bonnet. Mrs. Hutchins stood in the kitchen kneading bread dough on the counter. Her sleeves were rolled up high, and her arms were covered in white flour from her hands to her elbows. She smiled at Katie as she pushed down hard, deftly spinning and folding the dough.

"Kristoff's here," said Katie, reaching for the blue bonnet that was hanging by its long strings on a hook by the back door next to Mr. Hutchins' work hat. "He wants to take me on a picnic."

"What a good idea. The weather is perfect for it. You kids have fun."

Katie nodded and ran back to Kristoff as she tied the bonnet onto her head, her boots clacking loudly on the timber boards of the farmhouse floor. Kristoff and Katie rode silently in the wagon for a while, each quietly enjoying the company of the other and the warmth beating down from the sun high above them chasing away the last of the winter chill. A flock of ducks flew by overhead, their loud quacking echoing down over the couple. Katie tipped her head back to watch their steady formation flapping by.

"Happy?" asked Kristoff. His eyes crinkled around the edges as he smiled at Katie.

"Mmm." Katie nodded. She gripped the edge of the wagon seat to steady herself, and turned her head to survey the contents of the wagon bed behind her. She could see a picnic rug, a basket—no doubt full of food and drink—an umbrella and a large, soft cushion. It looked as though Kristoff had thought of everything. She wondered if he had always been this romantic.

"Do you ever miss Boston?" she asked.

"Yes, sometimes. I don't really miss the city itself much. I miss my family. But of course, my parents are gone and I don't have any siblings. So, mostly I miss my extended family—including Hannah, of course. I think it would've been different if I'd had immediate family living there. Perhaps I wouldn't have left Boston, but since I didn't really have anything tying me down—I thought I'd try my hand at being a Pioneer. It all sounded very adventurous and exciting at the time, and I was still so young."

"Are you glad you did it?"

"Yes, I am. I wouldn't change a thing. Although of course, there's always a cost to every choice we make in life, one way or the other."

"What was the cost—if you don't mind my prying?"

"I don't mind at all. The cost was loneliness. Until now, that is." He grinned at her, and tipped his hat toward her deferentially.

"Oh." Katie was taken aback by his bluntness, and his willingness to be so open and vulnerable with her. He hadn't seemed embarrassed to share such deeply personal feelings with her. Katie looked at him with admiration. She wished she could be so open and trusting with him. She just didn't know how to—she'd never been like that with anyone. Even with Nicholas, she'd always kept up something of a mask, to hide any pain or difficulty she might be experiencing, as though she were somehow protecting him from it. "I'm sorry."

"No need to be. I'm not afraid of loneliness. I prefer not to be lonely though, of course, that's why I'm so glad you're here."

Katie felt a warmth, that didn't come from the sunny day, drifting to her very core. It had been a long time since she'd felt so safe, secure and accepted. She relished the feeling, and fell silent again as the sound of the bay's hooves beat a steady rhythm amidst the twittering of birds, and the rustling of leaves in the late winter breeze.

The wagon trundled by several homesteads in a range of shapes and sizes, and in various states of repair. In one yard, children played hopscotch and several dogs roamed free, barking at the passersby while keeping their distance. The next property was still and abandoned looking, but Katie could see smoke winding from the chimney. She wondered who might live there. Soon after, they reached Kristoff's long, winding driveway. He jumped from the wagon to open the gate, then returned to drive the horse through it, before leaping out to close it again behind them.

"I don't remember us having to open the gate when we came over for the party the other night," observed Katie.

"No, I moved the cattle to another field that night so I could prop the gate open."

Katie realized there was a lot she would have to learn about living on a farm. She'd never even visited one before coming to Sacramento, and the whole concept of looking after animals and property was so foreign to her.

Chickens were scratching about in the yard as the wagon trundled in. They fluttered out of the way with loud squawks as the wagon passed. Katie wondered if she would be collecting their eggs every morning. She wasn't even sure how to go about doing something like that. There was so much to consider on a farm. She felt a stab of anxiety in the pit of her stomach. She wondered if she would ever learn to be useful out here.

The wagon continued through the yard, and down the edge of the field. A set of wagon tracks stretched out before them, and their horse carried on trotting as though he knew where he was travelling. Kristoff let him have his head.

"Where are we going?" asked Katie.

"There's a lovely hollow down by the lake. I thought we might sit there."

Before long, a small lake appeared beyond a patch of conifers. There were fir trees lining the banks of the lake, and a variety of waterfowl dotted its surface and shoreline. Behind it rose the mighty peaks of the Sierra Nevada, and Katie gasped in delight at the beauty of the scene laid out before her.

"Do you like it?" asked Kristoff, grinning.

"It's absolutely stunning. I've never seen anything so wild and beautiful."

"This is the edge of my property. The lake divides my land from Mr. Smythe's ranch, over yonder."

"Do you ever see the Smythe's?"

"Every now and then, they're good folk. They shop in my store whenever they come to town."

"What about the other neighbors, do you know any of them?"

He tipped his head to one side and narrowed his

eyes, "Of course, all of them. Didn't you know your neighbors in Boston?"

"Not many of them—Hannah, of course, but I knew her from school."

Kristoff shook his head in disbelief.

"Sure is a different life in the city, I guess."

"Yes it is."

Kristoff stopped the wagon beside a small patch of green grass. A large boulder marked the edge of the lake next to the clearing, and beyond it rose the edge of the dark woods.

"How about here?" he asked.

"It's perfect."

Kristoff climbed from the wagon, and helped Katie to the ground. He unhitched the bay to graze in the clearing, and then set up the picnic rug, driving the umbrella into the ground behind it to give Katie shade to sit in. She settled on the soft cushion he'd brought with them, and watched with delight as he unpacked a never-ending stream of goodies from the picnic basket.

There were ham sandwiches, slices of cheese, freshly baked ginger snap cookies and fruit slices. There was lemonade to drink, and pieces of decadent chocolate for dessert. Katie had never eaten such a lavish picnic before, and she ate until she could hold no more.

"That was delicious," she said, rubbing her full stomach with satisfaction.

"I'm glad you enjoyed it." Kristoff lay on one side, his hand supporting his head, as he watched Katie finish her meal with obvious pleasure.

"Did you make all of this yourself?"

"I wish I could say yes. But Mrs. Dane comes to help me out at home a few days per week. You'll get to meet her soon. She's a magician in the kitchen, and is responsible for most of my meals, including the food we ate at our engagement party. Although of course I'm sure you'll want to take charge of all of that after you settle in."

Katie nodded. She was looking forward to being Mrs. Kristoff Petersen, and couldn't wait to show him how well she could take care of him. He'd been taking such good care of her, she wanted to reciprocate, and soon she'd have the chance.

"Would you like to take a walk?" asked Kristoff, standing slowly and stretching his arms above his head with a yawn. "I might just go to sleep here if I don't get moving soon."

"That sounds nice. If I can walk after all of that food." Katie chuckled as Kristoff helped pull her to her feet. He tugged a little too hard, and she landed softly against his chest, her face tipped to meet his. He kissed her lightly on the mouth, and stared lovingly into her eyes.

"I'm looking forward to tomorrow," he whispered against her parted lips.

She smiled in response, and kissed him back, pulling his head toward hers with one hand. He groaned and kissed her harder, as he ran his fingers through her loose hair. Katie matched his passion, and their kiss grew deeper and more demanding. Kristoff lifted Katie from her feet, high above his head while their lips remained joined. Then he pulled away from her with a smile, and gently lowered her back to the ground. Taking her hand in his, he led her toward the woods.

"Where are you taking me, Mr. Petersen—do you intend to kill me and dump me in the woods?" asked Katie, laughing.

He turned to face her with a lowered brow and narrowed eyes. "How did you know that?" he asked in a tremulous voice.

Katie stopped, her eyes widening.

Kristoff laughed loudly, and swung her up into his arms, darting into the woods.

"You're mine now, Mrs. Pearson," he shouted. Katie squealed and the two of them giggled together as he ran.

When they were deep inside the woods, Kristoff set Katie's feet back on the ground gently, and took her hand in his again. The two of them explored amongst the trees and down to the edge of the lake, finding a duck's nest buried in leaves and twigs, with six large, white eggs in the center. Just as they bent to admire the nest, the mother duck came flying at them, quacking and flapping her wings.

Katie and Kristoff jumped out of the way, and dashed back toward the wagon laughing. Katie felt her foot slip on something. She stopped running to turn back investigate. It looked to be some kind of nest.

"Is that a bee's nest?" she asked. "It must have fallen from one of the nearby trees."

Kristoff bent to peer at it. Just then, a swarm of bees emerged from the nest, surrounding them quickly.

"Yes it is, run!" shouted Kristoff.

He took Katie's hand, and pulled her behind him,

the bees buzzing after them. Katie felt a sting on her arm, and another on the back of her neck. She squealed and ran faster. Then her ankle twisted in a hole, and she fell to the ground with a thud, letting go of Kristoff's hand. He turned and ran back to her.

"Are you all right?" he asked, swatting at bees.

"I think I twisted my ankle, it hurts," sobbed Katie.

"Can you stand on it?"

Katie tried to stand, but the ankle was too painful. She cried out and fell back to the ground.

"No, I don't think so."

"OK, hold on."

Kristoff lifted Katie's arms to place them around his neck, then he drew her into his arms and carried her quickly from the woods and back into the clearing. The bees gave up their pursuit, and the couple collapsed relieved onto the picnic rug.

"Well, that was exciting," said Katie.

Kristoff laughed, "I'm glad you thought so. Are you ready to go back home?"

Katie nodded, "Yes, I think I've had enough adventure for today. I only hope I'll be able to walk down the aisle tomorrow."

Kristoff frowned, "I'm so sorry, Katie."

She lifted her hand to cup his cheek gently. "Never mind, Kristoff. I will be fine, and I've had the loveliest time."

"I'm looking forward to many more fun picnics in our future, minus the bees and the twisted ankles, of course." Kristoff grinned at her ruefully.

"Me too," said Katie.

"Well, let's get you home then."

Chapter Seventeen

Katie lifted her foot and lowered it gently into the wooden bucket filled with water and chunks of ice purchased in town by Kristoff and delivered, as quickly as he could manage, to the Hutchinses' farm. Katie grimaced as her swollen ankle sank into the frigid water. She lifted her dress out of the way, to keep it dry. She was sitting on the bed in her bedroom at the Hutchinses' farm, and Mrs. Hutchins hovered over her with concern written across her round face.

"How does that feel, dear?" asked Mrs. Hutchins.

"Cold."

"Well now, while you're sitting there, I have a few things to show you for the wedding."

Mrs. Hutchins opened the closet door and her upper body disappeared into it as she foraged around on the top shelf for something. She soon emerged with a long package wrapped in brown paper.

"Here it is," she said with satisfaction.

She lay it on the bed beside Katie, and then returned

to the closet. She pulled out another package, this one smaller than the first, and lay it on the bed too.

"What's this?" asked Katie.

"My wedding dress and veil, I thought you might like them."

"Oh, do you mean that I can wear them for my wedding?" asked Katie, her mouth dropping open in surprise.

"Yes, that's what I was thinking. If you'd like to. Mind, the dress will be a bit big for you, dear, but I'm sure you'll look beautiful in it, just the same."

"I would like to. In fact, I would love to. Oh, please can I see it?"

Mrs. Hutchins beamed, and reached to open the package. She tore it open gently, and pulled a long, cream dress from within. The dress had a high waist, and a low neckline. The bodice was decorated with fine lace and hand-sewn pearls. The skirt was full, and swept down to a short train. Katie gasped, and threw one hand to her chest.

"It's wonderful! Oh, I can't wait to try it on."

"Yes, well it may need some adjustments, but I think it will work quite well for you."

Katie's eyes filled with tears, and she took Mrs. Hutchins' hands in her own.

"Thank you, Mellie. You have no idea how much this means to me. I thought I'd have to wear my green velveteen dress, or the brown corduroy one. And even though I wouldn't have minded that so very much, having a proper wedding dress to wear—well, it makes everything more real, don't you think?"

"Yes, I do. I'm glad you like it, dear."

"I do. I love it. And I'm so grateful for your friendship, Mellie. I don't know how I would have coped with all of this if you weren't here. Thank you."

Mrs. Hutchins ducked her head, and her cheeks flushed pink.

"Well, well. It's nothing at all. We're glad we can help you, my dear. And dear Kristoff as well."

Katie held the dress up in front of her, and stared at her reflection in the mirror. She almost didn't recognize the woman staring back at her. The rich food and relaxed, outdoors lifestyle of the past days in Sacramento had filled out her cheeks and brought color back to her face. Her hair shone, and her eyes sparkled. Even as she regarded herself, she felt a pang of guilt over her deception. Tomorrow, Katie would be walking down the aisle to become Kristoff's wife. And yet he still didn't know that she carried Nicholas's unborn child. How could she go through with it? How could she wear this beautiful dress, and say those ardent vows in front of all their guests, knowing that she wasn't being honest with Kristoff? She watched in the mirror as her eyes clouded over, and her face grew glum.

What would Hannah think of her? Keeping this secret from Kristoff was a betrayal to him, but also to Hannah. She sighed, and lay back on the bed, her foot going numb in the cold water. What could she do? If she told Kristoff the truth now, he might back out of the wedding. Now that she had gotten to know him and care about him that was the last thing she wanted. She was afraid he wouldn't want anything more to do with her, and she couldn't bear the thought of it. She was so confused, and each passing day seemed to muddy the waters more and more. She had to go through with the wedding, there was really no other option. And when she told Kristoff her secret, she could only hope he would be understanding.

Chapter Eighteen

The day had arrived and she was sitting in her small bedroom on the second floor of the Hutchinses' farmhouse. Katie sucked in her cheeks and blew out a full breath. She was feeling anxious, and her stomach was in knots. It was her wedding day, and Kristoff was waiting for her at the chapel with a host of his friends and colleagues. The only problem—she was having a crisis of conscience. She didn't want to marry Kristoff without telling him the truth. She dreaded seeing his face after the wedding when she revealed her pregnancy to him. He would feel betrayed, and rightly so. The thought of causing him any pain was making her dizzy with worry.

Did she really want to be married to someone who felt as though he'd been tricked into it? What if he held it against her for the rest of their lives together? Or worse still, what if he abandoned her and the baby—tossed her aside and sent her on her way? She had to face him and come clean about the whole situation. Her timing certainly could have been better. Sixty of

Kristoff's closest friends were crammed into the small chapel, no doubt excited about the coming nuptials. Katie closed her eyes to picture them, chattering and laughing, the women scrutinizing each other's gowns, hairstyles and hats, the men discussing the weather or their latest business deal.

Fanning herself with her hands, Katie glanced at the white gown hanging behind her bedroom door. Mrs. Hutchins wedding gown was beautiful. They'd made a few adjustments the previous evening after Katie had tried standing on her sore ankle and found it bearable. Then, Mrs. Hutchins had helped her into the dress. A stack of pins between her lips, she'd pinned here and there until the dress fit perfectly, and then they'd sat before the fire together while Mrs. Hutchins finished working on it.

The style was old fashioned, but becoming to Katie's fine features. She was grateful for the larger size and the high waist. When she got up this morning it seemed as though her bump had grown overnight. It bulged outward through her thin nightgown, unable to be concealed any longer. She wore a shawl over an old housedress at breakfast, even though it wasn't nearly cold enough in the well-heated farmhouse. After breakfast, she ascended the stairs slowly, savoring her last minutes living in the Hutchinses' farmhouse. They had been so kind to her, she was sad to leave, although she knew she'd see them often since they lived so close by.

After breakfast she wandered back into her room and sat on the bed. The window was pulled shut, to keep out the cold night air. She leaned over to open it, and felt the brisk breeze fan her face. She turned to look again at the wedding dress hanging on the back of her bedroom door. Its short train brushed against the floorboards, and the lace bodice shimmered in the morning light.

"It's almost time to go, dear," called Mrs. Hutchins from her bedroom down the hall.

"Yes, Mellie."

Katie stood and removed her shawl and housedress. Standing in front of the looking glass, she studied her protruding belly, rubbing it gently with her hands. She felt a sudden rush of butterflies.

That was odd.

There it went again. Almost as though something were tickling her from the inside. Sudden realization dawned. It was the baby. She was feeling her child moving within her. Katie's hand flew to her mouth, and she gasped with pleasure. Tears shone in her blue eyes, and her face broke into a large grin.

What a special gift for today.

Katie narrowed her eyes to regard the corset hanging on the end of the bed. She stood and shook her head, then slid it back into a drawer in the dresser. There would be no corset worn today. The thick petticoats Mrs. Hutchins had given her to go with the gown slipped over her head easily and she managed to fasten them in place thanks to their roominess. Next, she reached for the dress. When it fell into place around her, she again studied her reflection and saw that the high waist and full skirts hid her secret well. She smiled with satisfaction, and fastened Hannah's locket around her neck. Then, remembering the task ahead of her, she slumped back onto the bed, crushing the back of her dress.

Mrs. Hutchins bustled into the room carrying a bouquet of wild flowers. Delicate milkmaids, wild pink roses and burnt orange poppies were pushed together in a vibrant bunch, their scent wafting about the small room and filling Katie's sensitive nose with their smell.

"Now, my dear, are you ready to go? Oh dear, you'll wrinkle your dress. Up you get. Let me do up your buttons." She helped Katie to her feet, and nimbly buttoned the back of the gown. Katie felt morose, as though the wedding was a farce, since Kristoff didn't know the truth about her situation. And the idea of facing him, of telling him the truth, saddened her. She sighed, and reached to smooth her hair back into a braid that twisted elegantly around her head and settled into a full bun. Mrs. Hutchins helped her secure it with pins, and before long the style was complete, giving Katie an air of graceful poise.

Mrs. Hutchins lifted Katie's chin with one finger and peered into her blue eyes with her own grey ones.

"What is it, child? It's your wedding day. You should be full of joy, yet look at you. As though the cat stole your breakfast. Tell me, what is wrong?"

Finally, Katie could contain her secret no longer. She burst into tears, blubbering without restraint. In between gasps and sobs, she told Mrs. Hutchins about her troubles. When she finished, Mrs. Hutchins wrapped her arms around Katie and shushed her crying.

"There, there. Everything will work out in the end. You mark my words. There, there. No more crying now."

When Katie had finally calmed down and Mrs. Hutchins had wiped her face clean of tears, she said. "Katie, I know it will be difficult but you have to tell Kristoff."

"What if he doesn't want me anymore?"

"So be it. You aren't without friends, my dear. Mr. Hutchins and I won't allow you to go hungry. You can stay with us for as long as you need to."

"Truly?" Katie's tears welled up again as she hugged the older woman tightly, and cried into her shoulder.

"Yes, yes. Don't you fret, my dear. What matters most is that a kind and good man is waiting, with all of his friends, for you to marry him. You have to tell him the truth. You don't want to marry him with this hanging over your head. Whatever you decide to do though, you have my support."

"Thank you, Mellie. You're right," said Katie, taking a deep breath and setting her face toward the door with resolve.

Katie walked into the hall, and turned to smile at Mrs. Hutchins through watery eyes.

"Thank you again, Mellie. You've been so kind to me."

Then, she descended the staircase, finally ready to face her fears, and Kristoff.

Chapter Nineteen

Kristoff stood at the front of the church, his hands crossed solemnly in front of him. The chapel was packed to the brim with townsfolk dressed up in their finest suits and gowns. He smiled grimly at the crowd, and turned to face the back of the church. Where was she? Where was Katie? What was keeping her? He hoped she hadn't changed her mind and run off somewhere.

Just then, Katie came slinking through the door in a beautiful white dress. The bodice was covered in fine lace and pearls, and settled on a high waist. The skirt was full and voluptuous, tumbling to the floor like a waterfall, and ending with a short train. Her neck was delicate and white, graced only with a simple silver locket. Ringlets of blonde hair framed her stunning features, and a veil fell daintily over the back of her head. Kristoff's breath caught in his throat as he watched her. He coughed, and held his hand out to her as she moved toward him. That was when he noticed her blotchy face and red-rimmed eyes full of unshed tears.

"What's wrong, my darling?" he whispered gently, pulling her toward him. He stared deep into her eyes, and saw the pain there. She was vulnerable beneath his gaze for the first time since she'd arrived, and he wondered what was causing her so much angst.

"I have to speak with you."

"All right."

"Outside, if you please," she said, walking to the back of the church and out the door. The crowd murmured as Kristoff passed them, no doubt wondering what was happening.

"Back soon," he called to the group with a forced smile, then followed Katie out the door and into the sunshine.

It was a beautiful day. Spring was almost upon them, and had come early to California this year. Flowers were blooming all about them, birds were singing as they went about their day, and new buds of grasses and scrub were shooting forth to greet the season. Katie stood to one side of the church, her head bowed and her nose buried in the bouquet of flowers she held in her hands. She turned to watch him approach. He stood apart from her, waiting in silence for her to speak.

"I have something to tell you," she began. "As you know, I was married when I lived in Boston."

"Yes, I realize that."

"Well, there's something you don't know. I'm pregnant."

Katie stopped, waiting to see what Kristoff's response would be. He stared at her, shock registering on his face. Then his features clouded over with anger.

"You're pregnant?"

"Yes."

"And you didn't think you should tell me that?"

"I did—I mean, I wanted to. But I was scared."

"Scared? Of me?"

"Scared that you wouldn't want to marry me if you knew."

"Regardless, that's the kind of thing that people who are about to embark on a life together share. Isn't it?" Katie could see torment written all over his face.

"Yes, of course it is. That's why I'm telling you now. I couldn't keep it to myself any longer. I had to tell you. Even if it means you walk away from me. Even if I lose you. I just couldn't marry you without being completely honest."

"Well, thank you for that. But it's just a bit too late. I knew you were keeping something from me, and I asked you over and over to tell me what it was. But you refused. How can I marry someone who would keep something so important from me? All I wanted was for you to trust me, to open up to me. I tried so hard to get to know you, but you kept pushing me away. You don't trust me. Do you trust anyone?"

Katie stood in silence, unable to answer without choking on her words. Her throat was tight and full of tears, and she felt a sob rising in her chest. She held it back and stood quietly, watching Kristoff's distress, unable to do anything to comfort him. Just then, he turned on his heel and strode off into the scrub, disappearing from view.

"Kristoff, wait!" cried Katie, but he didn't turn back. She dropped to the ground, covered her face with her hands and finally let the tears run freely down her cheeks. He didn't want her. She knew this was how it would go. It was why she had waited, not saying anything, wanting to hold on to him for as long as she could before he turned her away. She realized then that she'd never truly had him—that it had all been a lie. She had lost him completely now; completely and forever.

As she cried, she remembered something—Mrs. Hutchins had offered her and the baby a place to stay. She didn't need Kristoff to take care of them. And yet, her heart was grieving over losing him. The pain that welled up from the depths of her soul, the sorrow she was feeling—she loved him. She didn't want to let him go. It wasn't because she needed him to take care of her and the baby, it was because she loved him. She wanted to be his wife, and for him to be her husband—loving each other until they were old and grey. She wanted to share her life with him; she wanted to be his everything.

Leaping to her feet, Katie gathered up the skirts of her wedding gown with both hands and ran after him, limping on her tender ankle. She was sobbing hard. Great racking sobs that tore at her body, and filled her lungs with pain. Tears slid unhindered down her face, dropping from her chin as she ran.

"Kristoff," she whispered, her throat hoarse. Then again, this time more loudly, "Kristoff!"

There he was. Standing in front of her. He turned to face her, his shoulders slumped in defeat.

"Kristoff, please don't leave. I need you. No, I want you. I want to be your wife. Please. I love you. I'm sorry. I'm so sorry. You're right—I don't trust anyone. I never have, ever since my parents died. I haven't been able to trust people, even the people I love. But I want to start trusting again—I want to trust you. I do trust you. Please, can't you forgive me?"

She stood before him, her gown dusty and her hair falling from the pins that had secured it in place, dropping long tendrils about her face. Her cheeks were covered in red splotches, her nose was running and her eyes were red and watery. Kristoff walked toward her, his blue eyes filled with anger and pain.

"You love me? Do you truly mean it?"

"Yes."

He stepped closer, and reached for her cheek, cupping it with one hand. His thumb rubbed her skin lightly. His face changed, and a happy smile pushed the anger away.

"Oh, my darling. How I've longed to hear you say those words. I love you too. I don't care that you're pregnant—so much the better. We'll have a child to share our happiness with. Only, promise me that you'll never keep anything from me again."

Katie laughed for joy, a bubble of laughter that buried her sobs and brought a smile to Kristoff's face.

"I promise. Yes, I promise to share everything with you."

He knelt down on one knee, and took her left hand in his.

"Katie Pearson, my sweet Katie, will you do the honor of being my wife?"

"Oh, yes dearest Kristoff—I will."

Kristoff swept Katie into his arms, lifting her feet

from the ground and kissing her on the mouth with a hot intensity that took her breath away. Lowering her down again, he said, "Well then, shall we?"

He offered her his arm, which she took with a smile, and they walked back to the chapel each thanking God for bringing them together, even through all of the misunderstandings and turmoil.

Chapter Twenty

Kristoff gazed down at the sweet face that beamed up at him through the redness and tears. He grinned at her as the minister read out the vows, which they each repeated after him in turn. He had finally learned her secret, and the veil of secrecy that had been guarding her heart and keeping her from him had dropped. He looked into her face and saw her standing before him—vulnerable and full of joy. She had shared herself with him, the way that he'd been hoping she would from the first moment she'd walked into his store. His soul was full to overflowing with delight.

He scanned the crowd of friends for a moment, and his eyes landed on Mr. and Mrs. Hutchins, who were grinning from ear to ear at the happy couple. Mrs. Hutchins' eyes sparkled with tears, and she dabbed at them with a handkerchief.

Kristoff returned his gaze to his bride, and listened intently as she completed her vows. Then it was his turn to promise to spend his life with her, to protect her and provide for her. To be faithful to her always, and to stand by her side through sickness and health.

"I now pronounce you husband and wife. You may kiss the bride," finished the minister, smiling warmly at them both.

Kristoff drew Katie close to him. His eyes found hers, and they sparkled with pleasure. Slowly, he dropped his face to hers, his eyes never breaking the connection. Their lips met, and he felt a jolt of rapture pass through him. His heart felt as though it might burst with contentment. Ending the kiss, he took her face between his hands and kissed the tip of her nose.

"So, Mrs. Petersen. Are you ready to go home?" he whispered.

She nodded, her eyes full of love.

"Well then, let's go."

The couple faced the audience, fingers woven together, and received a great cheer in response. They moved through the crowd, accepting congratulations and shaking hands as they made their way down the aisle. Children threw a colorful and sweet smelling mixture of flower petals and rice at them. Strangers hugged Katie's neck. And as they strode through the door, the brilliant sunshine glanced off their golden heads. They turned to face each other with a smile, and holding tightly to the other's hand they stepped forward into their new life.

Epilogue

August 1871

The trotting movements of the horse beneath Katie made her catch her breath as they bounded across an open field. She caught her bottom lip between her teeth, and held it there. They were going so fast, the ground was flying by beneath Merry's trotting black hooves, and Katie didn't know if she could stay balanced for much longer. Widening her eyes, she felt her body drifting to one side—further and further with each bounce.

Just as she was about to slide right off, Kristoff came riding up beside her with a wide grin lighting up his tanned face.

"Everything all right there, Mrs. Petersen?"

Katie flashed him a nervous smile. "I think I'm falling!"

Kristoff leaned toward her and pushed her back up into the saddle with one, strong hand.

"Better?"

Katie nodded, and took a firmer hold of the reins, pulling them tighter with both hands.

"Try moving your body with the horse. Push down into the saddle, and rock your pelvis like this." Kristoff's muscular physique swayed with the motion of the horse, his rear never leaving the seat of the saddle.

Poking the tip of her tongue out one side of her mouth in concentration, Katie tried to mimic him but it was hard to do while riding side-saddle, and she found herself bouncing even harder on poor Merry's back. Kristoff laughed with delight at her, a full bodied, contagious laugh that almost made Katie smile.

"I can't do it," she cried, pouting.

"Keep trying, my darling. In a few years we'll be teaching little Nicky how to ride, and you'll need to be able to keep up with us. We won't want to leave you behind."

Katie felt her heart warm at his words. Every time he spoke of their child, it still gave her a thrill. Less than a year ago, she'd been so anxious about her and her baby's future. But now, everything was so very different. Nicky had been born without complication at their home, with the help of Mrs. Hutchins and a local midwife two months earlier. He was a beautiful, well-settled baby, and Katie found herself falling more and more in love with him every day. And as for Kristoff—their love had blossomed, and grown, until she could no longer imagine her life without him. Since their wedding, eight months earlier, he had courted and wooed her in every way a man could. Katie found herself trusting and leaning on him like she had never been able to do with anyone before. He was her rock, her signpost and her true love. She would never forget her first love—Nicholas—but with Kristoff's help the wounds in her heart had been healed, and she had opened it up to welcome Kristoff in without reservation.

"I know that I promised I'd take you riding on the night of our engagement party," called Kristoff as King took off at a gallop, soon separating the two of them, "but it's better late than never!"

Katie laughed at her wild husband, and leaned forward in her saddle, urging Merry to go faster. Merry took up the challenge and leapt forward into a gallop, her ears back and her legs flying as she followed in King's shadow. Pushing into the saddle, Katie willed her body to move with the horse. All of a sudden, everything smoothed out and Katie's world stopped jolting.

"I'm doing it! I'm doing it!" she cried.

Kristoff peered back at her over his shoulder, and beamed. "I knew you'd get it," he called.

Katie's hair came out of its braid, and drifted out behind her in a wave. She stayed low and snug over Merry's neck, her hands gripping the reins and a smile fixed to her features. She watched as ducks, geese and other waterfowl rose up in fright from the waters of Kristoff's lake as their horses thundered past. The blacks, whites, greys and browns of their feathery plumage highlighted against the dark green of the fir trees, then the lighter colors of the Sierra Nevada rising up at the edge of the valley like a troop of sentinels keeping watch over them. Kristoff pulled King to a stop at the lake's edge, pushing his hat back and lifting his face to absorb the afternoon sunshine. Katie leaned back in her saddle, and tugged gently on the reins, bringing Merry to a halt beside him.

"It's beautiful," said Katie, turning about in her saddle to admire the length of the lush, green valley.

"As are you, my darling wife," said Kristoff, a twinkle in his eyes. "Any regrets, dear?"

Katie shook her head and urged Merry closer to King's side. Standing in her stirrups, she leaned into Kristoff and kissed his full lips, her eyes wide open and meeting his with love.

"None," she replied. "And you?"

He scratched his head thoughtfully, and twisted his mouth into a wry smile. "My only regret is not getting a bigger bed. I mean how much space can one tiny woman take up? Really? You sleep like you're attached to a spinning wheel or something. I get kicked all night long up and down my side, it's most aggravating."

Kristoff laughed heartily and Katie pummeled him on the arm with her small fists.

"I'm teasing. No regrets at all. I'm happier than a man has any right to be."

He lifted his arms and wrapped them around Katie's shoulders, pulling her closer for an intimate embrace. Tilting her chin toward him with one finger, he looked deep into her eyes, then kissed her gently. A short, sweet kiss, followed by a longer, more passionate one that closed Katie's eyes and filled her body with a heat that flowed from her lips to her toes. She soaked it all in—the beauty of the landscape surrounding her, the husband who loved her, and the healthy baby boy who brought her daily joy and thanked God for his bountiful provision.

* * * * *

Historical Note & Author's Remarks

This book was inspired by some time I spent in California during my years living in the United States. It's a wonderful state with such a wide variety of landscapes and wildlife, from the Mojave Desert in the south, to the redwood forests of the north. From the Sierra Nevada mountain range in the east, to the Pacific coast which forms the state's western boundary. California also has as a very interesting history. Ruled separately by first the Native Americans, then by Spain and Mexico, it was finally admitted into the United States of America in 1850 after the Mexican-American war.

In the early 1800s California was considered by those on the more refined east coast to be a wild and untamed country. It wasn't heavily populated by European settlers until the Gold Rush which began in 1848, and then it grew at an enormous pace over a very short period of time as California embraced its statehood. This book, set in 1870, comes along after a series of tumultuous events in the state's dramatic history. Sacramento was coming into its own as a city. The Gold

Rush was over, the city's problems with flooding had been dealt with, and business was booming. It really was the land of opportunity, and many fortunes were made there during that time period.

I hope you've enjoyed following the journey of Katie and Kristoff as they learned to embrace love and their bright future together in a story that spans the country, from Boston to Sacramento.

Warm regards,

Vivi

About the Author

Vivi Holt was born in Australia. She grew up in the country, where she spent her youth riding horses at Pony Club, and adventuring through the fields and rivers around the farm. Her father was a builder, turned saddler, and her mother a nurse, who stayed home to raise their four children.

After graduating from a degree in International Relations, Vivi moved to Atlanta, Georgia to work for a year. It was there that she met her husband, and they were married three years later. She spent seven years living in Atlanta and travelled to various parts of the United States during that time, falling in love with the beauty of that immense country and the American people.

Vivi also studied for a Bachelor of Information Technology, and worked in the field ever since until becoming a full-time writer in 2016. She now lives in Brisbane, Australia, with her husband and three small children. Married to a Baptist pastor, she is very active in her local church.

Follow Vivi Holt
www.viviholt.com
vivi@viviholt.com

HOLLY

Chapter One

August 1877
Kansas

Kurt Sawyer clicked his tongue and watched the sturdy horses pull the plow, his brow furrowed. The lines weren't straight. Perhaps they needed a little more speed. "Hiyyup! Get on there, Sam! Giddyup, Sal!"

The animals leaned hard into the leather straps across the front of their chests, heaving the plow forward. Its sharp blades cut through the soil, leaving freshly dug earth behind them. Kurt smiled and adjusted his grip on the reins as he walked behind the plow. In the distance, he saw a swirl of gray and black clouds gathering on the horizon. They soon filled the sky, hurrying toward him. He'd have to move fast if he was to finish this field before returning the plow to the Drake farm.

Monday would mark his first full year on his ranch, and he was glad to see the end of it. It had been a tough year, one of the hardest he'd ever experienced. But looking back, he couldn't help feeling proud. He'd managed a summer crop and now he'd be planting wheat to harvest next spring. And with the horse-drawn plow to help him, it might be a decent crop.

He'd written his folks back in New York state a couple of weeks earlier to let them know how he was doing. His mother had been concerned about him going west, certain something terrible would happen to him. But nothing had, and he was beginning to believe this ranch was his chance to make something of himself.

His brother Angus, ten years his senior, had moved to Wichita first. He and his wife Beatrice set out with their nest egg, intending to make a name for themselves. He'd started a flour mill in the growing town a few years ago and had done well. Now they had two children, were planning on opening an adjoining mercantile and had written Kurt, telling him he should come join them. It hadn't taken him long to make the decision—he wanted adventure and a chance to make his mark. And this was it.

He smiled wider as the neat furrows formed behind him. It would've taken him days to do this by hand. His neighbor William Drake had bought the plow in the spring and offered to let him borrow it. He'd jumped at the opportunity and couldn't have been happier with his decision. He'd have to do something nice for Mr. Drake to make up for the man's generosity. It was one of the things he loved about Kansas—even in these hard postwar times, every farmer shared and supported others as best they could. There was even talk of banding together to buy a harvester next spring.

When he reached the end of the field, the plow

bounced off something hard, jolting the reins from his hands. He stumbled forward and grabbed the straps of leather as they wriggled free through the grass. "Whoa there, boys." He pulled the horses to a halt and hurried forward to examine the plow, kneeling in front of it to study the blades. With care he ran his fingers over the sharp steel edges, his chest pressed to the ground. Aha—there was a nick near the front of one where it had likely hit a rock.

Kurt frowned and began to back out from under the plow when a crack of thunder made him start. The horses leaped forward and stumbled back again, spinning around in their traces. "Whoa!" he called—just as Sam's enormous hooves landed on his back. The horse stepped forward, then back again, and he screamed in agony as the Clydesdale's hooves crushed him into the ground.

The assault lasted only moments, but it seemed like an eternity. As quickly as they were spooked, the horses calmed and stood silently between the traces, ready to get back to work.

Kurt rolled onto his back with a groan, his face covered in muck, his head throbbing and his vision blurred. He had to get up and out of the way before it happened again, but his left arm lay limp at his side and he feared he might never be able to lift it again. With his right hand, he pulled himself forward and away from the plow, then scrambled onto his knees and slowly crawled one-handed.

Once he was a few feet away, he slumped to the ground again, moaned and ran his right hand over his head. It felt wet and warm to the touch—blood? He shut his eyes tight as a wave of nausea swept over him. He needed help, but there was no one around for miles—Mr. Drake was the nearest neighbor, but his house was a mile away.

Kurt rolled to his hands and knees again and a fresh wave of pain crashed over him, bringing out a band of sweat across his forehead. He groaned and took a quick breath as blackness descended. He collapsed on the soft earth as fat drops of rain pelted his head and back.

The sound of crickets pierced Kurt's consciousness and his eyes flickered open. It was getting dark and he could see the horses out of the corner of his eye. They stood patiently, their ears flicking in an attempt to dislodge the gnats and mosquitoes that appeared when day turned to night. The ground around him was wet, and he could see the storm clouds moving off in the distance.

With a loud moan, he set his right hand beneath him and pushed up, struggling slowly to his feet. His entire body ached and a sharp stabbing pain in his shoulder made him grimace. He didn't know how badly he'd been injured, but he knew he needed to get to town to see the doctor as quickly as he could. Whether he could manage the journey was another matter entirely.

He hobbled over to Sam's side and began the arduous process of unclipping traces and unbuckling leather straps one-handed. Soon Sam was free of Sal and the plow. Kurt took him by the bit and led him to the small cabin he'd built on the ranch as his temporary home.

He needed water, so he went inside, grabbed the water jug from the kitchen table with a trembling hand

and gulped down great mouthfuls. With a loud sigh, he wiped some over his eyes and face, startled to see how much blood dripped from his hand. Cradling his left arm, he stumbled back out to where Sam stood, his head hanging low over the water trough, his whiskered snout bathed with droplets. "Let's go to town, Sam," he whispered, his head swimming.

With his right hand, he pulled himself up onto Sam's back with a grunt, his legs closing over the animal's round, damp sides. He kicked his heels into Sam's ribs until the horse stepped slowly forward. He tugged on the reins, turned Sam toward town and kicked harder, sending the creature into a slow canter. Blood ran in a steady stream down the side of his face and dripped from his chin onto his hand. He watched the rivulets trickle down the outside of his white-knuckled fist as his body swayed with the horse beneath him.

All the way to town, he lurched left and right, back and forth as Sam steadily followed the road to Wichita. By the time they reached its outskirts, stars twinkled overhead. The blanket of gray clouds was gone and the moonless night was full of the sound of crickets and other creatures as they scurried to and fro over the drenched earth.

Soon he was at Dr. White's house. Hemlock White and his wife had moved to Wichita six months earlier from Virginia. Kurt remembered the welcome party that had been held by the grateful congregation of the First Presbyterian Church on the Sunday after their arrival. He tugged gently on the reins, guiding Sam toward the small whitewashed cottage, a lantern burning within.

He lifted a leg over the horse's back, to drop to the ground, but lost his footing, his head still spinning and fell onto his rear with a cry. He lay still on the ground, trying desperately to get his eyes to focus on the dark branches of a tree overhead. Finally he managed to scramble to his feet and lurched toward the front door. Next to the door hung a brass bell with a string hung beside it. He stumbled, his left shoulder hitting the wall with a thud, but managed to stay upright, and rang the bell.

The door opened. Kurt saw Dr. White's bearded face. Then his eyes rolled back in his head and he fell in a heap at the doctor's feet.

September 1877
New York City

Holly Bristol poked the darning needle through the sock, then paused to study her progress. Darning was a way to pass the time, and these days it saved her a pretty penny as well. Raising five children alone wasn't something she'd ever thought she'd have to face. Every sock saved and handed down was another one she didn't have to buy.

She sighed, let the sock fall into her lap and stared out the window. Life hadn't always been this way. When Charles was alive, they'd had money to spare, at least in recent years. The first few years of their marriage, after the Civil War, they'd had to scrimp and save, but she didn't care, being so much in love and accustomed to a life of poverty. After his death, she discovered he hadn't saved a penny over their years together. But while he was with them, they'd lived the life she'd always dreamed of.

After growing up in the poor coal-mining town of Morgantown, Virginia, Holly Sweetman had longed to attend lavish parties, wear pretty dresses and have her hair done in the latest style. When she and her sister moved to New York after the war, she'd attended a church picnic, hoping to catch the eye of one of the eligible bachelors in the city, in an attempt to change their fortunes and put the past behind them.

And she'd succeeded. Charles Bristol was handsome, enigmatic and soon had eyes only for the pretty, vivacious Holly. He'd returned from the war with a new outlook on life, and though his parents didn't approve of the match he refused to heed their warnings. He and Holly were married on a Friday down at the courthouse—a great scandal at the time, but she sighed with pleasure at the memory. In her mind his rebellion had been spurred by love, and she could think of nothing more romantic.

After his folks finally recovered from the shock of their eldest son marrying an Appalachian orphan girl at the local courthouse, they told him he'd have to make do on his own—since he'd refused to listen to them, he wouldn't inherit a penny. But he didn't budge, just tipped his hat, smiled and walked away with Holly's hand on his arm. And the two of them never looked back.

She sighed as she returned to her darning. A fire crackled in the hearth, its warmth filling the parlor. She heard the cook in the kitchen banging pots and pans and humming a Gaelic tune. Her mind wandered while she worked. Dreaming of the past had become a way for her to escape the present, and she indulged more than she should.

She and Charles had it all. With the income from his job as a bank manager, he bought them a house in one of the most prominent neighborhoods in town. She had everything she wanted: a ladies' maid, fashionable clothing, a barouche to carry her to parties and events, even a cook to prepare their meals.

When Tripp arrived, a chubby baby boy whose hearty cries could wake the entire neighborhood, Holly felt her heart might burst with pride and love. He was a handsome little fellow and she had difficulty disciplining him—especially since he always knew his own mind, something Holly had rarely experienced. As a result, he usually got his way and was hardly ever reprimanded. His parents were grateful that he was generally cheerful and kind, and their home was a warm and happy one.

When Tripp was two, another bundle arrived. Sarah came into the world with a serious look on her heart-shaped face, and Holly and Charles often joked that she seemed to have been born a schoolmistress. Her goal in life was to make certain everyone did as they ought and that all were treated rightly and fairly. She was soon followed by Heather, the opposite of her sister—messy, unruly and forever covered in mud or jam or both. She seemed determined to never wear a pair of matching stockings or be found with shoes on both feet.

Two more years passed and their happy family of five became six when Edward joined their brood, and seven when Eleanor arrived. By this time, the house that seemed so large and spacious when Charles bought it years earlier suddenly felt cramped and crowded. The noise the children generated often left Holly with a headache by day's end, and though Charles hired a nanny to help her, many nights she fell into bed exhausted before he even returned home from the bank.

Charles worked long hours to provide for his family, though he never complained about it. When he was home, he smiled wide and roughhoused with the kids, chasing them around the house until, laughing, Holly had to remind him they needed to settle before bedtime. Those were happy times, and remembering them made her throat ache. The scarlet fever that took him from them last winter came so suddenly, there was no way to prepare.

Only after his death did she find that the ongoing financial panic had wiped out their savings. With no income, they'd lost their house soon afterward. She was grateful for her sister and brother-in-law, who'd taken her and the children in when they had nowhere else to turn. Her sister Eve visited the day before their eviction and offered a place in her and her husband Rodney's home until she could get back on her feet.

Holly ran her hand along a window frame in the three-story brick house and bit her lower lip. When would she be back on her feet, and how? She couldn't work, not with five children to care for. And even if she could, there was no way she could earn enough to house, feed and clothe them all. She ran a hand over her neatly combed blonde chignon with a sigh. There was only one thing she could do, and she knew her sister was counting on her to do it. Remarry. But who would marry a woman with so many children?

Through the window she saw Edward, now five, digging in the garden. His favorite thing in the world was to dig. And since he didn't have a spade of his own, he used anything he could get his hands on: sticks, rocks, even the gardener's tools (much to the gardener's dismay). She'd chastised him so many times, she couldn't bring herself to do it again now. Watching him so happy, mouthing the words to a song while he worked, she hated to interrupt.

When she'd been mistress of her own home, she'd let him dig in the pumpkin patch as much as he wished. He'd been as happy as a lark there, his small shovel clutched between chubby fingers and a mud-smudged grin on his round face. But now they were visitors in someone else's home and she couldn't make the rules any longer, couldn't give her children the freedom they longed for.

She stood with another sigh and set her darning on the small side table next to the horsehair settee where she loved to spend afternoons watching the children play in the garden. She'd better have a word with Eddie before he uprooted his uncle's prize rose bushes. She hurried through the parlor, past the roaring fireplace to the mudroom, tugged on her coat and scarf and stepped outside, rubbing her hands together in front of her mouth to warm them with her breath.

Just as she reached the staircase that led down to the garden, she saw Rodney, her brother-in-law and master of the house, marching through the gate. She gasped, realizing it was too late. She could tell by the black look on his rotund face, his reddening cheeks and the way his thick dark eyebrows were drawn low over his small piggish eyes. He'd spotted Edward's digging.

Rodney reached the boy in a few long strides and picked him up by his collar. "I caught you, you little beast!" he bellowed, his eyes looking as though they might pop from their sockets in his rage.

Edward cried out, a shriek of fear and pain that tore through Holly's heart. She lifted her skirts and ran down the garden path toward them. She reached them and raised her hands toward where Edward hung, his feet kicking the empty air. "Eddie, I've told you not to dig around Uncle Rodney's rose bushes. I'm so sorry, it won't happen again, Rodney, I can promise you that…"

Rodney's furious gaze landed on her. "You have no control over this child!" he huffed loudly. "I've seen your idea of punishment. There's no discipline! He needs a firm hand and you fail to employ it. Well, no more—this time, I'll set the punishment. He must stand in the corner of the parlor for the entire evening and go without his supper."

Holly's brow furrowed and she twisted her fingers together. "Now, Rodney my dear, it's just a small hole in the dirt, nothing to get so worked up about. Look, I'll just fill it in with my boot…see? There now, it's all fixed. I don't think we should take it so far. He's only a small boy, he doesn't understand…"

Rodney's face turned purple as it contorted. "That is the exact problem, right here! You spoil the child!" He set Edward on the ground, keeping a firm hold on his collar, and marched into the house. Edward staggered behind him, sobbing and crying out each time his uncle jerked him forward.

"Rodney!" Holly hurried after them, still wringing her hands. "Please, can't you see you're hurting the child?" Her heart felt as though a hundred horses were racing a circuit inside it, and sweat ran down her back, soaking the fabric of her bodice. What could she do? She couldn't bear little Edward's whimpering.

Rodney shoved Edward toward a corner of the parlor, then turned to her, combing his fingers through his beard until it looked wild. His cheeks burned like flames. "There—that's what he deserves! And none too soon as far as I'm concerned!" He brushed his hands together as if pleased with himself and marched from the room.

Holly glanced at Edward as she fought back tears. It was completely unfair to treat him that way—his entire life had been uprooted, his father was dead and now he was being punished for being a little boy. She wanted to leap onto her brother-in-law's back and pound him with her fists, but instead she folded her hands in front of her and scurried from the room in his wake.

He'd retired to his office, throwing himself into the oversized armchair behind the mahogany desk where his papers were neatly stacked beside a large ashtray. He pulled his pipe from the top drawer and set the end of it between his teeth.

Holly took a long breath. She should think before she spoke, lest she say something she'd regret. "Rodney…"

"Don't bother trying to petition me on the boy's behalf. He's done his dash with me."

She frowned, her nostrils flaring.

"And I'll ask you to leave me be, as I've a good mind to…no. I'll say no more on the subject now. But if you care for your own wellbeing, you should go." His eyes narrowed and he patted his vest pockets, one at a time, until he found a pouch of tobacco and removed the pipe from his mouth to stuff its round end full. Finally he lit the pipe and inhaled a mouthful of smoke with a satisfied smile.

Holly closed her eyes and pushed her shoulders back, tipping her head up until her chin jutted forward. This wasn't the end of the matter as far as she was concerned. She knew it was his house, but he had no right to discipline her children for her. That was her job, and though she'd had everything else taken from her and felt as though she couldn't sink any lower, the children were still hers. She spun on her heel and left the room. "Of all the pompous…" she muttered, gaining speed and steam as she went. "How dare he?"

But as she made it up the stairs and flung herself onto her bed, her anger dissipated and was replaced by fear. There wasn't anything she could do—she and the children were at Rodney's mercy. They had to take whatever treatment he deemed fit to give them. She rubbed her eyes and released a single sob. "Oh Lord, what shall I do?"

The question hung in the air, and she felt hopelessness descend over her. There was nothing to be done. She and her offspring lived off her brother-in-law's charity, and she was being ungrateful after all he'd done for them. Of course he had a right to insist Edward not dig up his garden, or Heather not whistle in the house as he'd done earlier that morning. It was his house, and his rules must be upheld.

She sighed and let her mind drift back once again to Charles. This time she was digging in the garden, kneeling on a rug beside the bed, pulling weeds with gloved hands. Her distended belly, Eleanor inside, made her back ache. She held her hand over it as the kick of a small foot brought a smile to her face, then reached down again to yank a particularly stubborn weed.

Charles snuck up behind her just as the roots gave way. She sent the weed flying over her shoulder, her eyes widening in dismay as she saw it smack her husband in the forehead. Dirt fell in his hair and down the collar of his shirt. He froze, his eyebrows low over sparkling blue eyes. She grimaced and shrugged…and he leaped at her, tickling her beneath her arms and up and down her sides.

She laughed hysterically and attempted to wriggle free, but he tightened his grasp. His own low chuckle only made her laugh harder. Careful not to bump her bulging stomach, he threw his arms around her and pulled her close as his lips closed over hers. Her eyes drifted shut and she relaxed in his embrace as a deep sense of warmth, belonging and love flooded her soul.

When he pulled away, he looked at her, the corners of his mouth twitching with glee. "You're a terrible gardener, Mrs. Bristol," he'd crooned. "Just as well I didn't marry you for that, but for other reasons entirely." She'd blushed beneath his gaze and giggled as he bent to kiss her again.

Holly sighed and opened her eyes, the memory fading as she stared at the vaulted ceiling above the bed. Charles was gone, and so was the home they'd built and shared. Now she had to rely on the fragile largesse of her family to care for her children.

A sharp rap on the bedroom door made her sit up straight with a start. "Yes?"

The door creaked open and her sister Eve peered around its edge. "Holly, do you have a moment?" she asked in her thin high-pitched voice.

Holly nodded. "Of course, Eve dear—come on in." She wiped her eyes with the back of her hand, hoping her sister hadn't seen.

Eve sat beside her on the bed and drew a long, deliberate breath.

Holly's pulse quickened and she glanced with worry at her sister's peaked face. "What is it, Eve?"

Eve faced her and took Holly's hands in hers, her cheeks growing pinker with each passing moment. "Holly, I don't know how to say this…" Her gaze dropped to the bed and she sniffled, then pulled a handkerchief from her skirt pocket and dabbed at her nostrils.

Holly waited, her breath frozen in her throat.

"I do wish you wouldn't fight with Rodney so." Eve sniffed again, looking up at Holly with bloodshot eyes.

"I'm sorry, Eve, I didn't intend to. It's just that… well, you know how protective I am of the children, especially after losing Charles and the house… I just want to take care of them and perhaps I overreact sometimes." She squeezed her eyes shut.

When she opened them again, her sister's glimmered with unshed tears. "Holly, Rodney says you must leave."

Holly frowned. "What?"

Eve burst into tears, covering her face with her handkerchief. "He says you've overstayed your welcome and you and the children must find somewhere else to live. Oh, I'm so sorry, Holly! I tried to talk him out of it, but he wouldn't listen…"

Holly's eyes widened. What was Eve saying? Leave…how could they leave? She had five children— there was nowhere else for them to go. Charles' family had disowned him, so they certainly wouldn't take her in. Her own family consisted only of Eve, Rodney and some distant cousins in Massachusetts she'd never met. "But Eve, what in Heaven's name do you mean? Where will we go?"

"Rodney says he doesn't care where you go, so long as you don't come back. Oh, my darling sister—what *will* you do?" Eve collapsed against Holly's shoulder, her tears wetting the wool of her dress.

Holly's heart thundered in her chest. She sat still, thoughts whirling in her head. She'd talk with the children, tell them to behave better. Surely Rodney would change his mind. Perhaps if they played more quietly, helped more around the house…maybe they could stay. Fear wove itself around her heart and curled into a lead ball in her gut.

Chapter Two

Kurt's eyes flicked open. He blinked. The room he was in tipped and swayed, out of focus. He kept blinking, and slowly his eyes adjusted to the dim light. He could hear rainfall pounding on the roof. He was in a small space, felt the walls closing in on him. He sat up quickly with a gasp, feeling as though something was crushing his chest.

"There now, Mr. Sawyer, just lay back down again. Yer hurt real bad and ya need the rest. Dr. White'll be right back—he just stepped out to get fresh bandages. We had to wash 'em after the Stanton boy got his leg run over a few days ago and had to be wrapped from ankle to hip." The woman who spoke chuckled and stepped closer to him, a cup of water in her plump hands. "Here, have a sip."

Kurt nodded, took the cup and swallowed a mouthful, then winced as the pain in his head rushed back. He'd hurt himself, but how? His head was foggy, and he found himself reaching for thoughts, but they kept swirling away. "What am I doing here?" he finally rasped.

The woman's eyebrows arched in surprise and she rested a hand on his shoulder. "Lay back down, Mr. Sawyer, and I'll tell ya all about it."

He complied, grimacing as more pain flooded his neck, shoulder and back.

"Ya came knockin' on our door a half-hour ago. Ya didn't say a word, just fell down soon as my husband opened the door. Wasn't hard to figger out why—ya had hoof prints on yer head, big ones. That jog yer memory any?" She reached for a damp washcloth on the edge of a porcelain bowl beside the bed, then dabbed his forehead, gradually working toward the crown of his head.

He shuddered as a wave of pain and nausea burst over his consciousness.

"Sorry. I'm sure that hurts. Just tryin' to get it clean—ya got all kinds of mud and grit in these wounds."

Kurt studied her face as she bent over him. She looked like a kindly grandmother—gray curls, blue eyes sparkling beneath thin eyebrows, a turned-up nose, dimples at the corners of her mouth. "Thank you," he mumbled.

"Don't mention it."

He heard footsteps and glanced at the foot of the bed. Dr. White was there, frowning. "Howdy, Doc." He tried to smile, but his mouth wouldn't cooperate.

"Mr. Sawyer. Glad to see you've recovered your senses. Can you tell me what happened?"

Kurt closed his eyes, feeling the room spin. He sat

up—and immediately threw up, right into a bowl the doctor swung in front of him at the last moment. Mrs. White wiped his mouth clean, then rinsed the washcloth in the bowl. "Sorry," Kurt mumbled, laying back down again with a gasp as another stab of pain shot through his head.

"Never mind that. I believe you have a concussion, young man." Dr. White returned the bowl to the side table and checked the pulse in Kurt's wrist, studying the pocket watch in his other hand and mouthing numbers.

"I think it's coming back to me," Kurt began, letting his eyes drift shut. "I was plowing and I hit something. I stopped to check the plow, seeing as it's Will Drake's—I'm just borrowing it. Then there was a clap of thunder and Sam backed up and stepped on me."

"Oh dear," murmured Mrs. White.

"Sam's a big horse, I'm guessing, from the size of these hoof prints," the doctor remarked.

"Clydesdale. Draft horse."

"Oh dear!" exclaimed Mrs. White again.

"Is there somewhere in town you can stay a few days?" asked Dr. White as he unwound a thick white bandage.

"My brother lives nearby. Angus Sawyer—he owns the mill on the other side of town."

"Oh yes, I've met Angus," the doctor replied. "He's a good man. Well then, as soon as I get you fixed up, I'll head over to his house to let him know you're here. I do believe you'll be fine, Mr. Sawyer, but please be more careful in the future. I can't say I'm certain how you managed to get yourself here alone in this storm

at night with a concussion, but thank the Lord you did.
Now sit up if you can—slowly."

Kurt did so, and considered Dr. White's words while
he fixed the bandage around his head. How *had* he
managed to get to town? He couldn't remember much
of the journey. And Sam…where was he? "Sam?" he
blurted.

"I guess that's your horse, eh? I found a Clydesdale
wandering around outside—he's in my stable around
back. And he's fine, don't worry about him."

Kurt sighed in relief. He couldn't afford to lose Sam,
even if the horse had almost stomped him to death. He
was a reliable, hard-working animal, and Kurt didn't
have the money to replace him anyway.

When Dr. White left to fetch Angus, Kurt lay back
down and stared at the ceiling, willing it to stop spinning.

"Someone was sure watchin' over ya tonight." Mrs.
White bustled around the room, straightening up and
wiping things clean. "Ya know, it ain't right for a young
man like yerself to be livin' out there all alone. If ya
had a wife and family with ya, they could've taken
care of ya. Ya almost died out there today, and who
woulda known it?"

He frowned and took a long breath. She was right.
He'd never felt so alone in his life as when he'd regained consciousness out on the ranch, with no one
to raise an alarm. Perhaps it was time for him to find
a wife. But where? There were few eligible women in
Wichita, that he knew for certain after a year there—
and those were either too old, too young, or "soiled

doves." And he had no intention of leaving Kansas just to find a wife.

But the thought of spending the rest of his days out there alone sent Kurt's heart into his stomach. He had to do *something*.

"You awake?"

Kurt's eyes flew open and he inhaled sharply. His brother Angus stood beside the bed, his usually neat hair disheveled and his button-down shirt only half-tucked into his pants. "Yeah." He sat up slowly, his head spinning. "Sorry they had to wake you to come get me."

Angus shook his head, his eyes dark. "It's fine. Are you okay?"

"Doc says I'll be fine. Just a bit dizzy still." He let his legs drop over the side of the bed and winced at the pain in his neck. The doctor had adjusted his arm, saying something about a dislocation, and it still radiated pins and needles.

"Can you walk?"

Kurt frowned. "I can try." And he succeeded, using Angus's arm for support. They walked out the door, waving goodbye to Dr. and Mrs. White, then headed south down Lawrence Street. Wichita was small but growing fast. Lawrence, one of its main streets, was quiet at this time of night, but during the day it bustled with wagons, buggies and cowboys on horseback. When Angus arrived there in 1871, the town had just been incorporated.

"We'll need to come back to get Sam tomorrow," Kurt said. "I left Sal standing in the field. I undid the harness so he can get to water, but he's still attached to the traces. I have to get back to the ranch to take care of him and the other animals…" His head swam with all the things left undone.

Angus nodded and sighed. "I'm worried about you, all alone out there."

"I'm fine," Kurt responded defensively. He knew his brother had hoped he'd set up a business in town, but that wasn't his way. He didn't like cities and never had. He wanted to be out in the open, watching the wind blow through the tall grasses and horses kicking up their heels or grazing in the field.

"Anyway, Mrs. White already gave me a talking-to, so I don't need it from you as well," he snapped, then immediately regretted it. "I'm sorry. I just don't know what to do about it. Mrs. White says I should marry and have a family, but marry who? There's no one here fit to marry. Maybe I could find a boarder, but who would want to board on a ranch?"

Angus chuckled and ran a hand over his black beard. "Not me, that's for certain. But I do have an idea about how to find you a wife."

Kurt's eyebrows lowered. What was his brother up to? "Do tell."

"Just leave it to me. But tell me this—if I find you a wife, are you willing to marry her?"

"You'll find me a wife?!"

"I will, and I'll make sure she's suitable. But you can't be fussy, you understand."

Kurt pursed his lips. He knew he'd given up the chance to marry whomever he chose when he'd moved west. But he'd hoped he might someday find someone he could love and spend his life with. If his brother was willing to do all the work to find him someone, he could hardly refuse. "All right—if you find me a suitable wife, I'll marry her."

"It's a deal."

Holly tied the string of her bonnet beneath her chin and studied her reflection in the looking glass. Her cheeks were paler than usual, and she leaned closer to study the dark circles beneath her eyes. She'd barely slept a wink since Eve told her of Rodney's decision. Even thinking about it made her tear up.

She could hear her nephew James coughing in his bedroom down the hall and the low murmur of Eve's voice as she comforted him. The coughing worsened, and Holly frowned. Poor James had always been a sickly lad. The doctors had told his parents they didn't expect him to live to adulthood given the sad state of his lungs, and his parents had wrapped him in cotton batting ever since. Holly didn't approve of how they coddled him—ironic, given Rodney's criticism of her parenting skills—but she'd never say so to him or Eve.

She adjusted her bonnet one last time, pinched her cheeks and left the room, heading down the hall toward James' bedroom. "Children, we're going!" she called.

She heard the stamping of five pairs of feet as her children hurried to don hats and boots. No doubt they'd been procrastinating getting ready, playing in their rooms. With a tight smile, she shook her head at their hurried whispers.

She stuck her head into her nephew's bedroom, focusing on where Eve sat on the edge of James' bed.

Even though the morning sun shone brightly through the windows elsewhere in the house, in James' room the heavy drapes were still drawn, keeping the room in melancholy darkness. "Eve?" she whispered, careful not to speak too loudly. She didn't understand why her sister insisted on everyone using hushed tones around the boy—it wasn't as though a loud noise or raised voice would cause him any harm—but she respected her wishes.

Eve stood and walked over with a warm smile. "Yes?"

"Ready to go?" asked Holly, smoothing her skirts.

Eve frowned and glanced back over her shoulder at James, who'd swung his legs off the side of the bed and sat watching them with a furrowed brow.

"James can come too, if you like," added Holly. It might do the boy good to get some fresh air once in a while.

Eve's eyebrows arched skyward. "Oh no, he couldn't do that. It might upset his lungs."

"If you're sure…"

"Yes, it's really out of the question. But I'm ready. I suppose I can leave him…" Another backward glance. "Do you mind if I go down to the church with Aunt Holly for a few minutes?" she asked James.

Holly wanted to roll her eyes, but didn't dare—she knew how sensitive Eve would be about it, and she didn't wish to upset her sister. But sometimes she wanted to shake her by the shoulders and perhaps rattle loose some common sense. Ever since their parents died, when Holly and Eve were only thirteen and nine respectively, Holly had taken care of her younger sister. Even now as adults, she sometimes felt she should give her sister advice—a feeling she resisted as best she could.

"No, you go ahead, Mother. I might try to take a turn in the garden while you're gone." James stood, lifted his hands over his head to stretch—and fell into another coughing fit. At eight years old, he understood just how to manipulate his mother, who treated him as though the Earth revolved around him. But otherwise he was a sweet boy and rarely took advantage of his mother that way. Most of the time, he did his best not to cause any inconvenience.

Despite her reservations about his parents' treatment of him, Holly truly did love her nephew. And he adored her children as well. He seemed to be in a better mood with them there, even though their raucous behavior only highlighted how his life was different from the average boy's.

"Oh dear." Eve rushed to his side and patted his back, helping him sit back down on the thick mattress. "I'm not sure that's a good idea, my darling—your cough seems a little worse than before. We won't be gone long. And Cecilia is in the kitchen baking bread, if you need anyone."

Tripp, Sarah, Heather, Edward and Eleanor all arrived at the door to James' room at once, amidst laughter, stamping of feet and general rowdy merriment. "Coming, James?" asked Tripp, bounding into his cousin's room without a second thought.

"I don't know…"

"Oh, come on—it'll be fun." Tripp launched himself onto the bed.

James looked up at his mother with a frown. "Can I, Mother?" Heather and Edward were fighting over a toy wooden soldier, so she couldn't hear what Eve said, but a few moments later James emerged with Eve and Tripp behind him. "I'm coming too!" he declared with pride.

Holly's eyes widened in astonishment. "Well, that's wonderful. Let's go then, shall we?" She glanced at Eve, her sister's face looking even more pinched and pale than normal.

Even with a simmering tension between the two sisters over all the things that hadn't yet been spoken and the uncertain future that lay ahead, the walk to the church was pleasant. An early fall chill was in the air and James coughed a few times, but still seemed to enjoy himself. The leaves had begun to turn orange and yellow, and birds twittered and chirped and dived between their branches overhead. The children laughed and chattered, and for a few minutes Holly could forget about their plight until they reached the tall stone church they attended every Sunday. They were here to pray.

Ever since Rodney told Eve her sister had to leave, Holly had hoped and prayed he'd change his mind. Surely he wouldn't toss his sister-in-law and her five children out on the street to make their own way in the world? He couldn't be so cold-hearted. And sure enough, he'd given them more time than he'd originally intended. His ultimatum had been a week ago, and he hadn't made them leave yet. But according to Eve, neither had he changed his mind.

Eve was just as upset over the situation as Holly, and seemed to grow more nervous with each passing day. As they walked arm in arm up the church stairs, Holly could almost feel her trembling through her sleeves. "We'll pray Rodney will change his mind, or that God will provide us some other situation. I just know we'll find a way out of this." Holly smiled at her sister, but really she was trying to convince herself as much as Eve.

Eve nodded and forced a frail smile. "Yes, something will work out, I know." She patted her sister's arm and sighed.

The children were playing a noisy game of hide-and-seek around the front and side of the building, between the columns, staircases, trees and gravestones. James watched from atop a gargoyle at the bottom of the stairs. Holly spun to reprimand the troublemakers. "Children," she hissed, "please be quiet. We're going inside to pray. No playing, no shouting. You must sit quietly and speak only to God. Do you understand?"

They all lined up quietly behind her, nodding in agreement, and Holly sighed in relief. She and Eve walked into the church, the children following meekly behind.

They knelt and prayed for half an hour, during which both of the women wept, pleaded with God and admonished any child who raised their voice above a whisper. Only after they stood and made their way outside did the children resume playing, shouting with relief at their freedom.

Eve sobbed beside Holly, whose innards felt numb

and heavy. "What will you do?" she asked, pressing her hands to her chest.

"I really don't know." Holly's voice sounded empty and dull to her own ears. Just outside the churchyard, beneath a large oak, was a park bench. She sat there, moving a newspaper to one side.

Eve sat beside her and took Holly's gloved hand in hers. "I'm so sorry, Holly my dear." She wiped away a tear.

"It's not your fault. It's no one's, really. I suppose we couldn't expect Rodney would put up with me and five rambunctious children in his otherwise quiet home forever."

Eve frowned, staring at the ground, then picked up the newspaper.

Holly watched the children chase each other, throw piles of leaves and frolic in the small park beside the church. What would they do? Where would they go? How would she feed so many hungry mouths? Her heart ached.

"Look at this." Eve's voice broke through her melancholy. She shoved the newspaper toward Holly.

Holly took it with a frown. "What?"

"Look!" insisted Eve, pointing at an advertisement near the bottom of the classified page.

Holly lifted it higher and read:

WANTED: BRIDE
Successful landowner in Wichita, Kan., in need of wife. Must be sturdy, of childbearing age & good temperament. Apply by mail: Kurt Sawyer, Wichita, Kan. c/o Wichita Western Mill.

Holly's eyes narrowed. A mail-order bride? Was that really something she should consider? Who knew what this man Kurt Sawyer might be like? "You think I should do this?" she asked, eyebrows arched.

Eve grinned. "Why not? It's perfect. You need a husband and you're not likely to find one around here. He doesn't say anything about previous children, so maybe he's not particular. And he's a successful landowner, so he'd be able to support you all. It's worth writing to him at the very least. If you don't like what he has to say, you don't have to follow through with it. What other options do you have?"

Holly had to admit her sister had a point. She hadn't been able to come up with a single thing that would help in her current predicament. She'd thought she'd probably end up working at some textile mill, though she'd never be able to support her entire family on what she'd make there.

Her heart chilled at the thought of writing to a man she'd never met about the prospect of marrying him. Maybe he'd be a kind, hard-working man who'd be happy to have a new family. Maybe he wouldn't. But she'd have to take a risk if she and the children were to survive. She tore the advertisement out of the newspaper and put it in her pocket. "All right, Eve, I'll write him and see what he has to say. Who knows, maybe this is God's way of answering our prayers."

Eve threw her arms around Holly and held her tight. "Oh Holly, I hope so."

A tear rolled down Holly's cheek, and she pressed her face against her sister's shoulder. Maybe this Kurt Sawyer was just what her family needed. She knew she'd never love again—to wish for that was like hoping to hold the moon in her hands. But even without love, a marriage could work, she was sure. And in that moment she didn't know what else to do.

Chapter Three

All the way home from church, Eve prattled excitedly about the prospect of Holly finding a husband via the classified ads. Holly remained silent, but the more she thought about it, the more her spirits rose.

When they reached the house, the children scattered around the garden to play while Holly bustled inside. She hung her coat and hat on pegs by the back door and wiped her boots on the mat, went upstairs and sat at the little desk in the corner nook of her room to pen a letter.

With a blank sheet of paper and a nib pen in hand, she sat ramrod-straight and stared out the window, watching the children in the garden below. What should she say to this man she'd never met? Perhaps simply introduce herself and express her interest—that would be easy enough. Likely they'd correspond for some time before they made a decision. She could always tell him about the children in a subsequent letter. And with a prospect on the horizon, surely Rodney would allow them to remain until things were finalized.

She put pen to paper:

> *Dear Mr. Sawyer:*
> *My name is Holly Bristol. I'm a widow, living in New York City with my sister Eve and her husband and son. I saw your advertisement for a bride in the New York Gazette and am writing to express interest in knowing more about you and your life in Wichita.*
>
> *I must admit, I haven't been so far west, having never traveled farther than the mountains of western Virginia where I was raised. However, I am open to living elsewhere for a suitable situation. I am sturdy enough and accustomed to hard work and the running of a household.*
>
> *There are a good many Sawyers in the New York area. Are you acquainted with them at all?*
>
> *I look forward to hearing from you.*
> *Sincerely,*
> *Holly Bristol*

Holly folded the letter, put it in an envelope and addressed it in her smooth, sloping handwriting, then sealed it shut. Describing oneself in a few brief paragraphs was more difficult than she'd thought. How does one sum up one's life, one's very self, in so few words?

On her way out the door, she stuck her head into the parlor and found Eve doing needlepoint before the fire, James sat beside her putting a puzzle together on the coffee table. "I'm just going to mail this letter—I'll be back shortly. Do you mind watching the children?" she asked.

Eve smiled, and Holly caught a glimpse of the beautiful woman her sister had once been. Carrying a child had worn her out, and she no longer wore the blush of youth that had drawn beaus to her side from near and far. "That's fine, my dear."

Holly nodded and hurried to fetch her hat and coat. She'd rather mail the letter now, lest she lose her nerve. It was best she didn't think too much about it. She had a habit of talking herself out of things if she dwelled on them too long.

Three weeks later...

Holly heard Rodney grumbling through the bedroom walls. Her room was only a few doors down from Rodney and Eve's, and his deep baritone carried. She couldn't hear what he said, but she could guess.

He'd caught Tripp smoking his pipe outdoors when he returned home early from work. He'd boxed Tripp's ears, then yelled at them all for a good hour before supper. Holly and the children chose to eat in her room to stay out of his way, and after supper she'd put them to bed. That seemed to mollify Rodney, but she still avoided him on the way back to her room from the children's.

She understood his anger—she was angry with Tripp herself. Even at ten years old, he knew better. But he'd lost his father not so long ago, and his behavior had suffered ever since. At bedtime, in bed with his covers pulled up to his chin, he looked so young that her frown had melted away. She'd stroked his hair from his face as he apologized, tearfully explaining that the smoke reminded him of Pa. Her heart broke at his words, and she'd cried into her pillow the rest of the evening.

A tap on the door made her sit up straight in bed. She hurried to the looking glass and wiped her reddened eyes, but it was no use—her face was blotchy and her eyes puffy and swollen. Whoever was at the door would see she'd been weeping. She smoothed her hair back, composed her features and pulled the door open.

It was Cecilia the cook. "Miss Holly, this came for ye earlier. I thought ye might like to have it." She put a letter in Holly's hand.

Holly glanced down at it in surprise. Who would be writing to her? "Thank you, Cecilia."

Cecilia patted her arm, a look of compassion on her lined face. "He'll stew fer a bit, but everythin'll look better in the mornin', Mrs. Bristol. Mark me words." She smiled, showing the gap between her bottom teeth where she'd lost one.

Holly swallowed the lump in her throat and nodded. "Yes. Thank you again."

Cecilia waddled off, her ample hips swaying, and Holly watched her leave before pushing the door shut. She raised the letter to the light of the lantern she'd lit beside the bed, but didn't recognize the handwriting. Finally she turned it over. It was from Kurt Sawyer of Wichita, Kansas.

Her hand shook as she slit the letter open with a fingernail. She sat on the bed and smoothed her skirts before pulling the single sheet of paper out of the envelope. Something smaller fell out onto her lap. She picked it up—a train ticket from New York to Wichita!

Her eyes widened. Had he already made up his mind about her, even knowing nothing about her save her short note? She moved closer to the lantern and read:

Dear Mrs. Bristol:
I was glad to receive your letter. I am the son of William and Gladys Sawyer of Mount Vernon, New York—perhaps you know them?

My brother Angus and I moved to Wichita to start a new life of limitless opportunity. We are both doing well in our endeavors. Angus is married with a family. I hope you will consent to join me shortly and begin our own family together. I have prayed for a wife, and hope you will be as happy with matrimony as I'm sure I will be.

I have enclosed a train ticket for you, and hope you will use it as soon as possible. I am anxious to meet you. Send word of when you will arrive and I will meet you at the station.
Yours sincerely,
Kurt Sawyer

She folded the letter and set it on the bedside table. What now? He'd written nothing about his business, his home or himself. She knew no more about him than she had before, other than that he was related to the Sawyers of Mount Vernon. She vaguely recalled an elderly couple called William and Gladys from her volunteer days at the New York Society for Improving the Conditions of the Poor—they'd struck her as being good people, but she didn't recall ever having met any of their children.

She frowned and lay back on the bed. How could he make up his mind about her so swiftly, so determinedly? She wasn't sure she could do the same, though what other option did she have?

Then another thought struck: he'd only sent *one* ticket. And she needed six!

"The letter is well written—he's obviously an educated man. And we know his family, or at least know of them." Eve folded the picnic rug over her arm and straightened the wrinkles in the fabric with gloved fingers.

Holly nodded. Still, it felt as though she would be traveling to the middle of nowhere to meet a man she knew nothing about. She pushed a stray lock of hair behind one ear. "Though it isn't much." She sighed and leaned over to brush leaves from the hem of her skirt.

The children were investigating a nearby ant's nest, long sticks in hand with which to safely poke the colony. The ants, hidden beneath the ground in preparation for the coming winter, hurried out of their hole in confusion, rushing in every direction. Holly watched from a distance, her brow furrowed. "Children, be careful, please."

"We could arrange to meet with his parents, see what they have to say and get to know them before you make your decision."

Holly picked up the picnic basket from the leaf-covered ground by her feet. "That's a good idea. But he seems to want me to come as quickly as possible, so we'd have to do it soon."

"I'll ask Rodney if we can use the buggy tomorrow and we'll pay them a call." Eve smiled and her nose crinkled. Holly loved it when her sister's nose crinkled that way—it reminded her of their childhood. Eve had been a bright spot in the darkness of those hungry, savage days.

She grinned at Eve and looped her free arm through hers, swinging the picnic basket in her other hand. "He only sent one ticket, though…"

"I'll buy the children's tickets with my own money. Don't fret about it." Eve smiled and squeezed Holly's arm.

"Thank you, my dear sister. You know, I have a good feeling about this. It's all going to work out."

"Yes, it will." Then Eve's smile faded. "Though if it does, we won't see each other…for a long time. Perhaps forever." Her gaze dropped to the ground, her chin trembling.

Holly's heart plummeted. She'd considered that, but had pushed the thought aside. It didn't do to dwell on future hardships, especially considering that there were plenty of present ones. "We'll just have to make sure we see each other again. I'm sure Rodney won't mind you visiting. I can't speak for my future husband, given I know nothing about him, but the chances of us paying a call to New York seem higher since his parents live here, don't you think?"

Eve's face brightened. "Yes, that's true."

Holly stopped and turned to face her sister, her heart full of fear. "Oh Eve, my dear, what do you truly think?

Should I travel all the way to Wichita to marry this man I've never met?"

Eve's eyes glimmered with unshed tears. "I can't tell you what you should do, other than trust in God. What else is there?"

The buggy headed down the busy street, stopping outside a tall Federalist-style house with a high wrought-iron fence. Rain pummeled the roof of the buggy, and Holly and Eve pressed back against their seats to avoid the drops. "Fred, will you go and knock on the door, please?" asked Eve, rapping her walking cane on the wall of the buggy.

The driver grumbled and hurried through the gate and up the wide stairs to the front door. He tugged his collar up higher around his neck and knocked on the door. When it opened, he exchanged words with someone inside, then ran back to the buggy and poked his head in, rain dripping from his hat. "Miss Eve, the maid says they ain't home and won't be for some months. They're travelin'."

"Thank you, Fred. Let's head home."

Holly's stomach clenched. She'd dreaded meeting Mr. and Mrs. Sawyer. How could she possibly explain to them that she was considering taking her children to Kansas to marry their son, whom she'd never met? And now she couldn't even do that. Could she marry their son? She squeezed her eyes shut and leaned her head back on the seat as the buggy lurched down the drenched street toward home.

How she longed to go back in time, back to when Charles was alive and they had a home of their own and everything was wonderful. But it was no use wishing—everything had changed. It would never be the same again.

Holly laid the last of her gowns in the trunk, pushed the lid closed and leaned on it, pressing it down as tightly as she could before she snapped the lock shut. "One never realizes just how many things one owns until one has to pack them all into trunks," she mused to herself.

"Excuse me?" asked Eve, peering through the bedroom door.

"Nothing, just talking to myself." Holly laughed and sat down on the trunk with a sigh.

"That's the last of it?"

"Yes, that's everything. I left a few things in the children's room for you to donate to the needy, since we couldn't carry it all."

Eve nodded. Her face was grim, her eyes rimmed with red.

Holly felt a pang in her chest. "It's going to be all right. We'll be fine, Eve dear. Don't fret so much about us. It's an adventure. 'Life is full of adventures'—don't you remember that's what Pa used to say? He never said much of worth, but that stuck in my head."

Eve nodded, her eyes filling with tears. "Yes, I remember. It's just that…all my life, you've been all I had. You raised me when Ma and Pa couldn't or wouldn't. You introduced me to Rodney and taught me how to behave in society. You stood up for me when anyone criticized or looked down on me. And when James was born, you helped me cope with…

well, everything. I wanted to be there for you when you needed it…"

Holly rushed to her sister's side and threw her arms around Eve's thin shoulders. "And you *were*. When Charles died, I didn't think I'd make it through, but you helped me, gave me and my children a place to live. I'll be forever grateful."

Eve wiped the tears from her eyes, then stamped her foot on the hardwood floor. "I'm so mad at Rodney—I can't believe he'd throw you out this way! I don't think I'll ever be able to forgive him."

Holly shook her head, tucked a strand of Eve's dark hair behind her ear and met her gaze. "Please don't be angry with him. He was kind to take us in, but it isn't fair to him or any of you for us to stay here indefinitely. There are six of us, and we're noisy and passionate and difficult at times—he held up under it as long as he could, but he needs his peace and quiet, you know that. It's only right that you focus on *your* family. I don't hold it against him—I just want you all to be happy." She stroked Eve's cheek, wiping her tears away.

"And I want you to be happy, my dear big sister. Who knows, perhaps you'll even find love."

Holly laughed. "Love? I don't imagine I will, but I can still do what's best for the children. If marrying Kurt Sawyer puts a roof over their heads and food in their bellies, I'll do it and gladly."

Eve sighed and her brow furrowed. "But what about you? What about your heart? If you close yourself off that way, you'll never find happiness."

"I've stopped concerning myself with happiness, dear sister. I had it once and that's enough. Now come, let's find the children. I heard the cab pull up outside and the train is due shortly. It's time we were on our way."

Eve burst into fresh tears. "But we haven't had enough time to say goodbye."

Holly chuckled. "There never is enough time. And anyway, I hate long goodbyes—"

A rap at the door startled them. Cecelia poked her head in. "Is yer trunk ready, Mrs. Bristol?"

"Yes, it's ready. Thank you, Cecelia."

Cecelia nodded at someone beyond the doorway and two boys appeared, caps pulled low over their eyes. They tipped them to the ladies, picked up the trunks and carried them out the door and down the stairs.

Holly watched them go. Well, that was that. It was time to say goodbye to New York, this house and Eve, perhaps forever. She took a long slow breath, grinned gamely at her sister and headed downstairs.

She called the children, expecting to hear the thunder of boots on the ceiling. Instead, she found them all standing in a circle in the entry, the boys with hats in hand, the girls with their bonnets hanging on strings down their backs, all with long faces. "Come now, children—it's time to say goodbye." She tried to sound cheerful and lively, but it came out strangled.

One by one, the children embraced Eve and James and told them goodbye. Even Cecelia was crying when it came her turn. Rodney had given her a nervous farewell before he left for work that morning, which Holly had appreciated. He wasn't a bad man, just not a man who could deal with noise or disorder. Thinking about it, she held back tears.

By the time they were all packed into the cab like beans in a can, her eyes were swollen and her chest ached from suppressed sobs. She blew her nose, then leaned out the window to wave goodbye as the cab pulled away from the curb in a flurry of hooves, flicking mud and cracking whips. Eve and James looked so small standing in front of the gate. James' arm was threaded through his mother's and both had faces as pale as milk. They waved goodbye and Eve hid her mouth with her hand.

Holly's stomach turned, the bitter taste of bile in her mouth. Beside her, Sarah squeezed her hand, her eyes watching her mother closely. "It's going to be fine, Ma," she whispered, her large brown eyes wide. "Please don't be sad. We'll see Aunt Eve and James again."

Holly forced a smile but couldn't answer. She kissed Sarah's forehead, then held her close as the cab bumped and weaved through the streets of New York, headed for the train station. The other children drew close too, faces drawn, as they sat in silence.

Chapter Four

Kurt Sawyer held the letter from Holly, re-reading the words as he broke into a cold sweat. She had children. Five children.

She wrote it so casually. He hadn't thought of "what if she had children?" when he'd agreed to let his brother advertise for a bride for him. He was twenty-five and had assumed his bride would be younger, never married—and childless. Why hadn't he considered the possibility she might be none of those?

He rubbed his mouth and frowned. There was nothing to be done about it—she was not only on her way, but due to arrive in Wichita within the next hour. He was at the saloon across the street, waiting for the train to pull in. He wasn't much of a drinker, but he reckoned this particular situation called for it.

Five children. Heaven help him. And why hadn't he thought to ask her age?

He took a gulp of beer, spilling a little down the front of his best black waistcoat. He dabbed at it with one hand, then sighed loudly. Well, there was nothing for it but to marry the woman. She'd come all this way to do just that. He supposed he could send her back if it came down to it, but doubted he could bring himself to. He swallowed another mouthful and wiped his mouth on his sleeve.

This was all Angus's fault—he'd suggested the idea and written the advertisement for the newspaper. Kurt hadn't even seen it—he'd been too busy planting his crop, with one arm that still pained him. He should've included something about existing children. But it was too late now…

The hoot of a whistle in the distance made him choke on the next swallow of beer. A man walking by slapped him hard on the back, and he coughed it up on the bar. "Sorry," he muttered, shaking his head as the scowling bartender took a towel from his shoulder to wipe the bar dry.

He stood and cleared his throat. The tie he'd donned that morning squeezed his neck, and he stuck a finger beneath it and tugged to loosen it—he felt as if he couldn't breathe. He slapped his hat onto his head and strode out the door. It was time to meet the woman he was to spend the rest of his life with. And her five offspring.

Holly stared out the window. The train rushed toward a small, lively town perched in the middle of a great plain on the banks of a wide brown river that crawled downstream carrying riverboats of all shapes and sizes with it.

"Is this where we get off?" asked Edward with wide eyes.

"Yes, my darlings, this is it. Gather your things, please."

The train slowed, brakes screeching on the steel tracks and whistle sounding. The children all jumped, and Eleanor climbed into Holly's lap and buried her face in her mother's bodice. "It's just a whistle—nothing to be afraid of," Holly assured her, patting her back before she reached for her own straw hat and reticule.

She pinned her hat in place as the train shuddered and jolted, finally coming to a stop beside a raw timber platform. She stood, being careful to deposit Eleanor on her feet.

"Ma, are we going to get a pony?" asked Heather, her blue eyes wide. At seven, a pony would make everything bearable in her eyes. She fidgeted with her long blonde plait where it hung over her thin shoulder.

"I don't know, darling. Let's just wait and see. From what I understand, Mr. Sawyer lives outside of town, but he may not have room for a pony."

Heather frowned and flung her braid back between her shoulder blades.

"Let's go." Holly gently nudged the children toward the train's open doors.

Outside, she lifted her gloved hand to shield her eyes. The town was dirty and busy and the smell of dust, manure and livestock assailed her nostrils. Large yards holding hundreds of milling cattle lay to the east, and their baying acted as a backdrop to the noise of the train, wagons and pedestrians. She glanced around the station, watching passengers leave the train, locate their luggage and make their way off the platform. How would she recognize Kurt Sawyer? Would he even be here to meet them?

"Ma, what now?"

"I'm hungry!"

"Where are we going?"

"It smells. Are we gonna ride a horse to our new house?"

"Do I get a gun like those men, Ma?" That was Tripp, staring in excitement as he pointed to a pair of cowboys riding by the station, ten-gallon hats pulled low over their eyes and holstered pistols displayed on their hips.

"Heavens, no!" said Holly. "We'll eat soon—just stay close to me, children." She hurried them over to where the station master was taking stock of the remaining luggage on the platform.

He pulled his cap from his head to scratch it, mussing his thinning hair. "One of these yours, ma'am?"

She nodded. "We should have four trunks and a carpetbag. There they are...that one and those over there—those are ours. Thank you."

The station master pushed and pulled until all their luggage was neatly piled together, then ambled off to speak with a young man. Holly pulled her handkerchief from her skirt pocket and wiped her damp forehead beneath the straw hat. It was hotter than she'd expected for autumn, and that and her anxiety had left her bathed in sweat. Her heart pounded and her head buzzed with worried thoughts, hopes, plans, fears.

Above it all, the voice of the man speaking to the station master cut through. "...waiting for a woman. She has children with her...her name's Holly..."

Holly's heart leaped into her throat. The man looked so young. He wore an all-black suit with a white button-down shirt, and held a black Stetson in one hand. His dark blonde hair was neatly combed to one side, a stray strand falling across his face. He had chiseled cheeks and an earnest look that was immediately endearing.

She took a quick breath. "Stay here, children." She walked briskly toward him, her face burning. "Mr. Sawyer?" she asked, interrupting his discussion with the station master.

He glanced at her and his blue eyes darkened.

Nothing for it. She lifted her chin. "I'm Holly Bristol. Pleased to meet you."

Kurt wiped his sleeve across his brow and took a slow breath, but couldn't get his heart to slow or his mind to work. His thoughts had fled in the face of the beautiful woman on the platform. He should say something, try to set her at ease. She looked calm enough, but she must be feeling anxious given the situation. "Did you have a pleasant journey?" he finally managed.

"Yes, thank you," she replied. "We're ready to go if you are, though the children are hungry."

He looked behind her and spotted the five little ones huddled together by a pile of trunks. "I'll see what I can do about that," he said, trying to act nonchalant. He walked over, nodded to the children, lifted one of the trunks with a grunt and headed for the wagon. The children followed him, like a string of ducklings.

Sam and Sal waited patiently in front of the wagon, tails swishing and ears flicking back and forth as Kurt caught snippets of conversation between Holly and the children. She was older than he was, but stunning in a way he'd never imagined. With soft curves beneath a well-tailored gown, large blue eyes, silky golden hair and a wide smile, she caught the attention of every man passing by. And he hadn't been able to catch his breath since he met her.

Still, five children! Five extra mouths to feed! He felt a band tighten around his chest. Well, he'd just have to find a way.

"Where in town is your business?" she asked.

He frowned. What was she referring to? "My...business?"

"Your advertisement said you were a successful landowner. I assumed you had some kind of business." She watched him carefully, clasping tightly to her carpetbag.

He squinted, his head spinning. He wished, not for the first time, that he'd written that blasted advertisement himself. What had Angus done? "Well, I...actually, I'm a rancher. Or rather, a farmer working to become a rancher. It is a business—I'm in the business of raising horses, a few cattle, some crops. I've got a property just a mile outside of town. We'll head out there today after our, um, wedding."

Her face fell and she bit her lower lip.

"Does that mean I'll get a pony?" asked one of the girls.

He would have to make a point of learning their names. "Maybe," he answered, throwing the carpetbag into the back of the wagon. "Now, everyone in."

The children all obediently climbed into the wagon

bed, and he helped Holly up to the bench seat. The wagon was packed to the brim, and he swallowed hard at the sight. His life was about to change in every possible way, all at once.

Holly sat quietly beside him as he drove the wagon down Lawrence. The church was at Lawrence and First streets, on their way to the ranch. They'd stop in there, get married in front of the preacher and his wife, be on their way and arrive at the ranch in time for evening chores.

Kurt swallowed again. He hoped there were no more surprises.

Holly waited patiently in Rev. Martin's chambers at First Presbyterian. His wife Agatha stood with her, her hands folded in front of her simple dress, a warm smile on her face. "It's so nice to meet another woman my age," she said.

"A pleasure to meet you as well," Holly said absently. She couldn't think straight—she was about to pledge herself, her life and children to a man she'd just met. Conversation seemed impossible. She dabbed the sweat from her brow with her sleeve.

"I'm sure you're gonna love the Sawyer ranch," Agatha went on. "My husband says it's as close to Heaven as you can get around here—beautiful pastures, clean water in the creek, shade trees galore. You're a lucky lady."

Holly nodded.

Kurt and Rev. Joe Martin opened the door and walked in. Holly's children were all seated on chairs or the floor against the wall. They whispered and wriggled in place, but were otherwise behaving themselves admirably. She frowned—they *must* be hungry. She'd have to ask Kurt if they could find something to eat as soon as they were done here.

Her mind returned to her first wedding. It was held at the courthouse in New York. She'd worn a beautiful white gown with a long train. Charles had donned a top hat and a sleek black suit perfectly fitted to his slim form. He looked so dashing, so handsome, and she'd been overcome with the emotion of it all. She'd insisted they dress up, even if they weren't in a church in front of family and friends. And he'd gone along with her plan, just as he always did. She'd had to discretely dab at her eyes and nose throughout the ceremony to keep from leaking everywhere. It was beautiful. Even the fact that they'd done it alone, couldn't temper their excitement or their love for one another.

She'd been proud to become Mrs. Charles Bristol, having never thought she'd get the chance to marry a man like him. Never thought she'd become part of society, not after being raised by absent, drunken parents in the Appalachians. But she'd done it—married a Bristol and entered society (much to society's initial dismay). After years of parties, picnics and events, they'd finally offered her a grudging respect. Children had come, one after the other. And they'd been so in love. So blessed.

She knew she'd never have that again.

"Do you take this man to be your lawful husband?" asked Rev. Martin.

She nodded, swallowing the lump in her throat. "Yes," she whispered.

Within minutes, they were husband and wife. Holly let her eyes travel up the face of the man she'd just joined her life to. He watched her as if trying to read her thoughts. She managed a smile and braced herself as he leaned down to kiss her. Why did it seem so strange to be kissed by another man—almost as if she was cheating on Charles? But Charles was dead. He'd never be back. Still, she let her eyes drift shut as Kurt's lips met hers.

When she opened them again, his face hovered over hers. Was that concern she saw? Perhaps he was a good man. She hoped so, for her children's sake.

"We'd best get going," he said. "I need to get back to the ranch in time for chores."

She nodded in acknowledgement, took his arm and together they walked out of the church, the children following quietly behind.

The steady clip-clop of the horses' hooves on the road soothed Holly's nerves. She sat, straight-backed, on the hard wooden bench up front. A quick glance over her shoulder revealed the children were absorbed with their surroundings. They'd never spent much time in the country, and the chirruping meadowlarks, burrowing gophers and a herd of deer that startled and disappeared over a rise into the prairie grasses with a flash of white tails had them all looking goggle-eyed in every direction.

"So this isn't your first time being married?"

His question startled her. "That's right. The children's father, Charles Bristol, died last winter. We've been living with my sister Eve and her family ever since." She didn't want any secrets between them. Best to get everything out in the open right away as far as she was concerned. If he had questions, she'd answer them as best she could. She had plenty of questions of her own.

"I'm sorry for your loss," he murmured, adjusting the reins in his hands.

"Thank you. It was a shock, truth be told, but we're praying for a better future." She studied him. Tanned hands and face, muscular forearms beneath rolled-up sleeves. He had an easy, casual manner about him, and so far seemed quiet and steady enough, though time would tell. One thing she knew after years of experience on the subject was that men weren't often who they seemed to be. It took time to discover who they truly were beneath the surface.

"I hope you don't mind me asking…if you had a place to stay with your sister, why did you leave New York?" He turned to watch for her response.

She blushed beneath his gaze. There was something in his eyes that made her heart race. "Her husband gave us notice. He wasn't keen on having five children not his own in his home."

He grunted and pursed his lips.

What was he thinking? She'd been nervous about their meeting, since she hadn't told him about her children until after he sent her that ticket. She wondered how he felt about it—was the grunt one of discontent? Well, neither of them had been entirely forthcoming— "landowner" was a long way from "farmer."

And if she had told him she had five little ones, he'd likely have telegraphed that she shouldn't come. Most men would've. In fact, she'd been a little concerned he might turn her away at the station. But he hardly seemed to miss a beat when he saw them—she'd willingly give him credit for that.

It was too late for all that anyway—they were married. She was glad it had been in front of a preacher. From what she'd heard that wasn't always a possibility for a mail-order bride. She knew she couldn't have stomached the idea of moving in with a man she wasn't married to, but when it came down to it, she'd always put her children's welfare first.

"Thank you for lunch," she said. When she'd asked him about food after the ceremony, he'd pulled a picnic basket he'd packed that morning out from beneath the wagon seat. He parked the wagon under the shade of a cottonwood tree at the edge of town and spread the food out on a blanket. And she'd noted that though there hadn't been enough to go around, he'd gone without, quietly handing sandwiches to each child and herself before sitting back against the wide trunk of the old tree to watch them eat.

"You're welcome."

"What will we do for food on the ranch?" she asked. She had no experience on that subject. As a child, she'd had to scavenge for food where she could. Then when she'd married Charles, they had accounts at every store she needed supplies from.

"I have a garden out back. It's still small, though I was hoping you might get it going to where we have enough vegetables for the year and for canning and such. I'll hunt for fresh meat. There are plenty of berry thickets and wild apple trees around. Come fall we'll have beef to eat—at least that's the plan. My brother Angus will keep us supplied with flour and cornmeal and oatmeal. And I have a milk cow. Can you make cheese?"

She nodded. She'd never done it, but she'd seen it done and it didn't seem difficult.

"Anything else we need, I can charge for breeding horses, or trap furs and trade at a general store in town. Just let me know and I'll add it to the order when I go."

She chewed her lower lip. It sounded like there was plenty of food—she only hoped it would be enough. Five growing children could eat one out of house and home in no time.

"What about your parents?" he asked suddenly.

"Pardon me?"

"Your parents. Couldn't they take you in?"

Was he trying to be rid of her already? "They're dead, I'm afraid." She hoped he didn't ask how.

He didn't. "I'm sorry. Sounds like you've had plenty of hardships."

She gave a curt nod. "God gives me the strength to endure it."

"Sure enough." He nodded too, frowning.

She decided to change the subject. The sad story of her life always set people to pitying her, and she hated that—it made her chest ache. "What about you? You were from Mount Vernon originally—why did you leave?"

He cleared his throat and pushed his hat further back on his head. "My brother Angus came out here first. He's the real businessman in the family—he owns the Wichita Western Mill on the opposite end of town." He cleared his throat, as if that was a sore subject. "He said I should come, so I did. My parents weren't thrilled, but I yearned for adventure. And I've always wanted a ranch." He chuckled, as though to a private joke.

"Oh."

He coughed. "Just to get things out in the clear…my brother wrote the advertisement. I never actually saw it, as I spend most of my time on the ranch. It's new, you see, and it takes a lot to get things going. He suggested the idea of writing away for a bride. I went along with it because I trust his judgment. I didn't know he'd call me a 'landowner,' though—that's a bit high-hat for what I'm doing. Sorry about that."

Holly's mind whirled. It made sense, she supposed. Perhaps he'd never meant to mislead her, any more than she had him. She wanted to give him the benefit of the doubt—after all, he was her husband now. And he didn't seem the lying type. "All's well that ends well," she said, smoothing her skirts.

He glanced at her, curiosity filling his bright blue eyes. Then he nodded, once, in acknowledgement of her forgiveness.

Chapter Five

The sun made its way toward the horizon, a line broken only by the occasional tree or sloping rise. Kansas was flat, filled with wide-open plains of waving grasses. It was beautiful in a wild kind of way, and Holly began to relax as she watched the light turn gold and orange, tinting the lazy prairies. The road turned into a trail, then wagon tracks, brown lines in the grass.

Soon, she saw a structure, dark against the plains. Kurt had been silent for so long, his voice almost made her jump. "There's home, such as it is."

She smiled. Home. It'd been months since she truly had a home. But what would this one be like? The setting sun made the entire place look quaint, as if drawn from a fairytale. As they drew closer, she saw a large barn behind the house. It was bigger than the house itself, a cottage really, with two square windows out front and a solid door made from planks. In the fenced yard beside the barn, a cow lifted her head to watch their approach. A small herd of cattle grazed in the distance. A dog ran out, barking to greet them, its tail wagging.

The children had grown used to the journey, and began to chatter excitedly over the prospect of finally arriving at their destination. To a child, she supposed a ranch in Kansas might be a great adventure. But she worried it might turn into a set of shackles she hadn't anticipated, slapped on her ankles while she was looking the other way. She shook the feeling away, determined to find the best in the situation.

When the wagon stopped in front of the house, the children piled out, laughing and petting the dog, who leaped around with glee. Kurt chuckled and scratched behind the dog's ears. "This is Badger, on account of looking like one. He's friendly, as you can see—not much of a guard dog, but good with the livestock."

Holly smiled and reached down to caress the dog's smooth head. Badger's ears lay back against his head and he sat beside her, lapping up the attention.

"Everyone, go in and make yourself at home. I'll unload and get the horses settled in the barn."

Holly took a slow breath. "Come on, children. Let's go inside." They rushed ahead of her, barreling through the door. She followed more slowly, taking in everything as she went.

It was a sturdy structure, small but well-built. The first room held two chairs, a modest table and a cast-iron stove with a chimney. Another table near the far wall held several bowls and plates, jugs and cans—likely what passed for a kitchen. But it was cozy and tidy, and though she'd grown accustomed to a luxurious life as Mrs. Charles Bristol, she'd previously been acquainted with poverty. This didn't look like the poverty she knew—this was a home.

It was dark inside. She found a lantern on the kitchen table, a box of matches beside it. She struck one, lit the lantern and carried it with her into the second room— the bedroom, where a single bed stood against one wall. She pursed her lips. One bed. Seven people. And there was no third room. How would they work this out, especially on their wedding night?

Returning to the first room, she set the lantern back on the table. The children had explored the house, touching everything, picking it up, turning it over and exclaiming with excitement over it all. "May we go outside, Ma?" asked Sarah, standing on tiptoe, her eyes bright.

"Yes, but stay close. I'll be calling for you shortly."

They piled outside with whoops and hollers, and she couldn't help smiling at their enthusiasm. At least they were happy to be there. Perhaps this wouldn't be so bad. She'd been concerned she might be endangering them by bringing them to the edge of civilization, but now that they were here, it wasn't so frightening as she'd imagined.

Kurt pushed through the door, lugging a trunk with him. He hurried into the bedroom, set it on the floor, then came back out scratching his head. "Not sure where we'll put all this luggage," he said with a grin.

She grimaced. "Yes, we may have packed too much."

"Not what you were expecting?" he asked, leaning on the kitchen table, his eyes on her.

Her cheeks blazed under his scrutiny. "I honestly didn't know what to expect."

"I wasn't prepared for five…"

"I know. I'm sorry, I should have told you right away." She felt her throat tightening.

He gently rested a hand on her arm. "Never mind. There's nothing for it now. I just hope you don't mind things being a little…cozy." He laughed, soft and low.

Her heart leaped. She felt like she might burst into tears. "Thank you." With a cough to mask her strangled voice, she turned away. "What shall we have for supper?"

"There's a root cellar—I'll show you." He grabbed an iron ring in the floor beside the kitchen table and pulled, opening a trapdoor. "There. Help yourself to anything you need. I'm going to finish unloading the luggage."

She nodded. "Thank you."

He smiled and left.

Holly set her hands on her hips, looking down into the root cellar. She picked up the lantern and selected two bowls, then carried them down the ladder in the opening, stepping carefully backwards. When her foot hit solid earth, she turned and raised the lantern to eye level to look around. The cellar was small but functional, with timber walls and ceiling and a musty odor. It also wasn't quite high enough to stand in—she had to duck her head to move around as she scanned the stacks of food.

There was a pile of what looked to be smoked meat wrapped neatly in brown paper squares. Potatoes, yams and pumpkins were piled against the far end of the space, and onions hung in bunches from the ceiling. A shelf held salt pork, sugar, molasses, cans of baked beans, salt and other spices, all store bought. Against the wall to her right were sacks of flour, oats and corn-meal with WICHITA WESTERN stenciled on them— the promised bounty from his brother's mill.

It was only the middle of fall, but it looked as if Kurt had gathered enough food to last through the winter months. Though maybe not enough for seven. She'd have to take stock and make sure there was plenty for them to eat. And she looked forward to getting started on the vegetable garden—she'd never had one before. Her parents hadn't bothered, and there'd been no need once she was married. But she truly enjoyed garden-ing, and the idea that she could provide for her children by growing food filled her with a sense of satisfaction.

Holly opened a sack of cornmeal and scooped a good portion into one bowl, sliced some salt pork into the other and grabbed the jar of molasses before climb-ing back up the ladder. Time to make her first supper in their new home.

Kurt rubbed Sam's back with a cloth, then used the curry brush to groom him until his coat shone. Sam chewed contentedly on the corn in his feed box. Kurt talked to him all the while, a habit of his—it made him feel less lonely and seemed to soothe them as well. He chattered about the trip to town and the wedding, and his worries about all those mouths to feed.

He stopped all of a sudden as a thought crossed his mind: he wasn't alone anymore. He had an entire family with him now in that tiny cottage he'd built. He shivered, then smiled. Seeing all those children threw him at first. But now, once he'd mulled a little over just what would be required to support a family that size, he'd come to terms with it. After all, he'd dreamed of having a large family—it was just happening sooner than he'd expected. And all at once.

They'd have to expand the garden, that was certain. He'd have to hunt a little more frequently, and dip into his savings for clothes and other supplies. But otherwise, he should be able to continue on as planned. And once he got them into the town school, they'd be able to walk to the schoolhouse together, since it was only a mile away through reasonably flat land. Everything would work out just fine.

Holly…was another matter entirely. He still hadn't been able to settle his nerves about her, even though she seemed to have warmed to him a little. In fact, he was anxious about finishing the chores and going inside. Scared to go into his own house—what was wrong with him? That was no way for a man to live. He scowled, took a quick breath, set the curry brush back on the shelf in the barn and slapped Sam on the rump. "See you tomorrow, old boy."

Badger trotted along at his heels as he walked toward the cabin, his heart in his throat. He could smell supper cooking even before he opened the front door, and it brought a smile to his face. When he stepped inside, the happy sounds of laughing children met him and he paused a moment before pulling off his boots and hanging his hat on a peg by the door. "Evening, everyone," he called, then hurried into the bedroom to wash up in the basin.

When he returned to the front room, Holly was dishing corn cakes with salt pork and molasses onto plates. She set five of them along the kitchen table, then two more on the small round table he used for writing, reading or playing cards. There weren't enough chairs to go around, but the children happily stood at the kitchen table, waiting patiently to begin eating.

He sat in his chair at the little table. "Thank you. This smells delicious."

Her cheeks flushed pink under his praise. "You're most welcome. I hope it is." She sat across from him and bowed her head.

Kurt followed her example and said a blessing. While he prayed, he let himself glance at the children. Five little heads bowed, five pairs of eyes closed. Yes indeed, everything would work out just fine.

Kurt crossed his ankles, watching the flames in the fireplace leap and snap. The fire would burn out soon and it would be time for bed. He tapped out his pipe in the ashtray, set it down and stood with a yawn, stretching his arms over his head. He wandered into the bedroom, where Holly and the children were reading and drawing. Time to figure out sleeping arrangements.

He pulled a straw tick out from beneath the single bed. He'd made two of them before he'd fetched Holly and the children from the train station—the other was leaning up against the wall. He'd planned on making more, but hadn't had time. They were extra large, though—he hoped the children would all fit. He dragged one, then the other, out to the front room. If he'd set them in the bedroom, they'd take up all the floor space, and the only way to get to the bed would be to crawl over them.

Besides, it being their wedding night, he figured he and Holly would want some privacy.

Holly spoke behind him. "Would you like me to make up the beds?"

He faced her, his cheeks burning. "Yes, please. I'm afraid I don't have much…"

"I brought linens and blankets with me, since I wasn't sure what you'd have."

He exhaled with relief. "Good. I thought…"

"You should take the bed—it's your house. I'll sleep on the floor with the children." She rested a hand on his arm.

He glanced at her hand, feeling a spark of electricity run through him at her touch even as disappointment rose. "Yes, well…if that's what you'd like. I'll build some bunks when I get a chance. I'd already planned on adding a room in the spring. Does that suit you?"

She seemed surprised that he'd ask her opinion, then recovered her composure and murmured approval.

By the time he'd banked the fire, pulled in the latch key and readied himself for bed, Holly had finished making up the beds. The children were dressed in their nightgowns, the girls with nightcaps and their hair twisted into curls fastened with rags. Holly wore a nightgown as well, and her hair hung loose about her shoulders like a golden halo. He nervously hurried to his bed.

"Good night, Kurt," said Holly. Her words were echoed by a chorus of children's voices.

He nodded. "Good night, Holly. Good night, children."

He settled into his bed, pulling the covers up under his chin. Holly turned down the lamp in the other room, throwing it into darkness. The only sound was the rustle of the ticks as someone rolled over, a chorus of crickets and the bellow of the herd outside.

"Can we have a story please, Ma?" asked a small voice in the darkness.

"Yes, Eleanor," replied Holly. Then she began to speak, weaving a tale of an Indian woman and her papoose who were separated from their village and lost on the plains of the great prairie. They encountered an eagle, escaped a pack of hungry wolves and endured hardships of all kinds before finally being reunited with their family.

Kurt lay still in the night, his hands behind his head, his eyes fixed on the darkness, listening to her silken voice. The children seemed mesmerized by her words and soon he heard their breathing deepen as one by one they fell asleep on their freshly-made beds. And soon Kurt's eyes drifted shut as well.

Holly woke up just after sunrise, the small house bathed in amber light. Kurt was nowhere to be seen. Probably doing chores outside—he'd mentioned the night before that he had work to do morning and night. She had a lot to learn about what it meant to be a rancher. She dressed quickly and hurried to prepare breakfast.

By the time she had bread and bacon frying in a pan, the children were all awake. Tripp wandered over to the kitchen table, rubbing sleep from his eyes. "Good morning, Tripp. How did you sleep?"

He grunted, sat on the floor and rested his chin in his hands.

Holly pulled the crisp bacon from the pan with a fork, setting it on a tin plate. "Is something bothering you?"

"I want to go home."

She frowned. "Well, this is home now."

His eyes narrowed. "You never asked me if I wanted to move here. Why do you get to make the decisions about our life? Father would never have made us move here." His voice was tight and full of pain.

"I thought you were excited about living on a ranch?" She flipped the bread over in the pan.

"No, Eddie and the girls are. I never said I was. And you didn't ask."

"Well, I'm sorry, Tripp. But I'm the adult and I have to make decisions for our family. If you just give it a chance, I think you'll love it here. There are horses and cattle and so many things to explore. And if you ask him, I bet Kurt will even teach you to hunt."

"I'll never ask him!" shouted Tripp.

Holly took a step back, her eyes wide. What had gotten into him? "Tripp Bristol!"

"He's not my father. You shouldn't have married him. I'm the man of the house, you said so yourself. I would have gotten a job to support us!" He sobbed and ran from the cabin, slamming the front door behind him.

Holly watched him leave, her mouth open and throat tightening. She had no idea he felt that way. He was only ten, but he seemed to have taken the weight of the world onto his small shoulders.

Kurt stepped inside a minute later, stamping his boots on the mat by the door. "Is the boy all right?" he asked.

She wasn't sure what to say. "He's…just homesick, I think."

He half-smiled. "That's to be expected, I suppose."

Holly nodded and distributed bacon and bread onto the plates on the kitchen table. "Breakfast is ready," she said.

Holly raised a hand to shade her eyes from the sun's glare and studied the small patch of garden Kurt had marked off behind the house. There was plenty of space to expand. She walked around the square of land, calculating how much digging she'd need to do to grow the extra food they'd need.

She wanted to plant corn, beans, squash, more potatoes, tomatoes and carrots. Kurt assured her they could buy seed for everything she needed in town. He planned on going in a day or so to make some purchases, so she was putting together a list of things she wanted him to bring back.

Her gaze fell on the barn, and she saw Tripp seated against the side, his legs stretched out in front of him, a forlorn look on his face. Her heart broke for her eldest child. He'd always been so sure of himself, so headstrong and certain about what he wanted. She hated to see him downcast.

Just as she was about to go to him, Kurt emerged from the barn, stopped when he saw Tripp and put his hands on his hips. He said something, and Tripp stood to his feet and clenched his fists at his sides. She picked up her skirts and hurried toward them.

Kurt said something else to Tripp, pointed at the barn and turned away. As he did, Tripp rushed him, kicked him in the shins, then ran off as Kurt shouted. "Tripp!" Holly cried in dismay, but it was no use. He was gone.

She reached Kurt, gasping for breath. "I'm so sorry. I don't know what he was thinking."

Kurt, eyes narrowed, shook his head. "Never mind. I just asked him if he wanted to try riding one of the horses. I'm going out to check on the herd, and thought he might like to join me." He paused before adding, "The boy's angry about something, that's for sure."

Holly grimaced. "He's upset about us coming here. I didn't know until today—he kept quiet up until now. Are you hurt?"

He chuckled. "No, I'm not hurt. It's fine, I understand. I'd probably be sore myself if I were in his shoes."

"He just needs some time," said Holly, though she wasn't sure that was true.

"Uh-huh." Kurt didn't look convinced either.

"You're not going to…" She choked on the words.

"Turn him over my knee? No, I won't hit the boy. He's doing his best to figure things out—I guess I'll leave him to it." He nodded and turned to head back to the barn. "I'll ride out to check on the herd alone, I guess," he chuckled.

Holly sighed in relief and ran her hands over her

hair, feeling her throat tighten as he walked away. This was a fine change from Rodney's iron discipline. "Thank you so much," she called after him.

Chapter Six

With a gentle shake, Holly woke Eleanor, Heather and Sarah where they lay on their mattress, still covered in the thick blanket she'd brought with her from New York. She smiled at their sleepy faces and tickled beneath Heather's chin. "Time to rise and shine!" she sang.

"Good morning, Ma," croaked Sarah, rubbing her blue eyes with closed fists.

"Good morning, my sweet little cherubs. It's time to get up—we're going to church." Holly had never been so excited about going to church before, but spending an entire week secluded on a small ranch made her crave a crowd. She was looking forward to seeing the town again, this time without a ball of anxiety in her gut. And she hoped she'd meet some other women she could befriend. Perhaps the children would make friends as well.

She pulled the makeshift drapes back from the window. She'd hung a sheet over the square hole in the wall and planned to sew something more permanent as soon as Kurt made that trip to the mercantile he'd been promising since she arrived.

The girls sat up straight, blinking at the bright morning sunshine. Heather made her way into the bedroom. "What will I wear, Ma?" she asked, pulling a trunk out from where it had been stowed under the bed and peering inside.

"How about your blue poplin?" suggested Holly, standing with a groan and rubbing her knees.

"What's wrong, Ma?" asked Eleanor, her eyes full of concern.

"Oh, nothing, my dear. I'm just getting old and it hurts to sit on the floor too long." She grimaced, then laughed out loud.

They dressed quickly. Holly wet each of the girls' hair and parted it down the middle, braiding it into two long braids on either side of their parts. Then, she helped the boys get dressed and wet and combed their hair. By the time she was done, Kurt had set out bread and milk for breakfast, having dressed and groomed before anyone else woke. Now he sat at the kitchen table, reading from the Bible he kept on the mantel. "Ready?" he asked, looking up.

"Yes, thank you." Everyone ate quietly, and after the children finished Sarah wiped their dishes clean and stacked them back in place under the kitchen table.

Holly ate more slowly. "I'll take a piece of bread with me in the wagon," she said when she noticed everyone else was done.

"No need," Kurt responded. "Take your time eating your meal. I'll bring the wagon around front and load everyone in. There's coffee in the pot as well."

Her eyebrows arched in surprise. "Thank you, Kurt." She buttered a piece of bread and poured a cup of coffee, then sat at the kitchen table again. By the time she'd finished and wiped her plate clean, Kurt had finished packing all the children into the wagon. She rinsed out her cup, then picked up the picnic basket she'd packed the previous night and left beneath the table. They'd eat a picnic lunch on the way home from church.

The morning was fine, without a cloud in the sky. A sparrow called, followed by the wistful song of a meadowlark. The children, seated on bales of fresh hay, listened in delight, challenging each other to find the birds in the trees that lined the trail along the creek bank on Kurt's ranch.

Holly let her gaze wander over the landscape, marveling at the beauty of the place. Cottonwoods, poplars and sycamores dotted the pastures. Beyond the creek there were birch and elm then an expanse of waving prairie grasses that swept to the horizon. Leaves of various hues carpeted the earth beneath the trees, and the golden sunrise lit them up so it looked as if the ground was on fire.

When they'd journeyed from town to the ranch a week earlier, she'd missed so much, so busy had she been inside her own head. Now she could discover each piece of scenery, every aspect, and digest its beauty as carefully as she pleased. It had seemed such a long way, a mile on a hard wagon seat. But today, with the sun rising at her back and the beautiful vista ahead, she found it didn't last as long as she'd like.

Beside her Kurt whistled a happy tune, and the

sound brought a smile to her face. She caught his eye, and he paused the melody to grin and tip his hat, his blue eyes gleaming. "Will your brother be there today?" she asked, adjusting her bonnet as they bumped over a particularly deep pothole.

He nodded. "He should be. He's generally there every week."

"Good. I'm looking forward to meeting him." She wanted to ask him what he'd been thinking about when he wrote the advertisement for his brother in the New York *Gazette*, but she knew propriety wouldn't allow her to.

"I believe he feels the same way."

She watched him out of the corner of her eye. He did everything so easily, fluidly, as if nothing was too difficult. The way he hitched the horses to the wagon, or mounted up and rode away across the prairie, or held the reins loosely in his hands. The way he fetched her fresh water from the creek or carried luggage in from the wagon. He was strong, confident and at ease with himself in a way she'd never seen in a man so young.

When Charles died, he'd been forty-three. Kurt was twenty-five, and the difference seemed more obvious to her with each passing day. He was so vibrant and full of life. She felt almost old next to him and had to remind herself that the difference in their ages was a mere five years—nothing, really. Though it didn't feel that way.

He caught her staring and raised an eyebrow at her, which made her blush. She quickly looked away and focused on the trail ahead of them. She could see the town in the distance, each step the horses took drawing them closer. The children, growing tired of the journey, were quarreling over who could sit where, how much space should be between them and who was poking, touching, or humming beside whom. She turned, admonished them, then returned her focus to the road ahead.

"There's the church," said Kurt as they made their way into town. She could see wagons and buggies parking around the clearing in front of the building. And before long, they were winding their way up the rise to join them. The church itself was pretty, a brick cruciform building with a tall steeple and a bell. According to Kurt, it had been finished earlier that year, and the congregation was justifiably proud of it.

As their wagon pulled in front of the building, she saw a young couple with a baby open the door and hurry through it, letting it swing shut behind them. "Are we late?" she asked, smoothing her skirts and feeling her pulse accelerate.

Kurt pulled out his pocket watch as he set the brake. "No—just in time." He got down, helped her out, then settled the horses with feedbags while she lined the children up and smoothed flyaway hair and wrinkled clothing.

When they walked into the church, fiddle music and voices raised in worship greeted them. Kurt found a pew they could squeeze into and ushered them one by one into place. Her heart thumping, Holly couldn't help feeling nervous in the crowd of unfamiliar faces. She felt dozens of eyes fix on them as they sat. They certainly drew plenty of attention. She knew just what they must be thinking—who was this woman and all

her children, and what were they doing with Kurt Sawyer the bachelor rancher?

Kurt watched Holly's face with curiosity. Her cheeks
and neck were bright with red spots. She studied the
preacher attentively, only looking away to shush the
children or make them sit up straight, or stop fiddling
with their sleeves or skirts.

She looked so pretty today, in a white dress with
blue pinstripes. It fit her figure precisely and had ruffles, frills and lace aplenty. He didn't know fashion,
but could tell it was something few other women in
church could afford, and noticed some envious looks
directed her way. It was like she'd stepped right out of
one of his mother's fashion magazines back in New
York, the ones she'd leaf through while sipping coffee in the parlor.

Kurt was proud to call Holly his wife. But he still
wondered how she felt about him.

Holly stood and rubbed her damp palms against her
skirts. The service was over and people were leaving
the pews, milling around or heading for the back door.
The murmur of conversation filled the space, echoing
against the walls and roof, making it difficult to hear
anything in particular over the din of dozens of voices.

"I'll see you outside," said Kurt, close to her ear.

She spun around, wide-eyed. He was leaving her
alone? But by the time she opened her mouth to pro-
test, he'd disappeared into the crowd, the children following him. They ducked beneath arms and around
wide skirts, and soon she was by herself.

She swallowed and smiled at a woman to her right, but the woman stared through her. She ran a hand over her hair, smoothing it back into place. She lifted her chin, stepped out of the pew and spied three women conversing to her left. They looked to be about her age, and small children flitted between their skirts, laughing, hiding and clutching the fabric with pudgy fingers.

With a smile, Holly inched closer, joining their circle. The conversation ceased and their eyes locked on her. One woman frowned. "Hello," she began, her throat tight. "I'm Holly Sawyer."

"We know who you are," responded the frowning woman.

"Oh. Er…"

"Just so's you know, we don't approve of your type."

Her heart lurched. "What do you mean, my…type?"

"The type of woman who tricks a young man into marryin' her just to take on her children," another woman, blonde hair pulled back into a severe bun, contributed. She shook her head and the other women nodded and sniffed in agreement.

Holly's stomach twisted. Is that what they thought of her? "That's not what happened. I answered an advertisement Mr. Sawyer placed in the newspaper in New York. He needed a wife and I a husband, and…"

The first woman, whose brown hair hung in bangs down the sides of her face, arched an eyebrow and interrupted her. "Mr. Sawyer is an upstanding member of our community. There are plenty of young women who'd have made him a good match." She glanced at her friends smugly. "Including my niece, Jane. She'd have been far more suitable for such a fine young man." She sniffed again, looking Holly up and down in disdain.

Holly's spine stiffened. "I'm sorry to hear you don't approve of our marriage. But truth be told, it really isn't any of your business. Who we marry and what we do is between Mr. Sawyer, myself and the Almighty, and none of us give two hoots what you think!" Her cheeks burning, she spun on her heel and strode out of the church.

When she reached Kurt's side, he'd already hitched the horses to the wagon and settled the children into the wagon bed. He and another man turned to face her as she approached. "Holly, this is my brother Angus. Angus, this is my wife Holly."

Holly was still wound up from the encounter with the women inside. "Pleased to meet you, Mr. Sawyer," she said sharply. He nodded and shook her outstretched hand with a compliment of some kind, but she couldn't focus on his words.

Finally Angus' voice cut through the buzzing in her head. "…my wife's getting close to her time, so she couldn't be here today, but I know she's dying to meet you."

"Of course. I can't wait to meet her. I hope she's well."

"Oh, well enough, though she says she feels like an elephant. She doesn't look it to me, though." He grinned. "See you soon." He left with a wave.

Holly crossed her arms, forcing herself to smile until he was gone.

"Ready to leave?" Kurt asked.

"Very." She frowned.

His brow furrowed. "Is everything all right?"

Her nostrils flared. "Just fine and dandy, thank you," she replied sarcastically.

He looked confused, but offered an arm to help her into the wagon. "Well then, let's get going, shall we?"

She nodded and climbed aboard, even as her stomach roiled. How dare those women speak to her that way? They knew nothing whatsoever about her. They'd judged her before they even met her, likely based on some snippet of gossip that made the rounds. She didn't know how it could've happened so quickly, since this was the first time she and the children had visited town since their arrival a week earlier. Apparently the tale-bearers in Wichita were even more efficient than New Yorkers!

She could feel Kurt's questioning eyes on her. She'd been short with him and he no doubt wondered why, but was afraid to broach the subject. And she wasn't sure she wanted to talk about it.

She sighed and her shoulders drooped. It would be harder than she'd realized to find her way here. She'd dealt with the rejection of society women before, but hadn't been expecting it from the country folk of a frontier town. Tears stung her eyes, and she sat in silence listening to the buzz of conversation amongst the children. It seemed they'd enjoyed their trip to town, and a couple of them had even made friends at the church.

Sam and Sal clopped steadily on, heads high and tails swishing. She studied the open plains, saw a pocket gopher disappear with a flick of its small tail into a hole in the ground. A shadow sailed over the landscape and a dozen more gophers darted underground. She shaded her eyes with a hand to peer upward as a hawk soared overhead, its wings outstretched on an updraft, one eye angled downward to search for lunch.

She'd known it would be hard to start afresh, but she hadn't anticipated this hollow ache in her heart that never left, as if there was no place in the world for her to belong. The ranch was Kurt's place. Even though they were married, she still felt like she and the children were visitors, guests. At any moment Kurt could change his mind and rescind the invitation.

She stole a glance at him. He sucked on a blade of grass and squinted ahead, the reins loose in his hands, his hat tipped low over his face. Her husband was a stranger to her.

They passed a thickly wooded copse where birch trees mingled with orange-, red- and brown-leaved oaks and maples. The air was cooler there, the birdcalls echoing in the darkened air. Kurt turned to face her. "How does this look? For the picnic."

Holly nodded, one quick bob of the head. "This is fine."

He followed a side trail into the woods until they heard the tinkle of cool water over rocks. "There's a creek here—it's a nice place to sit," he said almost to himself. He stopped the wagon, and the children wasted no time in disembarking to explore the creek banks, searching for flat stones to skip across its glassy surface.

After Kurt helped her down, Holly unfolded a picnic rug and spread it on the ground close to the bank where she could keep an eye on the children. She sat and unpacked the picnic basket Kurt had carried from the wagon bed. There was a distance between them. She felt it crackle with the tension of things unspoken. He sat next to her, opened his mouth as if to speak, then shut it again and ran a hand over his beard.

She took a long breath and saw Eleanor was venturing too far into the water. "Eleanor Bristol! Don't you ruin your Sunday dress!"

Eleanor pouted and stepped back out of the stream to stand beside the row of small shoes with socks tucked neatly inside. "Yes, Ma."

Edward shrieked and leaped out of the water and onto the shore. "What is it?" asked Holly, her eyes narrowed.

Kurt hurried to Edward's side, then laughed as he saw what was in the boy's hands. "It's nothing but a crayfish. You should see if you can catch more for supper—they're tasty."

Edward gazed up at Kurt with wide eyes and grinned. "Yes, sir!" He rushed back into the creek, looked around, then pounced with both hands. He pulled another wriggling, clawed creature out of the water and shouted in delight. "I got another one!"

"You sure did—good work!" Kurt called.

As Edward carried his prize over to show Holly, the girls jumped around him in fear and glee. "Eddie, will you share it with me?" asked Sarah excitedly.

He shook his head. "Catch your own."

She pouted. "I will, then." She spun on her heel and strode into the creek, water splashing up to her thighs and soaking her skirts.

Holly closed her eyes tight and groaned. There would be no stopping them now.

Edward deposited a crayfish on the rug beside the first one and headed back for more. Holly sighed, unwrapped a pack of sandwiches and used the string to tie the creatures' claws together, then stuck them in the empty picnic basket. She returned her attention to the children, who were all now splashing in the creek, soaked to the bone, squealing in delight as they chased small fish and hunted crayfish.

Kurt went to join them, laughing over near-misses and cheering successful catches, and Holly smiled despite herself. He looked like one of them, clambering in the creek as though a child himself, his hat, boots and socks left safely on the bank.

Sarah emerged after a minute, grinning from ear to ear, a writhing crayfish in each hand. She set them down in front of her mother with a flourish. "I caught two, Ma!"

Holly chuckled and hurried to unwrap another pack of sandwiches. "Well done, my dear. You're quite the fisherwoman."

Sarah glowed beneath her praise and returned to the water.

Holly scanned the area for Tripp. Her eldest had taken to separating himself from the group, and today was no exception. She spotted him, seated alone on the ground behind her, his face drawn, faintly scowling. He watched the revelry before him with a flash of anger in his eyes.

Her heart fell. She ached for him and the pain he was feeling. As the oldest, he couldn't shake the memory of their family, whole and happy as it had been. Her teeth clenched and she swallowed the lump that formed in her throat. She'd have to talk to him, but not now. He needed time to work things out in his own mind. He was much like her that way.

She turned back to the creek to discover they were playing a new game. Heather and Edward were pursuing Kurt in a wide circle, squealing and shouting. Sarah pounced in his path and splashed him. He shouted and rubbed his eyes to clear them, then grabbed Sarah, threw her in the air and watched her land with a splash in the creek. The rest of the children watched in silence.

Holly's breath caught as Sarah struggled to find her footing and emerged from the water coughing and spluttering. She scrubbed her eyes with the back of her soaking wet sleeves…then burst out laughing. Heather, Edward and Eleanor all leaped at Kurt with cries of laughter. He dunked each one, making them all hoot and holler in delight—and come back for more.

Holly discovered she'd been holding her breath since Sarah's head disappeared under the surface. But seeing their joy, she released it in a single burst and smiled widely. When she laughed out loud, Kurt spun to face her, his eyes sparkling, and motioned her over. She frowned, but complied. As he made his way toward her, her eyes narrowed—what was he up to?

She soon found out. He scooped her up with a grin, one hand around her back and the other beneath her skirts. She held onto him, screaming "Kurt, put me down!" as he carried her back toward the creek. "Don't you dare! Kurt Sawyer, I demand you put me down this instant!" Surely he wouldn't. He couldn't.

He feigned dropping her into the frigid water and she shrieked, making him throw his head back in laughter. "You should see the look on your face," he chortled.

She sighed and managed a wan smile. "I thought for a moment there you'd lost your senses and were about to throw me into the stream."

A mischievous glint in his eyes made her catch her breath. "Who says I wasn't?" he teased.

Suddenly she was very aware of his arms around her and the feel of his sturdy chest against her through his sodden shirt. Her heart skipped and her gaze landed on his lips, full, parted and half-smiling. She licked her own lips and took a quick breath. When her eyes found his again, her pulse quickened.

"Don't fret, dear. I wouldn't—" Before he could finish what he'd set out to say, he was shoved in the back. He stumbled forward, tripped and fell, landing them both with a great splash in the middle of the creek.

As the cold water soaked through her clothing, Holly gasped for air, clawing for the surface with both hands. Finally she set her feet on the bottom and stood, coughing and hacking up creek water from her lungs. Thankfully, the deepest part of the creek was barely five feet. Kurt slapped her on the back, then wiped the water from his own eyes. He laughed, coughed, then laughed again.

Her nostrils flaring, she marched out of the creek and up the bank, her fists clenched. She glared at the four children, who still stood in the creek looking contrite.

"Sorry, Ma," said Eleanor, breaking the silence. She was always the first to speak.

"I just… I can't imagine what you were thinking! I'm soaked…" Holly could barely form a sentence between her chattering teeth and racing mind.

"Sorry, Ma," added the other three children.

"Sorry, Holly," added Kurt. He'd also climbed out and stood close by, his hands on his hips. "Not that I planned it, but, well…"

She shook her head at him, then flounced back to the picnic rug. "Well, lunch is ready. Not that any of you deserve it."

Deserving or not, they shouted with glee and raced over to the blanket to eat.

"Blessing first," Kurt stated firmly, just as they were each about to thrust a sandwich into their mouths. And as Holly watched him lead her children in a prayer of thanks, the rage she'd felt dissipated like the creek water running from her clothing. She let herself smile just a little at the thought of how amusing it must have seemed to the children when she'd landed in that creek. And the memory of the looks on their faces when she emerged from the water sparked a giggle that she hid behind her hand.

Chapter Seven

Holly kilted up her skirts, rolled up her sleeves and squatted beside the washtub, then took a shirt from the dirty laundry in the basket next to her and soaked it in the warm water. She picked up the chunk of soap from the pannikin sitting in the grass and began scrubbing.

The rhythmic work of laundry day always put her in a good mood. She hadn't had to do laundry when she'd lived with Charles, nor with her sister. But after a childhood of soiled clothing and linens stiff with age, she enjoyed the sweet feel of the soap on her hands and the smell of sunshine in her clothes. Cleanliness was something she took great pleasure in after the darkness of her past. She wiped the back of her hand across her forehead, pushing a strand of hair from her eyes with a sigh.

Tripp sat by the barn, playing with something in the dust at his feet. He'd been even more sullen recently, especially since the picnic at the creek after church the week before. She hadn't had an opening to speak with him about what was going through that bright, sensitive mind of his.

He stood, kicked the ground with a bare foot, and wandered off toward the pasture beyond. She called out to him. "Tripp!"

He swiveled slowly to face her, eyelids at half mast.

"Can you come here, please?"

He paused, glanced up at the sky as if hoping for guidance on whether or not to mind his mother, then meandered over, his brow furrowed. He stopped beside her, his arms crossed over his thin chest.

She stood and wiped her wet hands on her apron. "Tripp dear, I must know what's wrong. You've been moping around the place like a bear just come out of hibernation and there's no call for it."

His scowl didn't move. "I don't want to be here. And you shouldn't either, Ma. He's not your husband. Pa was. And this is *our* family." His lips pursed, he glared at the grass by her feet.

She put a hand under his chin and tipped it up until his eyes met hers. "Tripp Bristol, Pa will always be your father. But he's gone. I'm not trying to replace him—that can't ever happen. But we need a place to live, food in our stomachs, someone to care for us. If it were just you and I, I could find a job to support us. But there are six of us! I couldn't make ends meet no matter how I tried and then I'd lose all of you."

He huffed, tightening his grip on himself.

"Don't huff at me, young man. I'm still your mother and what I say is final. I want you to buck up and smile. And you treat Kurt with the respect he deserves. He's my husband now and this is his home."

Tripp's eyes narrowed. "I won't…"

"You *will*. I'm doing the best I can, son, and I'll make mistakes along the way. But we're in this together and I need you to help me. Can you please do that?" She caressed his cheek with one still-damp hand.

He brushed her hand away. "I'm the man in our family. I could've taken care of us!"

She tipped her head to one side, her heart aching for her son and his pain. "Oh darling, I know you could. But that's not what I want for you, not if I can help it. I want you to have the opportunity for a life of your own someday, not have you saddled with a mother and siblings to care for. One day you'll thank me…"

"Thank you?" he snarled "No, I won't. I hate it here!" He spun away and ran across the yard, disappearing behind the barn.

Holly's heart lurched. He'd never spoken to her that way before, and it cut her to the quick. She took a long, slow breath, waiting for her pulse to slow back to normal. Well, she'd have to speak to him again later, perhaps when he'd calmed down. But in the meantime, she wasn't sure what to do.

He'd seemed fine with the plan to move to Kansas when they were still in New York—though now she thought about it, she hadn't ever asked him and she couldn't remember him openly supporting the idea. In fact, she did recall a couple of incidents involving yelling and slammed bedroom doors when they were packing. Perhaps that had been his way of showing his displeasure at the decision.

Her eyes drifted shut and she chewed the inside of one cheek. Well, there was nothing to be done about it now—surely he could understand that. She was married and that was the end of the matter. She could hardly abandon her new husband and flee back to New York.

And she didn't want to leave, not now that she'd finally found a little peace. At long last she didn't feel as if she was intruding on anyone else's life. She could see a pinprick of hope at the idea of spending her life with this man. As much as he was a stranger to her, everything he'd done and said so far seemed to make things more certain in her mind—he was a good man, a kind man, and hard-working too. And there was nothing to go back to in New York.

Holly lowered herself onto her haunches again to continue the laundry, frowning at the tumble of dark thoughts in her troubled mind.

Kurt lifted the tin cup to his lips and slurped the water down. The day had been a hot one, and he'd spent most of it plowing another field for oats. Plowing was hard work. He'd borrowed the plow from Will Drake again, but while it made the work easier, there were still stumps to be pulled up and rocks to carry away. Not to mention slashing weeds, some as high as his shoulder, and the constant threat of snakes.

He'd thought he'd have plenty for winter, but he hadn't reckoned with how five growing kids could eat. He'd need more crops, more livestock, more of everything. His head hurt thinking it all through.

He set the empty cup on the table in front of him and glanced around the house. Where was everyone? He'd spied a few of the children playing in the field, but where the rest of them were was beyond him. And he hadn't seen his bride since lunch. Just thinking of her made his cheeks burn and his stomach churn. He bit his lower lip. He hoped she was adjusting to her new life. It was hard to say—her face didn't betray her feelings. Holly was a book he'd have to learn how to read, though he looked forward to doing it.

He was concerned about the boy, Tripp, who glared daggers at him every chance he got and refused to join in the fun and games he had with the other children. The others were no problem at all. He smiled at the memory of Holly in her sodden dress stomping up the creek bank and scolding them. He really shouldn't have carried her into the stream—it was too tempting for the children, and while they thought it was a hoot, he didn't think it earned him any favor with her.

He stood with a groan and stretched his arms over his head just as Holly rushed in the back door, a pile of dry clothing slung over one arm. "Oh, there you are," she said, her cheeks reddening.

"Yes, I am."

"Have you had a nice day, then?" She studied his face with what seemed like curiosity.

He swallowed. "Thank you, I did. And you?"

She nodded. "I was just about to prepare supper. Are you hungry?"

"Famished," he replied. He wondered what she'd spent her day on—he wanted to know everything about her—but he didn't dare ask. That was something he'd learned from Pa at a young age: a man never asked his wife what she did with her day. His father had shaken his head ruefully and rubbed his bearded chin when he said it. Instead, he took a step toward her and reached out a hand.

She startled and moved out of his reach. "I'll just put these things away."

As she left for the bedroom, he frowned. Was she so afraid of him? Or perhaps she liked him even less than he'd realized. Was she having second thoughts about the arrangement?

He sighed deeply and left the house, donning his hat with a frown. He'd come inside early to spend time with her, but if she'd rather not be around him, he'd just as soon get the chores finished now. Badger fell into step behind him, his ears flopping as he ran.

Between Tripp's attitude and Holly's distaste for his company, Kurt wondered if he should ask whether she preferred to go back to New York. He wasn't sure how it could be done, but there must be a way for them to annul the marriage and move on with their separate lives. If that's what she wanted, he wasn't going to stand in her way.

June 1860
Morgantown, Virginia

Holly ducked behind a large barrel and watched the boy searching for her. He wouldn't find her—she was well-practiced in the art of disappearing. She'd had to be. He looked between the barrels stacked against the outside of the store, but didn't spot her.

The store owner came outside, his hands on his wide hips, his red-rimmed eyes narrowed. He was looking for her too, though he couldn't maneuver between the new stock that had just arrived. Nor would he venture into the mud that caked the street after the winter deluge that'd flooded the town earlier that day. Finally he shook his fist, looking around through the spectacles perched on the tip of his nose. "You stay away, you little urchin, and don't come back! You hear me?" The stock boy went back into the shop, scampering through the narrow door as the man clipped him behind the ear.

As soon as they were gone, Holly stood, shuddered, then smiled and shoved the apple she'd nabbed into her mouth. She checked first one skirt pocket, then the other. They were both crammed with food, and her stomach growled at the thought of a real meal for once. She could still hear the drips of rain from sodden roofs and leaking eaves as she turned and wove her way through the narrow streets of Morgantown.

She reached the Monongahela River and stopped to watch a coal barge drift toward the shore, its hull empty but blackened with the remnant of a load long since sold by its owner. Now the coal was likely heating the parlor of a wealthy family in New York or Philadelphia, powering a train as it shuttled across the country, or sending bilious smoke skyward from the chimney of a factory in Boston. She loved to watch the barges come, be piled high with coal from the mines, then set off again into the world.

She took another bite of apple, filling her cheeks to capacity. It wasn't often her mouth was full, and she enjoyed the sensation.

Pa worked at the mine, though not as often as he should. She frowned and sighed, so soft that even she didn't hear it. She knew he hadn't risen in time for his shift this morning. She knew his schedule better than he seemed to, though it didn't do her or anyone else any good. He showed up to work when he liked, and she'd heard his boss threaten more than once that his place would be filled should he miss another shift.

She headed for home, still eating the apple. He couldn't afford to lose his job. There weren't many around Morgantown that didn't involve the mines or a farm, and if he upset the coal bosses, he might as well give up working entirely, since they'd make certain no one else hired him.

The alley behind the blacksmith's was smoky and dirty. Refuse spilled from doorways set up above the muck, and her boots were swallowed by thick suck-ing sludge. She tugged one foot free, only to lose the other in the dark muck. With a grunt, she broke free and made her way along the edge of the alley. She hated when it stormed, since the streets became difficult to navigate and the rodents and insects emerged in force.

Finishing her apple, she tucked the core in a pocket to stuff with cloves later. She'd seen her teacher Mrs. Sullivan do that once and filed the idea in the back of her mind to do the first chance she got. Mrs. Sullivan was the most glamorous, beautiful, talented woman she'd ever laid eyes on. She'd taken Holly under her wing from her first day at school and spent hours, even after school was done for the day, teaching her how to read and write. Holly had soaked it up, even borrow-ing readers and other books and magazines from the kindly teacher.

Mrs. Sullivan had awakened the desire to know more, to know everything she could, about the wide world that existed beyond the muddy streets of the mean little town. She'd spent hours imagining that one day she might be just like Mrs. Sullivan and have her pick of beaus in some distant and exotic city. She'd travel the world, and men would vie for her affection.

She smiled at the thought and skipped through a doorway at the foot of a two-story raw timber building. She smoothed her hair into place and drew a deep breath. If Pa was awake and had found enough money for whiskey, she'd have to be careful how she approached him.

Holly pushed the second doorway open a touch and poked her head in. The stench of the disheveled room always made her step back whenever the door had been shut for any length of time, and she'd left it that way when she went out earlier that morning. Usually by now, Ma would have stirred and opened it, and would be smoking on the step or visiting one of the neighbors.

She crept through the doorway, listening for any sound. It was quiet—perhaps they'd both gone out. But where was Eve? Her sister rarely went with either parent, and that morning she'd had too bad a cough to leave her bed, so Holly had left her behind. She crept through the living room on tiptoe and peered into the bedroom. A form was lying on the bed and she frowned. It looked like Pa. He must have drunk through his supply of whiskey already and it wasn't even dinner time.

The room was dark, dank, and the shabby drapes that hung over the single high window hadn't been opened. She stepped closer and peered at his face, then noticed a damp patch on his brown nightshirt. He hadn't even dressed yet, so how had he gone out drinking? She poked him in the side, but he didn't move. She leaned closer still. Usually she could smell the liquor on his breath from this distance, but not this time. Finally she pulled aside the drapes, letting a brilliant ray of sunshine in…and her heart dropped into her gut.

Pa's face was pale. Too pale. She covered her mouth, reached out with her other hand and shoved him. He barely shifted beneath her touch, and didn't awaken. She gingerly touched the damp spot on his nightshirt—and her fingers came away red with blood!

With a shriek, Holly stumbled back, wiping her fingertips against her skirts furiously. She tripped over something and landed on her rear, smacking the back of her head against the wall with a loud thud. When she reached up to rub her head, she felt blood there as well. Her stomach roiled and she closed her eyes tight. Then she shifted her skirts aside to see what she'd fallen over.

That's when she screamed, but the noise was dampened by a fog that covered her mind and made her vision shrink to pinholes. *Ma!*

She scrambled to her feet and stared down at her mother with round eyes. Her throat had been slit. Her skirts were pulled up around her waist, her pale legs sticking out like two bare sticks. Her fist was clenched around something. Holly bent down and forced Ma's fingers open. A gold coin fell from the stiffened claw and rolled in a circle on the dirt floor, before landing on its side with a dull clink. She scooped it up and stuck it in her pocket, still staring at Ma's cold, stiff body.

Blinking rapidly, she backed away, then turned and ran into the other bedroom, where she barreled right into Eve. Eve had her thumb in her mouth, and her eyes looked glazed. Holly caught her with both hands before she could fall to the ground from the impact, and looked her in the eye. "Eve! Eve, what happened? What's going on?" Her voice was calm, but to her it sounded a long way away.

Eve just stared blankly, sucking her thumb.

"Eve, wake up, girl! What happened to Pa and Ma?"

Eve blinked once, then her gaze met Holly's. "Three men came." That was all she'd say, though Holly drilled her for more. It was no use. Eve was only nine, after all. A nine-year-old couldn't be brave like Holly could at thirteen. Everyone knew that.

After a few minutes passed, the fog began to lift from Holly's mind, the panic subsided and her thoughts slowed until she was able to catch them. They couldn't stay there—what if the men came back? They'd discover that gold coin was missing and they'd return for it, wouldn't they? She couldn't be sure, but she wasn't about to wait around to find out. Eve was her responsibility now, and she knew she had to take her sister and get as far away from there as they could.

She scurried back to the bedroom, keeping her eyes averted from her mother's body. A small chifforobe leaned against the far wall, and inside she found a ragged carpetbag. She grabbed as many of her and Eve's things as she could find and the few valuables she knew her parents kept hidden, and shoved them into the bag. She carried it to the kitchen and added some bread in a cloth, a couple of cans of beans and some cheese.

Eve just stood there with her thumb in her mouth,

not moving or making a sound. Holly frowned. When did Eve start sucking her thumb again? She was far too old for that. Ma never let her do it. She'd had her hide tanned more than once by Pa when he caught her at it, and she had to wear one of Pa's old socks on her hand to sleep. But Holly didn't have the heart to punish her now. "Let's go," she said, grabbing Eve by the sleeve of her soiled dress.

The thumb shifted from Eve's mouth and her eyebrows arched. "Go where?"

"I don't know yet. But we have to get…"

A man came through the door quietly and stood with his hands on his hips, regarding them with black eyes that shone in his broad face. His nose was crooked and his forehead flat, making his features resemble a tin plate. He tipped his hat back and grinned, revealing gaps where teeth should've been. "Wot have we here?"

Eve's lower lip quivered, but otherwise she froze. Holly's mind raced. He'd come back for something, but what? The gold coin? Something else? "What do you want?" she said coldly, even as her heart hammered against her ribs.

He stepped closer. "Yer Pa took sumpin' from me, 'n I wannit back. Didja see a box? 'Bout yea high…" He held his hands ten inches apart.

She shook her head. "No. I ain't seen it."

He snarled. "I bet ye 'ave." He lunged for her, but she leaped adeptly to one side, pulling Eve with her. They sidestepped the brute, his long arms closing on air, and ran down the alley. Holly, the carpetbag bouncing on her shoulder where she'd slung it, was grateful

Eve had responded quickly. She turned her head to check on Eve running beside her...

The man scooped them up—first Eve, then Holly, one in each muscular arm, his eyes flashing in triumph. Holly's heart lurched at the look of utter fear in her sister's eyes. Then Eve screamed, a blood-curdling scream that sent a chill down Holly's spine...

Chapter Eight

Holly woke and sat bolt upright on the straw tick, her heart thundering in her chest. Sweat ran down her face and she turned her head from side to side in the darkness, looking for the man with the tin-plate face. He wasn't there. Of course he wasn't there—it was just a dream, one she'd had many times when she was feeling unsettled or fearful about something.

She exhaled and rubbed her forehead, then stood slowly, smoothed her nightgown over her legs and crept from the room. There was no point in trying to sleep now—she never could once she'd had that dream. She wished she could see Eve, have her sister hold her and tell her that their nightmares were all in the past, that the man with the crooked nose would never find them again.

At the kitchen table, she lit the lamp and searched Kurt's things for a piece of paper and a quill. He'd said she could use anything she wished, and she knew she wouldn't be able to still her pounding heart until she'd written down her thoughts. She tucked her night-

gown around her legs, sat down and began to write,
the shadow of the pen falling across the paper, away
from her hand in the flickering lamplight:

Dearest Eve,
I hope my letter finds you, Rodney and James
well. We all miss you very much. We've arrived at
the home of Kurt Sawyer and he and I are mar-
ried. He is technically a landowner—he has a
ranch just outside Wichita. The oversight in the
description, it seems, is because his brother, who
owns a flour mill in town, wrote the ad. Kurt says
he didn't know what his brother had written. I
have decided to see it as a small indiscretion,
one that can be overlooked. Especially consid-
ering my failure to tell him just how many chil-
dren I was bringing with me until after he sent
me a ticket.

I know, you'll shake your head at me when
you read this. You told me to be completely hon-
est with him and I should have told him that from
the first. But he has come to terms with my fail-
ure, as I have with his. We both find ourselves
in a situation different from what we expected.
But it doesn't follow that we should be unhappy.

So far, we are getting along well. He is young
but a hard worker, and I believe he will be able to
provide for us. He seems good and kind, and he
has a way with the children that warms my heart.
He has a very pleasing look about him as well.

My concern is that Tripp is so unhappy here.
He feels I have betrayed his father's memory by

*taking a husband, and that we could have made
it on our own without Mr. Sawyer. He is blinded
by his rage and refuses to even try to accept the
change. Have I made a mistake, dear sister? Perhaps we should have attempted to make it on our
own, but I was unable to see how—not after the
way Ma and Pa raised us. I couldn't do that to
my children, couldn't force them to live in that
kind of squalor and neglect.*

*Part of me thinks of coming home to you, that
perhaps we should simply get on the next train
and return to New York. I'm homesick and anxious about the children, and I don't know what
is right or wise any longer. My head is churning
with thoughts, hopes, decisions and doubts. And
none stand out to me. Tell me what I should do.*

*I had the bad dream just now, the dream
where the man with the tin-plate face is coming
after us again back in Morgantown. I wished
you were here to remind me it was just a dream.*

I look forward to hearing from you soon.
Your sister,
Holly Sawyer

The blade fell against the log, splitting it in two,
and Kurt let the head of the axe rest against the ground
while he caught his breath. He had all the wood he
needed to build the smoker. Once it was completed,
he'd head out and shoot a deer. The smoker would be
big enough to cure a good portion of the beast, provid-
ing them with a supply of meat for the winter months.
He ran the back of his hand across his damp fore-

head and squinted into the afternoon sunlight. Summer was over, but the heat still lingered. It wouldn't be long before the days were cool and the nights frigid. He'd noticed Holly using the supplies he'd purchased in town at her request. She'd been crocheting blankets and stitching quilts every spare moment in preparation for the change of weather. There was a new set of curtains on the bedroom window, and a cozy brown-and-blue-patterned wool blanket at the foot of the bed.

Once he had enough food stocked or in process, he intended to build bunks for the children. He scratched his head beneath his Stetson. When would Holly share his bed instead of theirs? He'd known it would take time, but it had been weeks since her arrival and still she kept her distance. She was polite enough, even kind in her attentions toward him, but there was a space between them he couldn't breach, no matter how he tried.

He noticed movement out of the corner of his eye and turned to see Tripp disappearing over a rise in the distance. The boy was alone, striding with purpose through the tall grasses toward the bull pen where Kurt kept Sheridan, the ornery bull he'd purchased from William Drake in June. The animal wasn't well behaved enough to be with the rest of the cattle, though he made forays into their pasture without Kurt's approval by simply leaping over the fence whenever he fancied.

Kurt rubbed his beard with a frown. Surely the boy wouldn't bother Sheridan. If he did, the bull might not take kindly to the intrusion. He'd warned all the children about the animal, but it was an open question whether Tripp would heed it. He set the axe against the stack of split wood and hurried after Tripp.

That boy really was a frustration to him—he moped around the place and gave him lip his own father would never have stood for. He knew Tripp needed some time to come to terms with the changes in his life, but he wasn't sure how much longer he could put up with being disrespected in his own home. Still, his heart ached for all the children whenever he saw a lonesome or melancholy look on one of their little faces—and he'd grown to care for them more than he'd imagined he could in such a short time.

The long grass brushed his trouser legs and the setting sun seemed to cover everything in a white haze, burning his retinas. He blinked hard, hoping to spot the boy. If he could see him, perhaps he could call him back before he got much further. Then he might still have time to build the smoker before darkness fell.

He reached the barbed-wire fence he'd erected to keep the bull separate from the rest of the herd. It was a temporary measure—he'd hoped the animal would fit in with the group, but he'd caught it goring one of the young steers and chasing others soon after it arrived. So far, the separation hadn't seemed to temper his behavior.

He glanced around the enclosure to where the bull stood facing the far corner. He couldn't see what was there, but he could guess. "Hey!" he shouted, waving his arms over his head.

The bull turned and studied him, its eyes rolling back into its head. Sure enough, Tripp was cowering in the corner. He thought he could hear the child whimpering. Why didn't he just climb back through the fence? "Tripp! Climb through the fence!" he yelled.

Tripp straightened slowly, as though he didn't wish to provoke the beast. But it didn't work—the bull charged him, head down.

"Tripp!" cried Kurt, sprinting toward where Tripp was climbing back through the fence. But it was too late—Sheridan caught him anyway, sending him flying through the fence and the air. He landed at the base of a tall willow tree and lay slumped in a tangle of arms and legs. Sheridan snorted, then, his territory successfully defended, turned and trotted back across the enclosure.

When Kurt reached Tripp, he scooped the child up into his arms. "Tripp?" Tripp didn't respond. His eyes were closed, long lashes black against the pale skin of his freckled face. Kurt's heart fell. "Tripp, can you hear me?"

Still no response. He jogged toward the house with Tripp in his arms, his frown like a razor cut across his face.

Holly poured a spoonful of pancake batter onto the griddle, where it sizzled in the melted bacon grease. The songs of birds filled the air as they flitted outside the cottage, preparing for nightfall. Heather and Sarah set the table for supper, while Eleanor pushed a toy horse around the floor—a gift whittled for her by Kurt during evenings by the fire.

The air grew cool once the sun set now, and Kurt had assured Holly that winter would be cold, though not nearly as cold as New York. They would probably even have snow for Christmas. She'd been preparing for the new season and was satisfied with all she'd managed to achieve in such a short time.

She heard the rapid tramp of boots across the yard. Her heart leaped at the sound of Kurt's approach, and she wiped her palms on her apron. He must have finished his chores already, and no doubt he'd be hungry. She'd grown to enjoy their conversations at supper and after. During the day he was working out on the ranch, but evenings were their time together. She'd taken to settling the children on their pallets earlier and earlier, anticipating conversation by the fire with her new husband.

But when he burst through the door, the look on his face and the limp form in his arms made her heart drop. "Tripp's hurt," he called. He carried the boy straight into the bedroom and laid him on the bed, boots and all.

She rushed to Tripp's side and knelt, pressing a hand to his forehead. "What happened?" she asked Kurt.

He shook his head. "I told him not to set foot in Sheridan's pen. But he did it anyway and the beast sent him flying."

She gasped, her pulse racing. She couldn't lose her boy. She checked him gently all over with both hands, looking for any sign of injury. Finding no blood or broken bones, she turned again to Kurt, her throat tightening with each moment. "Where is he hurt? Did you see what happened?"

Kurt removed his Stetson and sighed. "Well, I trimmed Sheridan's horns back after he used them on some steers a while ago, so the boy wasn't gored. But the bull caught him straight on and flung him against a tree trunk. He might have hit his head pretty hard, and I'm sure he'll have some bruises."

His words brought her some hope. If only the boy would move. "Tripp?" she whispered close to his ear. Still nothing. She hurried to the washstand, poured water from the jug into the bowl, wet a cloth with it and carried it back.

As she gently wiped his face, he began to stir. "Ma?" he murmured, blinking his eyes.

She laughed with relief. "Tripp, where does it hurt?" she asked, resting a hand on his forehead.

He gripped the crown of his head with both hands. "My head's pounding something fierce."

She laid the wet cloth across his forehead. "I'll mix up a poultice—maybe I can find some herbs in the garden to help. You silly child, venturing into a bull's pen that way. You could've been killed."

He offered her a weak smile. "Sorry, Ma."

"Well, you should be glad Kurt was there and saw what happened. He carried you all the way back to the cottage, I'll have you know. I hate to think what might have become of you if he hadn't been there. That bull might've decided to jump the fence and have another try." Tears pricked the corners of her eyes and she fought them back.

Tripp glanced sideways at Kurt, who lingered in the doorway. "Thank you," he said.

Kurt nodded, his cheeks coloring and disappeared into the living room.

"I'll be back in a minute," she said, straightening and hurrying after Kurt.

She found him in the front room, pacing between the

girls as they watched him goggle-eyed. Holly watched for a moment too, then met him at the kitchen table. "Thank you, Kurt. I mean it—I'm glad you were there. Thank you."

He put his hands on his hips, his eyes flashing. "What about the next time?"

She froze. "I'm sorry…?"

"What about the next time that boy decides he's had enough and does something foolhardy? What then? I can't watch him every moment of the day." He frowned, rubbing his mouth.

She frowned. Was he angry at her about something? "I'm not sure what you mean…"

"He's doing stupid things because he doesn't want to be here. He hates me and he's determined not to accept this life." He groaned and rubbed his eyes. "I… I didn't know it'd be this hard, Holly."

Despite his concerns, her heart skipped a beat when he said her name. The word sounded like honey on his lips. She ducked her head. "I know. It's always more difficult when there are children involved, that's for sure. But…?"

"And you didn't tell me. That's what stings the most. You didn't say you had children until it was too late to turn back."

Her brow furrowed. "Now hold on just a moment— I *did* tell you, as soon as I knew we were coming. How was I to know you'd send me a ticket after one letter? Besides, you could've put us on the next train back to New York if you didn't want to take us on. And what about that advertisement your brother wrote—

"successful landowner," with the address of his mill? Hrumph!"

His eyebrows lowered. "I told you, that wasn't my doing."

"So you say." She crossed her arms, unwilling to let him push her around. She'd done what she had to in order to protect her family—she wasn't about to be shamed for it!

He sighed and closed his eyes a moment, and when he opened them she saw resignation lingering there. Her bravado faded and she sunk into a chair, resting her head in one hand.

"I'm sorry, Holly. I just don't know how to work this out."

Her gut roiled with fear. Was he going to ask them to leave? She could feel it coming and swallowed the bile that rose up her tightening throat. "So…what are you saying?"

He sighed. "Maybe you and the children *should* go back to New York. I mean, it's not what you expected, I know. *I'm* not what you expected. And I don't know if Tripp will ever accept me…" He trailed off and started to pace again.

She watched him, her thoughts in turmoil. They'd have to leave. He didn't want them here any longer. What would they do? Where would they go? The tears that had threatened for so long finally snaked their way down her cheeks. She sobbed, covering her mouth to quiet the sound.

But it was too late. He'd heard and came hurrying to her side, kneeling next to her chair, his face drawn. "I'm sorry. I've upset you. I didn't mean to—I thought

you wanted to go home. I just want you to be happy…
I don't know what to do." His words tumbled out as he
cupped her face in his work-worn hands.

She leaned her cheek against his palm and let her
eyes drift shut even as tears continued. "We've nowhere else to go," she whispered. A lump formed in
her throat and she tried hard to swallow it.

When she opened her eyes, he was studying her
with an intensity she hadn't seen before. "I just feel…"

"What?" she asked, lifting a hand to caress his
cheek.

He looked down at the floor and inhaled deeply.
"…like I'm not enough. For you, for the children…"

She frowned as his gaze met hers, but she didn't
look away. It was as if she was finally seeing him for
the first time: the faintest freckles across his strong
nose, the flecks of green in his blue eyes, the pain that
lingered behind them. "I'm sorry if I made you feel
that way." She raised a hand to wipe the tears from
her cheeks. "You're a good man. And I'm sorry we've
turned your life upside down this way. I understand
why you'd want us to leave…"

His brow furrowed, he caught her hand in his, raised
it to his lips and kissed it, lingering there a moment.
"I *don't* want you to leave. Not if you don't want to.
I just thought… I thought you weren't happy here—
you or the children—and I didn't want you to think
you had to stay."

She forced a smile. "Where else would we go?"

Chapter Nine

Sam and Sal stamped their hooves, seemingly impatient to begin the journey to town. Holly pinned her hat on her head as she walked to the wagon. Everyone else was already loaded up and waiting for her. Tripp sat glumly on the wagon seat with Kurt. He'd recovered well from his encounter with Sheridan—just a few bruises and a couple days of double vision—but still looked pale and sullen.

His siblings were crowded into the wagon bed, wrestling and arguing about nothing. Holly rolled her eyes and peered over the wagon rail. "Behave yourselves. We're going to town and I want to see company manners from all of you."

They righted themselves, looking sheepish. "Yes, ma'am," four little voices said in unison.

Kurt finished fixing the traces in place and hurried to help her up to the seat.

"Thank you," she murmured with a smile. As she settled beside Tripp, she couldn't help thinking about the conversation of a week earlier. Kurt had suggested they should go back to New York, but only if that was what she wanted. He hadn't raised the subject since, and she'd largely kept out of his way. She needed time to think. Perhaps they should return home, but if they did, she'd need a plan for when they got there. So far, she'd come up blank.

She supposed they could move to Morgantown, though it made her stomach lurch. It was the last place on Earth she'd ever want to go, but she knew people there and could conceivably get work, especially since the state of West Virginia had opened a university there. Likely they'd be able to board with one of her old friends for a reasonable rate until they got their own place. But she didn't wish to take her children to the very town where her own childish innocence had been dashed.

The wagon set off, the horses easily pulling their load. Tall, big-boned with shaggy manes and forelocks, the Clydesdales trotted sedately down the winding trail that would lead them off Kurt's ranch and directly to Wichita.

She glanced at him, back straight, his black vest buttoned over a long-sleeved white shirt. His town clothes—she'd ironed them for him the previous night, using a flatiron warmed by the fireplace coals. He looked dapper and handsome, with his hair neatly combed beneath the brim of his hat.

He caught her eye and smiled. "Nice day, isn't it?"

She nodded. "Indeed."

"I thought we might stop in and see Angus—if that's all right with you."

"Yes, of course. That would be lovely." She knew

she'd see his brother and sister-in-law sometime, but after the way the churchwomen had treated her the first time she'd attended First Presbyterian, she had kept to herself.

She gritted her teeth. There was nothing for it but to suffer her way through it. Granted, Angus and Beatrice hadn't mistreated her—Angus had been polite enough, but she had no way of knowing how they really felt about her—did they take the same unfair view of her as those women had?

Unfair, but not completely incorrect—she had married Kurt in part to have someone to care for her children. She wouldn't deny it. What other way was there for a woman like her, without a penny to her name, to support her family? She had to marry, and she wasn't about to apologize for doing what was necessary, nor let her children go hungry if there was some way to prevent it. Those busybodies could go hang for all she cared.

Her brow furrowed as anger burned in her gut. What business of theirs was it? And if Angus and his wife dared to say anything like that, she'd make sure they knew her side of things.

Kurt's eyes narrowed. "You look like a snake with a frog stuck in its throat. Are you all right?"

She frowned. She hadn't told him about the churchwomen. He'd likely find out on his own what people were saying about them. That's how gossip worked—it always slithered to find the people it tore down. But all the same, she wanted to get it off her chest. "Do you remember the first Sunday we went to church?"

He nodded.

"There were some women there who were all in a lather about us. They said I had no right to marry you, like I was preying on you." Her cheeks burned and her stomach clenched at the memory of their words and the hurt they'd caused her.

"They said that to you?"

"Yes. I guess I'm concerned that your brother and his wife might feel the same way. Seeing as how those people are their friends." She stared at her hands clenched in her lap.

He coughed to clear his throat. "Well, now, that wasn't right." He scratched his beard and looked her in the eye. "They shouldn't have said anything, seeing as it's none of their business. And more importantly, they're wrong."

"They are?" she asked, hope stirring.

"Of course they are. We married each other because we wanted to. No one was taking advantage of anyone. I knew what I was getting into. And I'm a grown man, aren't I?"

She nodded.

"So there you have it. I decided to marry you, so I did. That's all. And if any of them have a problem with it, you can tell them to take it up with me, and you'd best believe I'll set them straight. Preying on me…hah! As if I was a prairie hen."

Holly laughed in relief. "Thank you. I'll make sure to tell you if they say anything else."

He nodded, his eyes flashing. "You do that. And don't fret about Angus and Beatrice. They're not like that—they're excited to see you. They told me themselves the last time I was in town."

Holly smiled. "I'm looking forward to seeing them as well." She took a deep breath as the anxiety that had weighed her down began to dissipate.

Kurt snuck a glance at Holly as they reached Wichita. She seemed to feel better after their discussion earlier—he was glad about that. He intended for them to stop at the mercantile first to get some supplies before heading over to Angus' house.

The town had grown so much just in the year since he arrived. The railroad brought new settlers every week. Businesses sprouted all up and down Main, Market and Lawrence streets, and new construction sites ran all the way down to the river and even across it. The sights, sounds and smells of the town always struck him the moment he left the peacefulness of the countryside, and every time he was grateful he could leave and go back home to the ranch. He'd embraced rural life the moment he moved away from New York, and happily so.

He stopped the wagon in front of the mercantile and leaped down to the dusty street with a grunt. He tied Sam and Sal to a hitching post and patted Sam's neck as the horses slurped water from the trough nearby, then helped Holly and Tripp down while the other children tumbled out of the back.

When they entered the mercantile, the children ran around, exclaiming over the barrels of candy, apples, flour, oats and more. There was a display of boots in one corner, some bolts of cloth behind the counter and pocket knives lined up in a small, lockable case on top of the counter. All as he'd hoped—he intended to surprise Holly.

He knew she'd been having second thoughts about staying; heck, he'd suggested himself that she take the children and go home. He wished he could take back those words—they'd driven a wedge between them ever since. He'd just been so upset by the incident with Tripp and the bull, and figured the boy would never accept their new life with him. But Tripp had actually been polite to him since then, and he'd begun to wonder if perhaps the boy's attitude had changed after all.

He ran his fingertips along the counter as a man wearing a black suit, white shirt and pinstriped apron smiled at him from behind it. "How're you doing?" he asked.

"Just fine thanks—and you?" replied Kurt. Then he looked closer. "I haven't seen you in here before."

The man nodded and chuckled. "That's right. I've just bought the place from Mr. Hungerford. It's my first week—still finding my way around."

Kurt arched an eyebrow. "Good for you. I'm Kurt Sawyer. Glad to meet you, Mr.…?"

"Brown, Handley Brown. Nice to meet you, Mr. Sawyer. You just let me know if you need help with anything—"

They were interrupted by a fussy-looking fellow standing behind Kurt—Mr. Werner, the postmaster. "Hold on… Sawyer, you say?" he remarked in a strong German accent. "I belief I have a letter for somevon named Sawyer…" He reached into his shoulder bag and pulled one out. "…*ja*, here it is. Goot thing I was here already delivering Mr. Brown's mail. It says it is for a *Holly* Sawyer. One of your relations?"

Kurt grinned. "That's my wife, over by the candy." He waved in Holly's direction.

"*Wunderbar*—here you go. You can give it to her yourself." Mr. Werner tipped his hat and bustled out.

"Thank you kindly," said Kurt to Mr. Werner's retreating back, tucking the envelope into his back pocket.

"Anything I can help you with?" asked Handley.

"Actually, could I take a look at that blue fabric with the black pinstripes?" Kurt pointed at the bolt leaning upright against the wall.

"Sure can." Handley lifted it onto the counter.

Kurt rubbed the fabric between his fingers, craning his neck to see where Holly had gone. She was whispering fiercely at Eleanor and Edward beside a barrel of red-and-white-striped peppermint sticks. "Holly? Could you come here a moment?"

She spun around, her cheeks flushed. "Yes, Kurt." She hurried to his side, nostrils flaring.

"Everything all right with the children?" he asked, glancing over her shoulder to see the two youngest standing on tiptoe to peer into the barrel.

"Yes, it's fine," she replied unconvincingly.

"Well, I just wanted to know what you thought of this blue cloth."

"It's very pretty." She frowned, running her hand over it. "But if you're thinking about a shirt for yourself, it really wouldn't suit. This cloth is for gowns."

"I know." He grinned. "I thought you might like to make a dress for yourself."

Her eyes widened and her mouth dropped open. "For me?"

"Yes. Really, I'd like to buy fabric for everyone— we all need winter clothes, and the children are likely to have grown out of theirs from last winter. They'll need new boots as well. So what do you think of this? I think it would look just about perfect on you."

She sounded stunned. "You're buying us all new clothes and boots?"

He nodded, his hands on his hips. "You'd best choose. Otherwise I'll have to pick for you—and I'm not known for my fashion sense," he chuckled.

She threw her arms around him with a cry, knocking him off balance. "Thank you!" she mumbled against his vest.

He caught her with one arm and steadied them both against the counter with the other, his heart skipping a beat. "You're welcome." When she pulled away, he straightened his vest, his cheeks burning.

Holly was in her element—she examined every fabric in the store, picking out a different one for each child. Then they all tried on boots, and she selected a pair for each of them, allowing some room to grow. She even selected cloth for a winter shirt and coat for Kurt himself, and insisted he get new boots to replace the worn ones with a hole in the left toe that he'd worn every day the past three years.

When they finally made their way back to the wagon with all their purchases, Kurt couldn't help but feel satisfied at how excited Holly and the children were over their new things. It brought a smile to his face. "All aboard," he called, donning his hat again.

Holly returned his smile, and he offered her his arm as she climbed into the wagon. Her touch on his shirt-sleeve made his skin tingle beneath the fabric and his heart sing.

It wasn't far to Angus' house—a spacious two-story structure just two blocks from the mercantile. The front yard was built around a large oak, and a rope swing hung from one of its branches over the straggly grass below. Holly studied it as her heart hammered against her ribs and internally she chastised herself. There was nothing for her to worry about—Kurt had told her as much. But she couldn't help feeling jittery.

Kurt parked the wagon and came around to the other side to help her and Tripp down. She gathered the children around her, and Eleanor and Edward, the youngest, clung to her skirts. "Now children, please mind your manners, and whatever you do, don't break anything," she murmured so only they could hear. They nodded, staring up at her.

Tripp, however, was watching the house, his brow furrowed. She hoped he wouldn't create mischief while they were there. She couldn't imagine why they were all so anxious—or why she was. Back in New York they'd rubbed shoulders with the richest residents and most well-respected families all the time. But this small town was mostly unknown to her, and that made her nerves twitchy.

Angus answered the door after the first knock and invited them in with a warm welcome. They followed him into the living room and he introduced his wife Beatrice. She sat in an armchair, her feet resting on a hassock, her enormous belly protruding like the prow of a ship on her diminutive frame. "I'm so sorry I can't get up, but we're so glad you could come. I do hope you'll join us for lunch. We've been so looking forward to seeing you all. My children are upstairs—Angus Jr. and Katherine, called Kate. With another on the way, as you can see."

Then she smiled up at Holly and held out her hand. "Please, come here, Holly." She patted the seat beside her. "Do sit down. I want to know everything there is to know about you. After all, we are sisters now."

Holly's cheeks flushed and she sat compliantly beside Beatrice, tucking her skirts around her legs and crossing her ankles modestly. "What would you like to know?"

Beatrice laughed, a warm, pleasant sound. "How about starting with where you grew up?"

Holly grimaced inwardly and cleared her throat. "I was raised in Morgantown, Virginia. West Virginia now, near the Pennsylvania border."

"Oh…that's coal country, isn't it?" asked Beatrice.

Holly noticed a young boy, about Tripp's age, emerge from another room and wave to Tripp—Angus Jr., presumably. He did resemble his father and his Uncle Kurt. Tripp followed him off into the house, and she smiled to herself. "There wasn't much to it—there isn't much to it now, from what I've heard. As soon as I was old enough, my sister and I moved to New York. She's still there."

"Oh, you have a sister? Kurt didn't mention that— though I can't say I'm surprised. The Sawyer boys, you'll find, are a tight-lipped pair. Getting information out of either of them is like forcing a full horse to drink from a river."

Holly chuckled. She knew just what Beatrice meant. She looked over at Kurt, who stood beside an upright piano against the far wall, deep in conversation with his brother. He caught her gaze and winked, making her heart flip. "Yes, her name is Eve."

"You must miss her," Beatrice replied, her eyes compassionate.

"Every day," whispered Holly, willing her voice not to break.

Beatrice set a dainty hand on Holly's. "Well, then, I'm so glad we have each other. I've never had a sister and always wanted one, and you've left yours behind, at least for now. Though I'm sure you'll be reunited. Life is too short to spend it entirely out of the presence of those we love, don't you think?"

Holly nodded, unable to speak around the lump in her throat that always arose when discussing Eve. She'd been all wrong about Beatrice Sawyer—she could tell the two of them would get along just fine.

When they left Angus and Beatrice's house, the sun was already low in the west, and Eleanor soon fell fast asleep in Holly's lap, her golden curls spread out and her hands tucked together beneath one pink cheek. Holly admired her and tucked a strand of hair behind the little girl's ear. She really was beautiful, and Holly was so grateful for her and her sweet personality.

In fact, there were so many things she was grateful for in that moment. She hadn't thought she'd ever feel peace or hope again after Charles' death. But here she was, riding on a wagon seat beside her new husband with a smile on her face and hope building in her heart that the future might just be better than she'd thought possible.

Kurt seemed to catch her mood and grinned knowingly. "That went well."

She nodded. "It did, better than I'd expected. Thank you."

He raised an eyebrow. "For what?"

"For reassuring me before we arrived. And for checking on me. I noticed you stayed close and made sure the conversation remained positive. I appreciate it."

He nodded. "They're good people—they wouldn't have said anything unfair. Still, I wanted to make sure…you know. I want you to be happy."

Her heart leaped. That was the second time he'd said those words. He seemed really to care for her, more than she'd believed, much more than she'd dared to hope he would.

"Oh, I almost forgot." He half-stood and pulled a creased envelope out of his back pocket. "Here, this is for you. Mr. Werner the postmaster gave it to me at the mercantile."

She took it and read the address in the dimming light. It was from Eve! She bit her lower lip and glanced at Kurt. What she really wanted to do was retreat to a quiet room alone to open it so she could savor every word. But she couldn't wait until they got home—she had to read it now, had to know what was going on in her sister's life since she left New York. She'd never been apart from Eve so long before. She'd practically

raised her after their parents' death—and missed her
even more than she'd realized she would.

She gently tore it open and extracted five full pages,
written on both sides in her sister's neat script. The first
pages were all about her daily life, Rodney and James
and James' new doctor. Then she addressed Holly's
situation in the sweet but firm way she always did:

> *My darling sister, you never knew what it
> meant to work at a marriage. Your own dear
> Charles was so in love with you, he gave you all
> your heart's desires and more. You never really
> argued or had him fuss at you. You aren't accus-
> tomed to marriage being anything other than fol-
> lowing your heart. But let me tell you—not every
> marriage is like that.*
>
> *Marriage to Rodney requires that I sometimes
> put aside my own wants, desires and dreams, for
> the sake of my family and my husband. Do I wish
> that I had a husband who catered to my every
> whim? Yes, of course. But it isn't so and I mustn't
> hold onto false hopes.*
>
> *And you mustn't either. You're married now
> and you must try to make it work. Kurt is your
> husband and you should do everything you can to
> support him. He needs you as much as you need
> him, and from what you've told me so far he's a
> good and kind man. Let that be enough for you.*
>
> *If you returned to New York, you'd find your-
> self alone and penniless, exactly the state you
> wanted to escape by marrying Kurt. I'd love to
> see you, of course, but I don't wish to watch you*

*fall into the destitution we escaped as children.
I don't think I could bear it.*

*Will you promise me you'll try? Give Kurt
a chance. I know you don't think you can love
again, but I believe in love and I believe in you. I
do hope you'll let Kurt into your heart. But, if you
decide to return home, I'll support you and do
everything I can to help you and the children...*

Holly let the correspondence rest in her lap and her
eyes wandered to the horizon. She ran over Eve's words
in her mind, considering their weight. She knew Eve
was right—and she'd already decided in her heart she
wanted to stay, at least as long as Kurt allowed her to.
She knew that her and her children's best chance of
building a new life was with him. And she'd grown
fond of him besides.

Could she let him into her heart, as Eve's letter im-
plored her to do? Her stomach clenched at the idea.
Vulnerability always resulted in suffering—that much
she knew after a lifetime of pain. With her heart still
aching from losing Charles, she wasn't sure she could
let down the walls that protected it to allow Kurt in.

Even as Holly pondered, she realized with sudden
clarity that she hadn't suffered the pang of grief that
usually accompanied thoughts of Charles. Her eyes
widened in surprise—she felt nostalgic and a little sad,
but wasn't overcome by the urge to collapse on the
ground in tears. Something inside her had changed.

Chapter Ten

The pelting rain hammered a dull staccato rhythm against the cottage's shingled roof. Kurt shrugged off his overcoat and hung it on a peg outside the door, then removed his hat, slapped it against his hand to knock some of the water off and set it on another peg. His muddied boots came off too, to be set on the porch near the dripping coat and hat.

He took a deep breath and let his gaze wander over the ranch. His view was obscured by the driving rain, but he could see the barn, dark and sturdy beside the house. The horses grazed in the distance, their blacks, browns and tans against the green of the sodden grass. He was grateful for the rain, though it made working that much harder. The crops he'd planted would benefit from a good soaking.

When he opened the front door, it smelled good inside, and the warmth from the fireplace made it feel cozy and snug the moment he entered. Several of the children sat before the fire, playing some game, he couldn't tell what. But they were quiet and well-occupied.

Heather glanced up at him, her blue eyes twinkling. "Howdy, Mr. Sawyer!"

He grinned at her precociousness—where had she picked that word up? "Howdy yourself, Heather."

Something was different about the place, though he couldn't quite put his finger on what. It smelled like baking and cinnamon and everything good, in a way that reminded him of childhood Christmases. The lantern light and firelight made shadows dance on the walls and furniture. He spied Holly at the kitchen table, a floral-print apron tied tightly around her trim waist, humming while she kneaded dough on a board he'd cut for her use. "Good evening," he said, wandering over to greet her.

She smiled warmly, and it lit him up inside. "Good evening, Kurt. Would you like some coffee? I just made a pot."

He nodded and sat at the table.

She poured it at the stove and set in front of him. "Here, that should warm you up. It's certainly blowing a gale outside."

"It sure is. And that rain is really coming down too." He frowned. Something was different about Holly. She almost seemed to glow as she buzzed around, putting together what looked like a blackberry pie. She must have gathered berries from the bushes over by the creek. He'd shown them to her the previous week, thinking the children would likely enjoy picking the fruit while they played. "Did you have a good day?"

She reached across the table to lay her hand on his and meet his eyes. "I did. And you?"

He startled at her touch, tipping his head to one side. The feel of her skin on his sent a buzz up his arm and he took a quick breath. "It's been well enough, given the wind, rain and a half-dozen runaway steers. And a leaking barn roof, which I'll have to deal with another time. But the day's done, and all's well that ends well."

She nodded, noting his use of the same saying she'd offered him when she first arrived. She pulled away to finish the pie's top crust. "True enough. Supper's almost ready—we're having roast veal with cornbread and greens, and blackberry pie for dessert."

He ran a hand over his beard. "That sounds delicious."

She hummed a tune while he watched her wipe her flour-covered hands on her apron, then slide the pie into the cast-iron oven. He saw the flash of glowing coals before she closed the door, using her apron to protect her fingers from the heat.

"I'm going to work on your garden tomorrow," he began, tapping the tabletop. "If it's not still pouring rain, that is. It's time to harvest the pumpkins and gourds, so I thought I'd do that for you and dig up the potatoes and carrots. I want to expand the space, but I'll probably wait until spring. There's not much point now, with the planting season passed."

"Thank you, I appreciate it. You know, that might be something the boys can help you with. Tripp needs something to do—it's time he started helping around here with the men's work. And Edward's only five, but he loves to dig." She wiped the back of her hand across her forehead, leaving a trace of flour on her fair skin.

Tripp's ears had perked up at the suggestion he could do "men's work."

"I don't mind," he said, trying to sound nonchalant.

Kurt smiled. "That sounds fine." But all his attention was on Holly. She really was beautiful, and though he'd noticed that the first moment he'd laid eyes on her, there was something about her now that drew him in. She made his heart feel warm and full. Once, facing his new family at the end of a workday filled him with anxiety, and a few times he'd even found extra chores to keep him away. Now he realized he couldn't wait to come inside and see her. Even the children's noisy play and hearty bickering brought a smile to his face.

Kurt turned his head around to look over his shoulder at the boys. Tripp tugged at a pumpkin still on the vine, and Edward was shoving a trowel two-handed into the earth, a pile of dirt growing beside him.

Kurt grinned, cut a small yellow gourd free from the vine and dropped it into a string bag he'd looped around his shoulders. The garden was overgrown with weeds, making it difficult to locate the actual vegetables. Some had begun to rot where they were hidden, and he chastised himself over the waste. He hoped Holly would be a more conscientious gardener than he'd been.

He stepped deeper into the tangle of foliage, foraging through it in search of pumpkins and gourds.

They made for good eating—he was looking forward to pumpkin pies and roast gourds with butter and brown sugar—and he smiled in anticipation.

A sharp pain in his hand made him draw it back with a furrowed brow. What was that? He kicked one boot at the weeds and saw a small thick snake pull back into a loop, its beady eyes watching him closely. He reached for his shovel close by on the ground, raised it high and brought it down hard on the snake's neck, severing its head in one swift movement. Then he hurried to the edge of the garden and slumped to the ground.

Tripp was stacking pumpkins into a neat pile, Edward having ducked back into the cottage. "What's wrong?" asked Tripp, coming over to Kurt and studying him with hooded eyes.

"Snake bit me," replied Kurt, holding his wounded hand in the other.

Tripp gasped. "What kind? Did you see it?"

"Copperhead, I think." Kurt's nostrils flared and he closed his eyes. Of all the thoughtless things…he knew not to poke around in undergrowth like that. He'd been distracted and should have been more careful.

"I'll get Ma!"

Kurt stopped him. "No. You can help me."

Tripp squatted beside him. "Yes, sir. What do I do?"

"Take my knife." Kurt leaned to one side, exposing the knife he wore in a sheath on his belt.

Tripp unclipped the sheath and carefully extracted the knife. The blade shone in the morning light.

"Now, you need to cut the bite like so." Kurt, teeth

clenched, drew an X across the cut with his finger. He hoped the boy was up to it.

Tripp's face paled and he took a quick breath. "Yes, sir." He brought the knife toward Kurt's hand and hesitated, his hand shaking.

Kurt met Tripp's gaze with a forced smile. "I'm glad you're here, buddy. Wouldn't trust anyone else to do this."

Tripp swallowed, nodded, then gently drew the knife across the bite wounds, then again across them.

Kurt watched thin lines of blood appear. "That's it. Well done." He gritted his teeth, brought his hand to his mouth, sucked out the poison and spat it onto the ground. "Thanks, buddy. Could you trouble your Ma for some water?"

Tripp nodded and sprinted toward the cottage, soon returning with a cup in his hand, water sloshing over the sides as he ran. Right behind him was Holly, her skirts swishing around her pumping legs. "Are you all right?" she cried, kneeling in the dirt beside him and taking his hands in hers.

Kurt sighed and extracted his undamaged hand to lay it gently on her head. He stroked her golden hair, feeling a longing he'd never before experienced. "I'll be just fine. A snake in the grass bit me, but Tripp cut out the poison. He was a big help." He grinned at Tripp over Holly's bowed head, and the boy's cheeks flushed red.

Holly turned to face her son. "Is that so? Well, I'm grateful you were here, son."

Tripp ducked his head and scuffed a boot in the dirt.

Kurt took the cup of water from Tripp, rinsed his

mouth and spat on the ground again. "Thanks." Tripp nodded as Kurt gave him back the cup.

"I'll get you a bandage," said Holly, standing to her feet.

"Just a moment. Do you think you could help me into the house?" Kurt's pulse raced. He knew the chances of being killed by a copperhead's bite were slim, but it could make you wish you were dead. Already he could feel the snake's venom making its way through his body. He began to shiver as chills ran over his skin.

Holly nodded and helped him to his feet. He slung his arm over her shoulder and walked to the cottage with her help. He chuckled to himself—he knew he could've made it alone, but he was enjoying the opportunity to be so close to Holly.

Inside, she helped him into a chair, then bent to remove his boots. "I'm sorry about tracking mud through the house," he told her.

She shrugged and smiled. "Nothing a mop and bucket won't fix. Are you feeling all right?"

He swallowed hard. Heat and searing pain radiated from his hand up his arm. The poison working its way through him felt like a steam engine that couldn't be stopped. "It smarts some."

Holly stood and wiped her palms on her apron. "Sarah! Heather!" she called, her voice ringing through the cottage.

The two girls dashed in from the bedroom, pine cone dolls in their hands. "Yes, Ma?" asked Sarah.

"Sarah, please boil some water on the stove. Heather, could you fetch the bag of clean rags?"

The two girls nodded and hurried to comply. Holly headed for the back door. "Where are you going?" asked Kurt, his wounded hand throbbing.

"There's an elderberry bush out by the barn. I'm going to harvest some leaves and berries for you. They'll help with the pain." She disappeared through the door with a rustle of skirts as his head fell back on the chair.

Sarah returned after putting the kettle on the stove to boil. She stood staring at him with wide eyes and a nervous frown, seeming unsure of what to say. "Snakebite," he informed her with a wry grin, and she nodded. Heather joined them, a small bag in her arms, and whispered to her sister before she too turned to stare at him.

Holly burst back in through the door, holding the edges of her apron up, then headed straight to the table and dumped a bunch of green leaves and berries on its surface. She rummaged beneath the table, found a pot and set it on the stove beside the kettle, then added the berries and water from the pitcher.

Finally done with that, she turned her attention to Kurt, Sarah and Heather. "Thank you, girls," she said with a quick smile and took the bag from Heather, who went to bring her mother the kettle. Holly poured some boiling water into a bowl, wet a rag with it and knelt again beside Kurt. "Your hand, please," she requested. Her voice was gentle, and when she caught his gaze her eyes crinkled around the edges. She took his hand and he flinched in anticipation of pain, but her touch was light as a feather.

She wiped the cut clean with the cloth, rinsing the rag several times until the water was pink from the blood. She extracted another cloth from the bag, laid it across her lap and grasped a handful of elderberry leaves from the tabletop. "These should help you feel a little better," she explained as she laid the leaves one by one across the wound, then wrapped the cloth around his hand to secure them. "And I'll make a tonic from the berries for you to drink as well."

Kurt held his breath and watched Holly while she worked. There was a crease between her eyebrows that spoke of concentration, and he wished he could kiss it. But she'd never given any indication that she wanted to be kissed, let alone there. Should he wait for that? They were married, but he didn't want to push her into something before she was ready.

How long might that take? He had so little experience with women. He'd courted one back in Mount Vernon, but she'd gotten engaged to someone else, and he'd never had a chance to kiss her. He'd been hurt, confused, and left with no more an idea of how to win a woman's heart than he'd had before.

"All done," said Holly, using the arm of the chair to push herself to her feet.

"Thank you," he replied, even as nausea made him wince. "I think I might be sick." Holly ran for the kitchen, but it was too late—he lost his breakfast all over the floor with one great heave. The two girls jumped back out of the way, their mouths agape in horror. "Sorry," he grunted.

Holly returned with a bucket. "Never mind, I'll take

care of it. But I wonder if we shouldn't go for the doctor?"

"No need…just a copperhead. I'm sure I'll feel fine in no time…"

"Still…" She wiped his beard and mouth with a wet rag, her face drawn.

"Who would go?" he asked. He knew he couldn't ride nor drive a wagon, the way he felt.

"I'll send Tripp."

He thought a moment. "Fine, if you think the boy's up to it." He wasn't used to having people take care of him. It felt strange and endearing at the same time.

She nodded. "Sarah, fetch Tripp and tell him to ride to town for the doctor."

"But Ma, Tripp doesn't know how to ride," Sarah objected.

"He may not be a *confident* rider, but he's learned how to saddle a horse and ride well enough over the last few weeks. Go."

Sarah went, and Holly turned to her sister. "Heather, I need more water. Will you fetch me some more from the creek, please?" She held out the bucket, and Heather took it and followed her sister outside. "Now, Kurt, let's get you into bed."

He liked the way his name sounded on her tongue. "Yes, Ma'am," he mumbled.

She leaned down to offer him her shoulder for support. He stood, looped his arm around her shoulders, and together they made it to the bedroom, where he fell on the bed with a gasp and a crackle of dry straw. She looked at him, hands on her hips, wisps of hair flying around her pretty face, her blue eyes flashing. "*Don't* call me 'Ma'am'," she said before walking out.

Kurt closed his eyes, wishing he had the strength to laugh.

By the time Tripp returned from town with Dr. White, Kurt had been asleep for hours, tossing and turning on the straw tick. Holly showed the doctor into the bedroom. "Thank you for coming, Dr. White. He says he was bitten by a copperhead and he was sure he'd be fine, but he vomited, and he's been sleeping since Tripp left to fetch you." She wrung her hands, her brow furrowed.

She'd carried on taking care of the house and the children since Tripp disappeared down the long winding drive on Sam's sturdy back. But she was tense the whole time. Kurt wasn't getting any better. Tripp had only taken the trail to town in the wagon a few times, never on a horse. Every noise made her heart drop into her stomach, every small annoyance caused her to snap at the children in aggravation. When Tripp finally returned successfully with the doctor, she didn't know whether to laugh or cry with relief.

Now she watched as Dr. White woke and examined Kurt. When he was done, he ushered her from the room, pinched the bridge of his nose and sighed. "It looks as if Kurt has developed an infection along with the bite."

Holly's throat tightened. "What can we do?"

"Honestly, there's not much we can do. Have him drink plenty of water, rest and hope for the best. I'm not sure what else would be of benefit in this situation.

He says he sucked out the poison, and he's talking and aware of what's going on, but his temperature's high."

"I'm making an elderberry wine and there's a willow tree—I could make some willow-bark tea for the fever." Her mind raced. What would happen to them if Kurt died? Her heart fell at the thought—how could she go on?

Dr. White nodded. "He'll need you most over the next day. By then you should know which way things will turn."

"Thank you, Doctor."

He nodded. "Sorry there wasn't more I could do—Sally May Watkins is having her first child down yonder, and I promised her I'd be there…" He tipped his hat and hurried out the door past Tripp, who was standing outside with his hands clenched in front of him.

Tripp watched him go, then stepped inside. "Ma?"

"He's going to be all right, Tripp. You were very brave going after the doctor that way. I'm proud of you, son." She gave him a hug.

He ducked his head and squeezed his eyes shut. "But if he dies…"

"He's *not* going to die. The doctor says he'll be just fine—he has an infection and needs to rest awhile, that's all." She wasn't entirely convinced herself, but she didn't need to worry her young son over Kurt's well-being, especially after losing his father. Her eyes sparked with tears.

"All right, Ma."

"It'll be dark before long. Do you think you could do the chores for Kurt?" She wiped her eyes dry with her sleeve.

"Yes, Ma." He pulled himself free of her embrace and hurried out toward the barn, wiping his cheeks as he went.

Holly watched him go and smiled through her tears, thoughts spinning in her head.

Chapter Eleven

Holly stared out the front window of the cottage, watching Kurt sit on a fallen log a hundred yards from the barn. According to Kurt, the oak had been split in two by a lightning strike years earlier, and half the tree still lay inert on the ground. He sawed a piece off for firewood occasionally, but mostly he liked to sit on it at night and stare up at the stars like he was doing now.

It was three days since the snake bit him, and he'd recovered just as the doctor said he would. She hadn't slept a wink that night—staying by his bedside, bathing his forehead with a damp cloth, trying to get him to drink water or willow-bark tea whenever she could. Then at noon the following day, he'd sat up and asked for something to eat. Her relief was instantaneous. Even the children, who'd been tiptoeing around the place while Kurt was ill, broke into shouts and squeals the moment he recovered. It was a happy day.

Yet now here he was, staring up at the black sky. She frowned—was he upset about something? Did he want to be alone? She understood that feeling, since she never got the chance herself.

She sighed, took the dishcloth off her shoulder and wandered back to the kitchen table. The children were all in bed, the older ones whispering to each other, Eleanor and Edward sound asleep. She was grateful the little ones had learned to sleep through their siblings' constant noise. Now what? The dishes had been wiped and put away. The fire glowed faintly in the hearth, already banked.

She blew out the candle she'd lit on the mantle, turned and marched outside. If he was so unhappy he needed to leave the house just to get away from her, she wanted to hear it from his lips. She was sick of fretting, of being scared they'd ruined his life, of worrying he'd send them all packing if she did something wrong or if one of the children got into mischief. It was time she asked him how he really felt. If he wanted them to leave, better she should know now.

But when she reached him, her resolve melted away. Badger had padded along silently beside her, and she leaned down to pat his head. Her hands were shaking as she pushed her hair out of her face and took a deep breath.

Kurt heard a twig snap beneath her boot and turned. "Oh, it's you."

She rolled her eyes in the darkness. He sure knew just what to say to melt a woman's heart. "Yes, it's just me."

"No… I mean I'm glad it's you." He patted the log beside him. "Come sit with me, won't you?"

She nodded and sat on the log, positioning herself

a foot away from him and smoothing out her skirts. "What are you doing out here?"

"Just watching the stars. There's nothing like a starry night, don't you think? In Mount Vernon, there were too many lights at night to see them clearly. I imagine New York was even worse…"

She frowned. Perhaps all the motives she'd ascribed to him were just in her mind—it was possible he wasn't trying to avoid her. But she still felt as though she didn't know him, not deep down. The person he truly was, seemed always hidden from her, just out of sight. "It's just that…" She trailed off in the stillness of the evening.

He scratched his beard. "Just what?"

She could see his eyes twinkling in the darkness, and decided to risk it. "I thought you were trying to get away from me. And I don't want to be the kind of wife who drives her husband from his own home. I just… why are you laughing?!"

He scooted closer to her on the log until their legs touched. "I'm not yearning to get away from you— quite the opposite."

She frowned. "Truly?"

"I am your husband, after all."

She felt her cheeks flush in the cool night. "Yes, but you don't seem to really like us. I mean, don't get me wrong, you're kind to us and good, but you're so quiet and you keep to yourself. I guess I wondered if you regretted everything and wished we weren't here…" As she said the words, she wished she could take them back. They sounded so much harsher than she'd intended.

His hand found hers where they were clenched in her lap and enclosed them. "I'm so glad you and the kids are here. You've brought life into my world and stirred things up." He chuckled. "I needed that—it was too quiet around here before. I don't want to go back to that."

She smiled, trembling. Her fingers tingled at his touch and she let her hands relax, threading her fingers through his. "I didn't know…"

"Now you do. What would I have done these last days if you weren't here? No one would've even known I was sick, let alone cared for me."

She sighed. "Yes, I suppose."

He seemed to sense her disappointment in his words. "But that's not the only reason. When you arrived, I got an instant family—a big, happy family full of love. Who wouldn't want that? And best of all, I got you."

Her eyes widened and she held her breath.

"I could never have imagined I'd meet someone so loving, kind, smart and beautiful as you, my darling Holly. You're everything I didn't know I wanted. If only you loved me the way I love you, I think we could be happy together…" His voice thickened with emotion until he couldn't speak.

Neither could Holly for a moment. Finally she managed to exhale, then swallowed the lump in her throat. "You love me? I…thought you'd never forgive me for saddling you with all these kids!"

He leaned closer, taking her breath away as he caressed the side of her jaw. "They're amazing—just like their mother. And one day, I hope we might have one of our own…" His lips hovered just above hers, making her pulse race. When they met, she closed her eyes and wove her fingers through his hair, the world spinning around her in a daze of joy, pleasure and anticipation.

She finally pulled away for breath, watching his face, the curve of his cheek and the strong line of his nose, the depth of his eyes as, full of love, they studied her every movement.

"Do you think you could learn to love me, some day?" he asked.

She bit her lip and smiled. "I love you already, though I didn't know it until this moment."

He took a quick breath, then reached for her again, his mouth devouring hers in a passionate kiss, full of the longing grown over weeks of hopelessness and fearful regrets. Now they were gone as hope and love collided in a soulful embrace.

First Presbyterian was packed tight with congregants as Holly adjusted her hat. A hatpin was scratching her scalp, and she reached up to move it to a more suitable location in the depths of her chignon.

Today, dressed in a modest mint-green gown, she'd actually looked forward to coming to the new brick building. Angus and Beatrice weren't in attendance— baby Ulysses Roscoe Sawyer had arrived the day before, so they were at home. Still, she felt the bond even though they were absent. They were on her side, and she didn't care what anyone else thought. She had friends, and a husband who loved her, and five wonderful children who that very morning managed to make it to church without a single argument. What more could she want?

She smiled as she raised her hymnal. The final hymn rang through the small space, echoing off the walls and ceiling with the swell of melody. She glanced at Kurt, and he smiled at her and patted her hand where it rested on his strong arm. She sighed as the last notes faded away. The minister thanked them all, dismissed them to leave and she watched the children rush outside to play. "Should we stop by to see Angus and Beatrice and the baby?"

Kurt nodded. "That would be nice. I'm looking forward to seeing him."

She chuckled. "I'm sure Beatrice is just relieved to have it done with."

"Well, I'll be right outside—as soon as you're done, we'll head over there." He hurried out the door, his hat in his hands.

Holly frowned—he'd done it again. He'd left her all alone in the church with folks she didn't know. She didn't wish to be left by herself there, and he knew it.

"Excuse me?"

She turned to see a petite, mousy woman with light brown hair staring at her through round spectacles perched on a thin, straight nose. "Yes?"

"Hello, I'm Alice Brown. Are you Kurt Sawyer's new wife?"

She braced herself. "Yes, I am—I'm Holly. Pleased to make your acquaintance, Alice."

Alice grinned. "Yours too. I've been wanting to meet you—I heard you were beautiful, and boy, you sure are. How do you get your hair to sit that way? Mine's always frizzy like this, rain or shine—I can't seem to do a thing with it."

Holly smiled. "I think your hair is lovely, but I'm sure we could fix it the same way. I'd be happy to help you sometime if you like."

Alice beamed. "Oh yes, please—that would be marvelous! I've just moved here and I don't know a soul, not really. My husband Handley bought a mercantile store here…"

"Oh, of course—I met Handley the other day when we came to town. He sold us the most darling boots and some really beautiful fabric I'm sewing our winter clothes from."

Alice looped one arm through Holly's and led her toward the door. "I just know we'll be good friends. I have a sense about these things."

Holly nodded with a grin. "I think so too."

"And these are your children?" asked Alice. All five were running circles around Kurt and the wagon, whooping and hollering.

Holly cringed. "Uh, yes, that's them."

"They're delightful! Handley and I have been trying for children for years, but God hasn't chosen to bless us that way, or not yet. Though we're so blessed in other ways that I just can't begin to count them." She squeezed Holly's arm, happily watching the children play. "So we've come to terms with it. I've learned life can be awfully miserable if you count the blessings you don't have, rather than the ones you do. Wouldn't you agree?" Her hazel eyes glimmered behind her glasses.

Holly patted her hand and tipped her head to one side. "Yes, indeed. You're very wise, though I don't know how you got to be so at such a young age."

Alice smiled wide and laughed. "Oh, you flatterer.

You know, all of you should come to the house for lunch today. I made a roast yesterday for the Sabbath meal, and it's big enough for all of us."

Holly pursed her lips. "Oh, I don't know. We have to visit Kurt's brother and the new baby…"

"You can do both—I insist. I have to get to know you better, since you live out of town and I don't know when I'll next get the chance to visit with you. I haven't been to the ranch, but Handley tells me all about his customers and where they're from and what they're like, so I feel like I know them all myself sometimes…"

As Alice kept talking, Holly led her toward Kurt to ask if they could dine at the Browns'. When he said they could, she let herself take a moment to look around the space in front of the church. Her children played with some of the other kids from town. Handley joined Alice, who told him to expect guests, an open smile on her face.

Holly felt the warmth of her husband's presence— his solid dependability, his strength of character, his goodness and his love for her. And peace like a river flooded her soul.

* * * * *

About the Author

Vivi Holt was born in Australia. She grew up in the country, where she spent her youth riding horses at Pony Club, and adventuring through the fields and rivers around the farm. Her father was a builder, turned saddler, and her mother a nurse, who stayed home to raise their four children.

After graduating from a degree in International Relations, Vivi moved to Atlanta, Georgia, to work for a year. It was there that she met her husband, and they were married three years later. She spent seven years living in Atlanta and travelled to various parts of the United States during that time, falling in love with the beauty of that immense country and the American people.

Vivi also studied for a Bachelor of Information Technology, and worked in the field ever since until becoming a full-time writer in 2016. She now lives in Brisbane, Australia, with her husband and three small children. Married to a Baptist pastor, she is very active in her local church.

Follow Vivi Holt
www.viviholt.com
vivi@viviholt.com

What on earth?

Suddenly, a shiny red Mustang came around the curve of the driveway at a speed far too fast for the dirt road, and when the vehicle slammed to a stop, it nearly hit the side of Avery's SUV.

Who drove that way, especially on unpaved mountain roads?

The man unfolded himself from the driver's seat and stood to his full over-six-foot height, let out a whoop of pure pleasure and waved his black cowboy hat in the air before combing his fingers through his thick dark hair and settling the hat on his head.

Avery had never seen him before in her life.

It wasn't so much that they didn't have strangers occasionally visiting Whispering Pines. Avery's own family brought in customers from all over Colorado who wanted the full Christmas tree–cutting experience.

So, yes, there were often strangers in town.

But this man?

He was as out of place as a blue spruce in an orange grove. And he was on land she intended to purchase—before anyone else was supposed to know about it.

Yes, he sported a cowboy hat and boots similar to those that the men around the Pines wore, but his whole getup probably cost more than Avery made in a year, and his new boots gleamed from a fresh polish.

Avery fought to withhold a grin, thinking about how quickly those shiny boots would lose their luster with all the dirt he'd raised with his foolish driving.

Served him right.

Just what was this stranger doing *here*?

"And didn't you say the cabin wasn't listed yet?" Avery said quietly. "What does this guy think he's doing here?"

"I have no idea how—" Lisa whispered back.

"Good afternoon, ladies," said the man as he tipped his hat, accompanied by a sparkle in his deep blue eyes and a grin Avery could only categorize as charismatic. He could easily have starred in a toothpaste commercial.

She had a bad feeling about this.

As the man approached, the puppy at Avery's heels started barking and straining against his lead—something he'd been in training not to do. Was he trying to protect her, to tell her this man was bad news?

Don't miss
Opening Her Heart *by Deb Kastner,*
available January 2021 wherever
Love Inspired books and ebooks are sold.

LoveInspired.com

LOVE INSPIRED

INSPIRATIONAL ROMANCE

UPLIFTING STORIES OF FAITH, FORGIVENESS AND HOPE.

———————————

Join our social communities to connect with other readers who share your love!

Sign up for the Love Inspired newsletter at **LoveInspired.com** to be the first to find out about upcoming titles, special promotions and exclusive content.

———————————

CONNECT WITH US AT:

Facebook.com/LoveInspiredBooks

Twitter.com/LoveInspiredBks

Facebook.com/groups/HarlequinConnection

HARLEQUIN

Heartfelt or suspenseful, inspiring or passionate, Harlequin has your happily-ever-after.

With new books published
every month, you are sure to find the
satisfying escape you know you deserve.